Unjustly Awarded
A Coswell Novel

Major Character List

1. Jefferson Ripley – Retired Army Master Sergeant, Call sign – Coswell,
Aliases- James Winchester and John McNally.

2. Walker Ripley – Retired Army Sergeant Major, Call sign Templar, know aliases Oliver Holmes and Liam McGregor.

3. Lt. Colonel Leslie D. Massengill – CMH award winner, and sadistic sexual deviant.

4. Louise Wilson- Estranged wife of Leslie D. Massengill.

5. Wilbur- Heroin Addict and Hotel Clerk at the Shady Elms Motel

6. Brandy Potter- Sweet, lovely, waitress at the Breakfast Nook and possible love interest to Coswell.

7. Lt. Colonel R. William Hand- Military Investigator assigned the CMH case involving Colonel Massengill.

8. Gunnery Sergeant Luis Juan "Jumbo" Lopez – Gunny in Massengill's squad.

9. Lance Corporal Willie Roosevelt – Corporal in Massengill's squad.

10. Madison and Cheryl Bridger- Twin girls that are long time friends of Brandy Potter. Girls caught in a web of deceit and the pressures of life.

11. Chaplain Timothy Michaelson- Retired Marine Chaplain who lives in Cedar Creek and is commonly at the local VFW.

12. Chastity Michaelson- The bright young daughter of Chaplain Michaelson.

13. James Willis- Owner of Willis Hardware store and friend of Leslie Massengill.

14. Kenneth Ripley- Grandfather of Jefferson and Walker Ripley and WWII hero.

15. Charles Alexander Thomas- Rich, powerful, Georgetown lawyer that has retained the services of Templar.

16. Catherine Louise Parker- Fiancée of Charles Alexander Thomas and target of sexual harassment.

17. Dr. Susan Stock - Professor and Doctorial advisor to Catherine Louise Parker.

18. Naomi Sanchez- Live in housekeeper of Charles Alexander Thomas.

19. Daphne Ambrose – Jazz singer in Richmond Va.

20. Rich O'Donnell – Blue Danube ticket taker.

21. Gracie Greathouse - local defense attorney and madam.

22. Dallas Bird- Fayetteville Detective working related case in which Colonel Massengill is a suspect.

23. Kelsey O'Quinn – former Jag assistant in Quantico that meets Dallas Bird on a cruise.

Chapter 1

Jefferson Ripley is sitting in his warm, paneled den surrounded by his most prized possessions, his books, records and WWII pistol collection. He reads quietly and slowly sips his warm cognac when his phone rings. He momentarily looks up from his book on custom Mauser hunting rifles and peers at the phone. He notices the number is from out of state. He activates the microwave jammer on his phone to secure the line from prying ears. One cannot be too careful. He slowly removes the receiver from the cradle and presses it to his ear. He speaks in a deep, firm tone one word, "Coswell." In his everyday life living in rural South Carolina he is Jefferson Ripley, mild mannered U.S. Army Master Sergeant, retired. In the cloak and dagger world that consumes most of his time and effort now, he is Coswell. The woman on the other end of the line informs him she was referred to him by Templar. Hearing this name, Jefferson knows this is a real and highly interested party.

The woman on the other end begins and says, "This is...." At that point she is interrupted and cut off.

Jefferson tells her, "No names. What are the job specifics?"

"My husband, or should I say estranged husband is the job. He is an evil man. He simply needs killing for the evil deeds of his life."

Jefferson stoically responds, "Just because someone is evil does not justify killing them, unless of course the appropriate fee can be negotiated. I will need to know all of the details about this individual to make my decision on whether or not to eliminate this target."

Jefferson continues, "Where is the target? What is his current station in life?"

"He lives in Cedar Creek North Carolina, just outside of Fayetteville. He is a retired Marine Colonel that was last stationed in Quantico, VA. He lives on a ten acre plot of land out in the rural area adjoining the forest. One last thing, and maybe the most important one, is he was awarded, albeit undeservedly, the Congressional Medal of Honor. Only a truly evil man could accept such an award knowing he was unworthy of it."

Jefferson inquires, "Who is the beneficiary of his life insurance and his will? If it is you, suspicion could be cast in your direction if he is killed."

"When I last saw him I was, but I do not know. I do know he was a great admirer of Madalynne O'Hare. He has no children, or anyone else to leave anything to. He is such an utterly unloved and hated man. We have not seen each other in over five years and I never want to see him alive again." She adds, "I will attend his funeral but only to verify he is dead because I do not know if evil like that can be destroyed."

Jefferson Ripley tells her, "As long as there is no recent connection, this should not be a problem. Although, if there are any problems because of your connection to the Colonel, know that I am in the business of eliminating problems. Do you understand?"

She gingerly mutters back into the phone an almost inaudible, "Yes."

Jefferson then repeats his question, "I asked do you UNDERSTAND? This work is going to be hard and most definitely final so this decision is not one to be made lightly or with little conviction."

Jefferson continues, "I need to understand your intentions. I need to know are you ready to deal or are you simply wasting the very valuable time of a dangerous man? That is unwise!"

Again she responds, but this time very definitely, and tells him, "Yes sir Mr. Coswell."

Jefferson tells her, "You stand to inherit a great deal from this and this man is a higher profile target because of the CMH. I will require a fee of $150,000 to be paid to me for this job, half by Friday, the other half upon completion. Wire the first half to 1st bank of Grand Cayman." He tells her to write down the following account number and once the transfer is made burn the paper she has written it on until it is cinders and ash. He reads off the account as follows: 2695492XS42595010. Jefferson tells her "I will contact you upon completion on a burn phone you will receive. I have access to this phone. If it is ever used for an outgoing call to me, or anyone else, the job is off and I keep the initial payment. Is this CRYSTAL CLEAR?"

She once again responds, "Yes sir Mr. Coswell!" and hangs up.

Jefferson sits and deeply sips some more warm cognac and thinks to himself, North Carolina is nice this time of year......

After Jefferson hangs up he picks up the phone again and contacts his old friend Templar. He informs Templar he needs a drop box at the Fayetteville North Carolina airport industrial parkway. A burn phone is also to be hand delivered to the employer's front door in a plain brown wrapper. He asks Templar "Are you sure she on the level? Does this man deserve killing or is this just another scorned woman lashing out at the cause of her pain?"

Templar responds in a relaxed tone. "As far as he can see Coswell, this man is a blight that needs to be removed from this world. It would be an injustice if he were to live a long and prosperous life."

Templar's opinion means a great deal to Coswell. They respect each other. They have worked together many times in the past and take care of small details for one another so their employers never have the opportunity to meet the 'mechanic' they have hired.

It is Wednesday morning and the payment is to be sent via bank wire by end of business on Friday. Jefferson needs more information about this job. He picks up his secure satellite phone and dials the number of the burn phone he had couriered to his employer. When he makes the call a woman nervously answers.

Jefferson Ripley immediately begins, "This is Coswell. I need a detailed dossier of everything. I need to know every detail you can think of that pertains to this target. Do not leave anything out no matter how trivial. Put the dossier in a large manila envelope, and take it to the Soman Aeronautics building at the Fayetteville Airport industrial parkway. There will be an old US mailbox there. You will know which one because it is tagged with graffiti, marked with CC on the side. Drop it in the mailbox and await my call on Sunday. The information absolutely required is a recent picture, the target's name, and current address. Also include any information about his military background, and any other pertinent information you might know of that would not be in public record. You have two days to accomplish this and make the initial payment."

Coswell continues, "If this is not done, and my instructions followed to the letter, I will see this as a problem. I will convey to you for the final time that I do not tolerate problems, as you know I eliminate them."

The woman adamantly responds, "I understand Mr. Coswell. I will see that everything is done by Friday."

Coswell tells her, "I hope you completely understanding me. You are to keep this phone with you at all times, as this will be the only way I will contact you in the future. There will not be a need for a lot of communication. If you do your part, and everything goes as planned, you should only hear from me two more times. Once you receive the final call, and verification that the job is complete, you are to remove the simm card from the phone and destroy it. You are then to dispose of the phone in a city dumpster."

After the line goes dead, the woman wonders to herself, 'Is this worth all of the danger to remove my estranged husband from this world? I know he is an awful man but does that make me awful for doing what I think is right?'

Jefferson begins to think his plan over. He goes to his safe and removes $8700.00 for traveling money and emergencies. He knows that once in the Fayetteville area, he will need to find a small, out of the way, cash only, motel. He gets out two of his clean I.D's. This includes a driver's license, passport, and forged credit cards for each. He looks over his choices and comes across two that seem to work quite well, James Winchester and John McNally.

Jefferson quietly ponders in the large, leather, stuffed chair in his den. This is the evening he will put together the master plan for eliminating this target. He puts together each piece in his mind like unscrambling a jigsaw puzzle. His plan needs to be seamless, well thought out, and logical. He cannot just show up in a new town, kill one of its chief citizens, and leave quietly without anyone noticing. One of the activities that relax Jefferson and allow his mind to flow freely is gun maintenance. He thoroughly cleans his Smith & Wesson model 18 22 long rifle revolver. It has a threaded four inch barrel and is made to attach a silencer. This is one of the possible weapons that would be an ideal choice for this plan. He may need something that is quiet, compact, and has the velocity to kill quickly. It does not always happen, but hopefully everything will go as planned. Jefferson knows that is always the hope, but rarely the case.

The next morning Jefferson arises early and continues to prepare for the upcoming job. As it is Thursday, and he will not be leaving for Fayetteville until the money is safely in the off-shore account, he double checks everything and packs what he believes he will need for this job. He wants to make sure this mission goes off as seamlessly as possible so he begins to break things down into a manageable, day by day, schedule. He knows he will need at least a day to read the dossier and absorb it, another couple days to recon the area and work out any possible difficulties that could not be accounted for, and one day for the execution of the target. Even with a day or two delay he should have the job completed, and be driving home, by the following Saturday.

Jefferson decides late Thursday night to drive up to Columbia and rent a Ford Explorer, leaving his car in Columbia at a hotel. The Explorer is a fairly mundane, everyday, vehicle that no one will notice. Jefferson checks in to a Holiday Inn in Columbia, South Carolina on a Thursday night. His timing could not have been any better. There is a home football game in Columbia on Saturday. The South Carolina Gamecocks are playing the Georgia Bulldogs. It will not look suspicious or uncommon for someone, even from in state, to get a hotel for a few days. He rents the room for a week and pays for it with a credit card of one of his aliases, James Winchester.

Jefferson walks from the Holiday Inn in Columbia, across the street, to the car rental agency. He rents a

2013 Ford Explorer and drives it back to the Holiday Inn, parking it next to his older Chevy Suburban. Late that night, actually about 2:30 am, he goes out into the parking lot and removes the license plate from his Chevy Suburban. He puts it under the passenger's seat of his vehicle and swaps the rental car's license plate onto the Suburban. Jefferson then proceeds to put a North Carolina license plate on the rented Ford Explorer. Sometimes, the police in rural areas will pay more attention to out of state tags. Once he arrives in Fayetteville, he wants to be sure to blend in, so as not draw any undo attention to himself during his visit.

After sitting all day, at the hotel, relaxing in the bar, and eating at the restaurant, he finally receives an alert on his phone from his off-shore bank. His payment of $75,000 is posted and now he can begin the job.

At 4 a.m. the next morning Jefferson Ripley begins his ride east on interstate twenty, heading towards the interstate ninety-five interchange. Once he reaches interstate ninety-five, and makes the turn north, he remains on that same road all the way to Fayetteville in North Carolina. Most people would not be calm and relaxed, but Coswell is definitely not like most. The

14

rest of the world would probably view the goal of this mission as something sinister. Coswell knows he must use every minute he has, including the drive time, to go over the details of his plan. Once he arrives in Fayetteville, the real work will begin, he will need to pour over the dossier and absorb every detail. If what his employer has told him is true about his target, he shouldn't have too much remorse when he completes his mission. Coswell does think about the Congressional Medal of Honor. What if this man really earned it and his estranged wife is just a bitter woman? What if this woman is jealous that his life, without her, turned out to be a better one and this is her motivation? What if it is all a lie and she just wants him dead? With most, Coswell would not even care, but a fellow serviceman. This may take an extra few days to make sure he knows all the facts and gets this job right. She says he is a loathsome, evil, manipulative man who doesn't deserve to be breathing the same air as everyone else. Is this the truth? Time will tell.

When he was in the Army, Coswell had been very good at stealth and recon. This led him to other fields that required a certain amount of, let's say, moral flexibility. He could not be flexible when it came to the

Medal of Honor. It demands two things, honor and the truth.

Coswell drives aimlessly along the desolate corridor of interstate twenty east for over an hour. He finally comes up on the interstate ninety-five interchange. It is a pleasurable drive that is comfortable, allows him to think about the job, and he concentrates on the details he knows are fact. Is this woman being a spiteful, scorned, estranged wife that wants revenge on a man because he could move on to a new life and start over? Is she telling the truth that this man is a coward and did not deserve anything he has received in life? Coswell still needs to know more and is anxious to arrive in Fayetteville, but at the same time needs to take his time and appear to be a common, vacationing tourist. He must show a great deal of restraint at this point.

After turning north on interstate ninety-five he drives to a point just beyond Florence, just before arriving at Dillon, he stops at a small tourist attraction area know as 'South of the Border.' This area is full of restaurants, strip malls, adult shops, and as seen on TV items. Basically, the whole town is nothing but a tourist trap, it sells good Mexican food, outlet priced clothing, and overpriced gimmicks. So that he will appear to be a visitor, he walks around and shops for a while. He aimlessly wanders from shop to shop, eventually passing several restaurants. The smells of the delectable foods floating through the air beckon him forth. He stops and walks past the bar and into the dining area of one of the many Mexican bar and grille restaurants. He sits and takes his time with a fine meal of enchiladas and refried beans. This is nicely accompanied by a fine Mexican cerveza. Once he has killed the appropriate amount of time, and is well fed, he walks back to his vehicle and is soon on the road once again. He turns onto the entrance ramp, and is within minutes, he is on interstate ninety-five heading to Fayetteville and 'South of the Border' is only a memory.

He enters the Fayetteville city limits, and after about ten minutes, takes the interstate right through the middle of town. He gets off on exit 46 near the airport where there is a rest stop, and heads east. Once on the two lane road, he passes several roadside motels. He chooses one of the motels a few miles from the interstate. He pulls into the parking lot and the neglected, not fully functional, neon sign outside reads

Shady Elms Motel. He parks and sits in the Explorer for a moment. He opens the door to the Ford and walks across the parking lot to the small building with the word 'OFFICE' lit above it. He walks to the desk to check in and a man is sitting in a wooden chair leaning back and asleep. Coswell knows this is the type of motel he will not have to have a credit card or show a driver's license to obtain a room, this is a motel mostly rented by the hour.

Coswell approaches the clerk who is a painfully thin man with long stringy hair and black plastic rim glasses. He looks like your classic heroin addict and wears a name badge that reads Wilbur. Coswell says "Hello." but he does not move. Again, Coswell repeats his greeting, this time in a much louder voice, "Hello Wilbur!"

The man stirs and in a painfully slow manner walks to the counter. Coswell asks, "Do you have a room available?"

Wilbur replies, "Uhh, yeah man. How long you need it?"

Coswell explains, "I am very tired and need some rest because I am touring cross country."

He pays in cash for a week and tells the clerk not to disturb him with housekeeping. Coswell tells him, "I will probably be resting for four or five days, I am going to pay for seven days, if I am not disturbed you can keep the extra two days fee."

The dead eyes of the clerk almost show a glimmer of life, he is thinking how much smack he can buy with an extra eighty dollars.

Coswell goes to his room which is on the end of the motel building. He parks his Explorer next to the building rather than in front of his room. After unpacking his clothes, he returns to his vehicle, and drives to airport industrial parkway road. This is where Templar set up his drop box. Many of the industrial buildings there are abandoned, so there will not be much of a chance someone will notice him. Templar set up an old U.S. mailbox for the drop box on this job. These old boxes are commonly used on street corners and at Post Offices and will blend in and not be noticed. Coswell has the key to the back of it, once he opens it he is able to retrieve the dossier left by his employer, as well as the copper jacketed hollow point sub-sonic ammo and new satellite phone he had requested from Templar. Templar also included the recon photos, and the name and address of the employer. If something happened to go wrong she will not be difficult to deal with. She is an attractive, mature, blonde named Louise Wilson and she lives in Wrightsville Beach, outside of Wilmington, NC.

Coswell drives back to the motel, and once there begins reading through the thick dossier about this Marine Lt. Colonel.

Chapter 2

According to the detailed dossier delivered to Coswell's drop box, the Marine button winner in question is Lt. Colonel Leslie D. Massengill. There is a recent picture of him as well as his photo from his military I.D. He served a long career in the Marine Corp dating back to the Vietnam War, and is a retired Lt. Colonel that is a shell of the man he once was. In Vietnam he was a strong virile man who was 6'1" tall, 195 lbs and as all marines claim, a deadly killing machine. The recent photo of the Colonel shows a slight, frail man who may still have the desire, but like older dogs or wolves no longer has the legs to run with the pack any longer. He is a target. From the looks of his current picture, Coswell believes it will not take much physical force to subdue and overcome him. Today he is still, of course, the same height but looks to weigh about 160 lbs which is thin and gaunt for a man of that height. According to the information in the dossier, he lives at 1313 Cedar Village Way in Cedar Creek North Carolina. During the Vietnam War, he was a Captain in the Marines. This is when the battle off the Ho Chi Minh trail occurred where he performed his "heroics" for which he was awarded the Congressional Medal of Honor. The official marine after action report of the incident is in the dossier, as is a copy of the file that can now be found in public record. One of the important facts Coswell is looking for and finds in the file is the name of the Lieutenant that was the investigating officer from the inspector general's office. His name is 1st Lieutenant R. William Hand. The official description states, that Captain Massengill was part of a probing scout squad to determine the VC advancement along that corridor of the Ho Chi Minh trail. The Captain, Gunnery Sergeant Luis Juan "Jumbo" Lopez and Lance Corporal Willie Roosevelt were dug in for the night in a shallow foxhole in a rice paddy along the Ho Chi Minh trail. A fierce night battle had broken out a few thousand yards away. This was a skirmish between NVA regular army artillery and a U.S. Army mobile artillery division. The two artillery divisions were trading deafening barrages in the night. The shelling was getting closer and closer to the squad's position, but this was no closer than it normally did so the Captain saw no reason to move his men. The shelling and constant explosion drove the Sergeant out of his mind. All three soldiers were armed

22

with the M-14 and the Sergeant's was an E3 full auto model. The Sergeant screamed uncontrollably to the Captain "We have to pull back. We are going to die." The Captain tried to calm Sergeant Lopez' nerves and show leadership by telling him, "We will hold our position until dawn when we can complete our mission." Still blood curdling screams came from the Sergeant and he grabbed his rifle and ran back toward the jungle. The Captain, surprised at his fear, yelled for him, "Get back here Sergeant Lopez." The Sergeant then turned and sprayed the Captain and Lance Corporal with fire. The Lance Corporal took the brunt with three rounds spanning the width of his chest and the Captain had been hit with two shots about an inch apart. One was in the ball of the shoulder, and the other was a small grazing flesh wound. Just then a small VC force armed with SKS rifles opened fire. The Captain returned fire and laid down a heavy barrage of suppression fire. When there was a lull in the attack, and the VC were back on their heels, the Captain ran after the Gunny to stop him and retrieve his weapon. He knocked him unconscious with the butt of his rifle and dragged him to safety near the trees. He went back for the Corporal who was in critical condition and

23

barely alive. If they were able to get him to the medics at battalion HQ there is a chance he might live. The Captain, risking his own life, saved his small unit of two men and fought off the enemy while protecting his men from extreme danger and eminent death.

Coswell finishes reading the official inquiry and thinks to himself, 'There is another story here.' Coswell has been in combat many times and not once was it glorified or pretty. War is ugly and treacherous and you only hope to survive, not flourish in it. It never works out as well as this story is all tied up. He reads on further, because there has got to be another account, CMH awards require a witness to give testimony.

The story continues, the Captain carried the injured Corporal to safety, but upon reaching the tree line, found the Gunny dead. He had apparently been killed by enemy fire. The remaining two soldiers, the Captain and Corporal, were rescued the following morning and the Sergeant's body was loaded on the chopper at the extraction point. An autopsy was performed on Gunny Lopez, and it showed that the Gunnery Sergeant had died of four 7.62mm rounds to the chest. The rounds were so mangled nothing else could be determined about them because the bullets had contacted solid bone. The two preferred rifles of the VC and NVA are the SKS and AK-47 both of which fire the 7.62mm round. It was assumed by the Medical Examiner that Gunnery Sgt. Lopez was indeed killed by the VC. The ME assumed this, Coswell will assume nothing.

The Corporal, although critically wounded, did survive and was sent to the intensive care unit for 3 weeks, and at this time Lt. R. William Hand had an opportunity to interview him. The records show that he died shortly after the interview of massive internal bleeding. This was attributed to the multiple gunshots he had suffered.

Coswell thinks that if Lt. Hand is still around, although he would be long retired, he might know the real truth. Coswell decides this bit of information justifies further investigation and he will start with a few calls, the first one being to the USMC retirement pension department to track down Lt. Hand. If Lt. Hand was a career man he must have at least been a Major, possibly a Colonel, upon retirement. Coswell closes the dossier and decides to let all these new facts soak in. He slides the dossier under the mattress between the box springs, and takes a long, hot, relaxing shower. In the shower he is thinking, there is just something wrong with the story about a Gunny freaking out, there is no way a hardened Marine Gunnery Sergeant would lose his mind and begin shooting at both of his squad mates. He knows something there is wrong, he cannot put his finger on it, but it is there. It has been a long day of driving. Maybe after a good night's sleep his mind will be rested and he will come to a better realization in the morning.

When morning breaks, his first call is to USMC pension department. A sweet, southern voice answers the phone with a sultry sounding, "Hello." Coswell knows he can get the information he needs because a little charm goes a long way in getting what you want. He tells her, "Well hello and how are you on this fine morning?"

She responds, "This is Brenda and I am just as sweet as honey on a hot, South Carolina night."

He tells the sweet, southern girl, "I am so happy to hear that darling. Is there any way you can help me track down an old buddy that lives in the area? I am only going to be here in town for a couple of nights and want us to get together and catch up." Coswell then asks, "Do you have a record of pension distribution for a man named R. William Hand?"

She tells him, "Yes we have him here. He retired as a Lt. Colonel in 1992 and still has his pension checks sent to the address in Lumberton, North Carolina." Coswell asks her, "Do you happen to have his phone number? I would like to contact him and let him know I am going to drop in." She falters for a moment but with a little coaxing, and the fact that they haven't seen each other in years, her heart melts enough to break protocol.

Coswell hangs up the phone satisfied with his performance. In a moment, he picks it up again and begins to dial the number for Lt. Colonel R. William Hand. The phone begins to ring and a deep voice on the other end answers the phone with a crisp, and defined, "Colonel Hand, how may I help you?"

Coswell begins, "I am a reporter for the Memphis Press Register, and I doing a story on honorable soldiers in an unpopular Vietnam War. This story is to show that among the ugliness there were heroes of Vietnam."

Lt. Colonel Hand exclaims, "Well it's about time! What does that have to do with me I was in the inspector general's office?"

Coswell explains, "The soldier I am researching right now is Congressional Medal of Honor recipient Lt. Colonel Leslie Massengill and his heroics along the Ho Chi Minh Trail." There is a dead silence on the phone. Colonel Hand says, "Do I have your word we are off the record?" Coswell agrees. Hand finally says, "Are you sure you don't want to pick someone else? Massengill is not the poster boy for what you are looking for. The investigation was a huge mess. It turned up details that we did not want the media at the time to have, we just had to clean it up to make it presentable."

When Coswell presses further, "So what was the issue? He received the Medal. Is this a conspiracy? Who all is involved?" Colonel Hand stops him, "You don't want to dig into this, which is for damn sure! Everyone who did look into this in the past isn't among the living anymore. They all became accident prone and their death seems to be expedited. If I were you I would step away from this all together."

The Colonel will not say anymore, only this "You shouldn't believe the official report. The one that I originally wrote was edited by the inspector general himself, so we could have the 'war hero' the country needed. I have never seen two witnesses to the same event tell such similar stories in all of my life. Hell of a lot of good it did. Let it alone......" Then the phone line goes dead.

This gives Coswell so much more to ponder, but it does give credence to the story told to him by Louise Wilson. That is a point for the home team. Coswell begins to read further into the dossier and reads the personal accounts written by Louise Wilson, the former Mrs. Massengill, who apparently has gone back to using her maiden name.

Colonel Massengill had been an abusive alcoholic after returning from Vietnam. He would go out drinking and causing trouble, and when he came home, sometimes assisted by the local authorities, he would smell of booze, cigarettes and often some cheap whore's perfume. If he was really drunk, he would move in on Louise, and beat her like he was tenderizing a cheap cut of beef. He would sober up, and he would lose his courage from a bottle, and once more he

29

became the coward she said he always was. He would sob uncontrollably and beg her forgiveness. He would swear he would never get drunk like this again. That would be true until the next weekend. One day, he was so drunk, that he began telling her things that were forbidden. He began telling her classified information and then breaking down and telling her the real truth of the night on the Ho Chi Minh trail.

According to the wife's description in the dossier this is what really happened.

Then Captain Massengill, Gunnery Sergeant Lopez and Lance Corporal Roosevelt were in a foxhole that they dug for the night just off the trail. The shelling was constant that night; there were almost no reliefs between explosions. The Captain was the one that was a coward in the face of danger as he sat with his knees pulled up in his chest rocking back and forth and screaming like a frightened child that wanted their mother. Gunny Lopez was on the M14 E3 and was keeping anything that moved suppressed and pinned down. Lance Corporal Roosevelt had been injured but only slightly. He was helping keep and VC stragglers at bay until morning when the squad was going to catch up and reinforce them. Gunny Jumbo Lopez had already killed 12 VC that night and had taken command because the Captain was petrified with terror and could barely function. He was gasping for air like an asthmatic child. The Gunnery Sergeant had laid down his M14E3 to cool and told the Corporal to reload it. He grabbed up the Captain's M14, which while a semi-auto, was more easily controllable.

Suddenly, and without warning, the Captain grabbed the freshly loaded E3 and took off running for the woods a couple of hundred yards away. Gunny Lopez ordered Lance Corporal Roosevelt to go after him and retrieve that weapon. As Roosevelt left the foxhole he was struck by three rounds from an enemy SKS. Gunny Lopez put down heavy suppressive fire and then went to the Corporal's aid. He picked him up and while carrying him ran down the Captain. He dove and knocked him down and the Corporal rolled along the ground. The Gunny stood up to get a hold on his commander and the distinct sound of the E3 pumping out lead was heard. The Sergeant had been hit four times in the chest by the M14E3 that was held in the hands of the Captain who was sitting on the ground. Just then the Corporal started to come to and the Captain emptied the clip of the rifle in the direction they had run from. The Corporal had assumed that he was firing at the enemy and the Gunny was killed by the same. They both hid in the edge of the woods until morning and the squad reinforced them and called the helicopter to airlift out the wounded. The next morning the Corporal who was critically injured asked the Captain what happened and he told him that he had dragged him into the woods after the Gunny was killed by the VC. The Corporal was in and out of consciousness and took this for the truth. So this was also his story that he told the investigator for the CMH award.

If this is really the truth then how did the Captain get wounded? There is no reference of it in the wife's story from his drunken confession.

Chapter 3

Coswell has read through the entire dossier, and has a handle on what it has in it, but there were still a few holes that need pieces to fit. He needs to be sure because he has his own code of honor. He is not a cheap thug for hire, yet someone who will have the courage to do what others will not when necessary. He is not just the weapon, but the Judge, Jury and Executioner. He has to make sure this is a job where justice is served.

Monday morning he leaves out early to do some reconnaissance, and observe some of the daily habits of the intended target. As with most retired military, Lt. Colonel Massengill still arises fairly early, but not at the 0500 when reveille used to play. He wakes up at about 0730 and Coswell is waiting outside his home on Cedar Village Way. He parks at the end of a long drive out on the country road. This is a rural community and each plot of land is at the least five acres. The Colonel lives on a ten acre plot, in a farm style house, with a big wrap around front porch covered by an over hanging roof. This is the type of farm house that has been built throughout the 19th and 20th century in the southeast.

One could find these all over the back roads in Tennessee, Alabama, the Carolinas, Georgia and all other farming communities in America. The houses are set at least ¼ to ½ miles apart and probably a quarter of a mile off the road. The front lawns are like a large pasture that one would see driving down a country road. They are green and rolling and have gravel paths leading down to farm houses and through hay fields or horse paddocks. This also greatly lowers the chance of Coswell being spotted by nosy neighbors.

Coswell thinks this is a perfect opportunity to try out his new Zeiss binoculars that are supposedly clear visually to fifteen hundred yards. He parks at the corner of Colonel Massengill's lot about an eighth of a mile away from the end of his long drive and about fifteen hundred feet from the Colonel's wrap around front porch. He sits and watches through his binoculars, and awaits movement at the Massengill house. He sees the Colonel come out onto his wrap around porch, and sit at his outdoor table sipping coffee in his pajamas and robe. He sits and quietly enjoys the morning without a care in the world. Meanwhile Coswell sits taking in every detail of the Colonel and his morning routine. Coswell thinks to himself, as is always true, the devil is in the details. Little did Massengill know his demise would soon befall him. If he did know this, would his routine still be so nonchalant and carefree? Did this man believe that he is always master of his own destiny? Coswell contemplates this as the Colonel sits sipping coffee and reading his morning paper until 0930. The Colonel goes inside at 0930, and Coswell reaches around to the floorboard, behind the passenger's seat, and picks up his Nikon Camera with the 1000 millimeter telephoto lens. It is a 16MegaPixel digital SLR camera that takes flawless photos from any distance. Since it is digital, it only uses a memory card to store pictures rather than film. As both surveillance and discretion are important in this business Coswell never keeps the memory card in the camera. However he keeps a blank one on him so all he has to do is slide it in, close the side panel and he is ready to shoot. He keeps the camera readily available on surveillance jobs and stakeouts, but always makes sure to tuck it up under the seat a little and covers it with a golf towel. This is in case prying eyes are peeking where they do not belong.

He loads the card into the camera and takes some base shots. He takes shots of the entire property, zooms in on the house, shoots the pasture, and horse barn off to the side, and a few Appaloosa horses in the pasture between the house and barn. Coswell also takes a couple of shots of the Colonel's vehicles, a Jeep Wrangler and a newer Chrysler 300. Coswell, of course, gets shots of the vehicle's license plates.

The Colonel reappears again about 1130. He comes out of the farm house fully clothed and gets into his Jeep Wrangler. His clothes are neat and well cut for him. They seem to fit the classic personality of a retired Colonel. He wears a nice pair of chino slacks and a plaid shirt, like the ones some hunters and lumberjacks wear. He wears chukka boots that are both comfortable and durable. His dress is simple, yet in some way, has a rugged elegance of manliness.

Coswell thinks to himself, 'This man has to have everything so perfect, in his daily appearance, and his life. What will happen when the ugliness oozes up from his past, and dark secrets both then and now, are exposed to the light of day?'

Once Massengill gets into his Jeep, Coswell starts the engine to his Explorer and drives about a quarter mile down the road to circle around. The Colonel backs out of his drive, and begins driving away in the opposite direction. Coswell simply keeps him in sight as he pursues him to his first stop.

Massengill enters the Breakfast Nook Restaurant and goes to the corner booth and takes his seat. Coswell enters a couple of minutes after the Colonel, and sits on a stool at the high bar. There are a few people on the stools, and Coswell knows he can blend in there. Coswell orders black coffee and cinnamon roll from a cute, slightly plump, but oh so sweet brunette waitress. She is about 30, maybe a couple years older, and has bright red lips, a glowing smile, and the most beautiful green eyes. Her name tag reads Brandy, and Coswell thinks he loves cognac and brandy can be just as good in a pinch.

He talks her up a little and she laughs, then she sees the old Colonel and his claw of a hand go up to beckon her. Instantly her gleeful smile turns to a sullen look of despair knowing he is at her station. When she approaches Coswell, it is with a carefree love of life. She greets all of her other customers with the same worldly outlook, a genuine virginity of sorts. She seems to have an innocence that nothing can dash, and a bubbly and truly attractive love of life. This all ends quite abruptly when she sees the old crusted, slightly

37

bony hand of the Colonel motioning to her. He holds his hand up, and with only his index finger extended, he slowly, and rhythmically motions to her. This is interesting to observe, because it is almost like a skeleton motioning to her and she has no choice but to obey.

Colonel Massengill orders and looks Brandy over from head to toe while doing so. He looks at her like a mongoose looks at its next meal. Coswell can tell this is a torture Brandy endures daily. He is literally salivating at her sweet curvaceous body and intentionally spills his water so she will have to mop it up and he can look down her shirt at her heaving breasts. This man is a megalomaniac, and a certified asshole. If he had shown interest in this girl, when he was Coswell's age, he would have been a pedophile.

The Colonel orders his runny eggs and limp bacon. Even his breakfast order fits his personality. Brandy turns to walk back to the counter to put in his order, and the Colonel swings his hand under her dress and slaps her on her round ass.

Coswell knows at this moment, he doesn't like this guy, not one bit. Coswell thinks about what the Colonel is having for breakfast and how fitting it is.

This man probably torments the young waitress because he has problems in that area, limp and runny like milk toast is so fitting. Coswell has to stay focused now because he cannot let the personal enjoyment of killing this bastard influence his dedication in finding out the real truth. Brandy brings Coswell his breakfast, and her beautiful green eyes are tearing up. He asks her, "Are you alright? I saw what the man in the corner did. Why doesn't your manager ask him to leave?"

Brandy responds, "You haven't been here before have you? That is the almighty Lt. Colonel Leslie Massengill, Medal of Honor winner, and Cedar Creek's most upstanding citizen."

Coswell quips, "He isn't acting like a pillar of society. He looks like a dirty old man."

Brandy says, "That's what he is, in fact that is an insult to dirty old men. He acts all high and mighty; he even wears his Marine dress blues when he goes to church on Sunday. He is so hypocritical. He is completely above board in the daytime but many people believe he leads a double life at night."

Just then someone yells at Brandy to go clock out, her shift was over at 12:30. Coswell looks at his watch, it is 12:43. He looks over and the Colonel is harassing the new waitress that has picked up Brandy's station, lucky her. Coswell sees his opportunity.

Before Brandy turns to leave he says to her, "I am so sorry I was rude, I didn't introduce myself. I am John McNally." He grasps her hand and smiles and she simply responds, "Charmed. My name is Brandy Potter."

Coswell, or as Brandy knows him John McNally asks, "Well, when is the last time someone treated you to a good lunch, and not here?"

She smiles and tells John it has been a long time because her hours there precluded her from being out late and most men aren't free during the day.

McNally says, "Well I am asking now, what do you say?"

She thinks a moment about how nice he was to her and how understanding he had been, could this just be a ploy? She looks at McNally for what seems like a long time. She is sizing him up from head to toe. He is a man just under six feet in height, maybe a couple inches shorter, and is a thick, strong looking man. He probably weighs about two hundred pounds and has big arms and large powerful hands. However, when she looks at him she only thinks of a gentle man, one who

40

has soft eyes, coal black hair and for some reason treats her only with a gentile attitude. Then she knows he is sincere and says, "Yes, anywhere but here."

McNally tells her, "It is your choice."

Coswell knows the Colonel is a man of habit, he has already been informed he is a night owl so he lets him go for now. He knows he will head back to Cedar Village Way and then be on the prowl tonight. That will give Coswell time to get some information from his new friend and maybe make another call to Lt. Colonel Hand as a follow up.

McNally and Brandy get into the explorer and it only takes a minute to get her talking about the Colonel again. She tells McNally that there are rumors that he goes to those 'special adult' theaters in the east side of Fayetteville. He goes to the kind of theater where someone can buy a ticket and stay all night. These are theaters that have two uses, to get charged up or sleep off a drunk. After he pumps her for a little intelligence, McNally thinks he should treat her well, she probably knows a lot more. After all, she is a waitress and has to take so much crap in life, especially from Col. Massengill. He asks, "Where would you like to go?"

She responds to him, "Are we going to get a burger or pizza?"

McNally smiles and tells her, "Anywhere you want is fine, you are worth so much more than that. Just choose a restaurant and we will go there."

She says, "Would the Tutwiler Café be ok, I love the Trout Almondine."

McNally responds with a smile and asks, "Which way?"

She tells him to make a right and at 13:37 they are sitting down in a nice dining room that one could tell was once a cafeteria. She seems to forget all about the Colonel and his harassment and is quite taken with McNally.

McNally knows she will be a good source if he plays this right. He gets up and excuses himself and she holds on to his hand as he pulls away. It is clear no one has ever been truly nice to this girl.

He steps away and walks calmly to the hall by the restrooms so he can make a call with some level of privacy. He phones the now retired Lt. Colonel Hand, and tells him that he is not going to pursue the story with Colonel Massengill but he would like to meet him for a drink and discuss it off the record. Lt. Colonel

Hand reluctantly agrees to meet tonight at 20:00 at a bar and grille outside of Lumberton. The Colonel tells McNally it is east of Lumberton out on 41, and the name of the bar is the Horse Pen. After the short conversation McNally returns to Brandy and they enjoy a nice leisurely meal and some dessert too. She has strawberry shortcake and he has a slice of apple pie a la mode. She spends most of the meal talking and McNally listens intently, absorbing every fact and adding it to the dossier in his mind. She tells him that everyone in town both reveres and fears the Colonel but she did not know why. He is an older, slight, and now a frail shell of the man he once was. She did not understand why people of this town hold him in such high regard when there are so many rumors about the seedy and deceitful life he leads. Both cannot be true.

She says, "He cannot be a pillar of the community and a perverted man at the same time. One has got to be a façade. No one tries to make people think that they are both a gentleman and a scoundrel."

He tells her not to get so worked up. He says, "I have found that people eventually get what is coming to them, the old adage of what goes around comes around seems to always come true in the end."

She smiles and softly says, "Well John I hope you are right."

Brandy and McNally leave together and go back to the Breakfast Nook restaurant where she works so he can drop her at her car. It is now 16:00 and the restaurant is closed because they only served breakfast and lunch and close at 14:30.

McNally gets out, walks around the explorer, opens the door for her, and walks with her the few steps around the side of the building to her vehicle. She hugs him and then, very surprisingly, reaches up and gives him a deep passionate kiss.

McNally is not expecting this and pulls away a little but then settles in and thinks, "What the hell?" He knows she is a good source and will do anything he might ask of her. Then he thinks to himself, he is not that kind of operator. If he feels anything for this girl it will be genuine. It has been too long and he has been without human touch or compassion because of his work. Maybe since she is far enough from where he lives, but close enough to be within driving distance, this might be the perfect situation. He could actually allow himself the pleasure of a woman's touch again.

They break their embrace, he brushes her hair out of her eyes and puts his finger gently under her chin, "How would you like to have lunch again tomorrow baby doll?"

Her gleaming green eyes dance and she tells him, "YES. John I had the best time I have had in years today and I would really like to see you again."

He hands her a business card that reads John McNally industrial equipment sales and has a phone number. He tells her, "If I don't come by at 12:30 give me a buzz at the number on the card." The number is one of the burn phones he had picked up for this job and couldn't be traced so there is no danger. He kisses her again as she gets in her car. He then gets in his explorer to go fuel it up. He wants to make sure it is topped off as he is heading straight from there to drive to Lumberton.

The drive is about an hour and he should be there by 17:40, which will give him plenty of time to recon the area to make sure he has more than one way out of the Horse Pen bar if things go wrong. Never have only one way out, McNally has a set of rules. The number one rule he lives by is that three is two, two is one, and one is none. He finds this is true for lots of things, but paramount for weapons, plans, and exit strategies.

Chapter 4

Coswell drives south and while thinking over everything that has become immensely more complicated, he realizes there is nothing simple and straight forward about this job. He wasn't just going to kill a target, but a man who was awarded the CMH. He still needs to find out more about that man. That is reason for the drive to Lumberton. He needs to find out who is telling him more of the truth, because no one ever tells the whole truth. It may be what they think is the truth, but from their point of view, even truth always has a bias and prejudice to it.

Something else is eating at the back of his mind, it is Brandy. He knows that he can tell himself she is just a source all he wants to, but that isn't the truth and as the old saying goes 'to thy own self be true.' He knows she adores him for his strength and character and of course he couldn't lie. He thinks she is very sweet and uncommonly attractive to him. Is it the distance? Is it the fact that he can see her from where he lives in just a few short hours, but still keep her at an arms length of distance because she didn't have the means to do the same? He can

47

figure that out later. Coswell needs to center his thoughts and get ready for his encounter with Colonel Hand. If this goes well he will know which story is the truth, and maybe find out that one thing that has been bothering him about Louise Wilson's story. Coswell hopes that this visit ties up all the loose ends but things always seem to unravel further down the line.

He pulls into the town of Lumberton at 17:50 and goes looking around at the local general merchandise store. He shops in the hunting and fishing area and decides to buy a short flip open buck knife, a ball cap and a field and stream magazine. He stops at a local pizza joint and has a slice of sausage pizza and a beer. Around 19:00, he drives out to the Horse Pen bar. He enters the bar at 19:30, wearing faded jeans, his camouflage cap, a pair of old boots, and a red flannel shirt. When he walks in to the small roadside bar he blends in like the wallpaper, which it looks like it has been there since the Eisenhower years. He sits at the short end of the bar facing the entrance with a full length mirror to his left so he can glance at it and view the whole bar. The pool tables are over his right shoulder and after having a cold one he goes and shoots a couple of games by himself.

Soon an older distinguished man, with his hair high and tight, comes into the bar and sits at the corner of the bar, right next to the spot where Coswell had been drinking. Coswell finishes his shot at the eight ball, puts the cue back in the rack on the wall, and walks over to the bar. Coswell sits beside the older man at the short end of the bar.

"Colonel Hand?" Coswell asks and the man looks at him for a moment and nods.

The Colonel asks, "How about we go to the corner table on the other side of the pool room where there will be more privacy and no one to eavesdrop?"

Coswell agrees and buys another round. The two men walk over to the dark corner away from the bar and the other patrons. The Colonel looks at Coswell and he can see the torment in the Colonel's eyes. There is a story to be told and Hand may have the missing pieces that help Coswell in his decision that has turned out to be not so cut and dry.

Coswell tells the Colonel, "From two other sources, not including you, there have been two distinctly different stories about Lt. Colonel Leslie Massengill." He asks Colonel Hand, "So what is the real story Colonel?"

Hand slowly drinks his double scotch on the rocks and before he begins he asks, "Are you sure you want to know? Most everyone that has known the truth in the past has conveniently seemed to pass away."

Coswell nods, "Go on."

Hand tells him, "I was green for an investigator put on a CMH case. It was the first one I had ever investigated and I wanted it done right. All along the brass wanted it wrapped up quickly. They wanted a nice neat story and they knew the outcome before it even started. At every turn when there was an issue, or something that didn't add up, my commander told me to streamline it. He said we need a wholesome American hero because the Vietnam War isn't being perceived well and the people needed a CMH award winner who doesn't have his widow accept the award for him posthumously."

Hand did background investigation on Captain Leslie D. Massengill and those who had served with him in the past did not speak highly of him.

Hand says, "Those that served under him gave vanilla answers to the questions asked, because they did not want their statements to get back to Massengill and create advancement issues for them. One of the

Gunnies did say something because let's face it they tell it like it is. One of the Gunnery Sergeants said he didn't know what the D stood for but if there was any justice in the world it was Douche. No one seemed to like Massengill, no one respected him, or had anything positive to say."

"Finally after doing the background I got to speak to Corporal Roosevelt because he was well enough to give his testimony. Roosevelt told me a carbon copy of the official story. It was so similar to Captain Massengill's story that I know the story had been rehearsed."

Coswell sits and thinks while he listens then asks, "What about the Captain's wound to his shoulder?"

Hand continues, "That was what bugged me. I asked Roosevelt about that. He told me that he was unconscious when it happened but it must have been the same enemy fire that wounded him. He did comment that the Captain's wound did seem to be much more traumatic for an SKS rifle wound but he didn't know what to think of it."

The Colonel had already finished his double scotch so he waved at the bartender to bring him another.

Coswell asks Hand, "Are you sure you don't want to slow down?"

The Colonel responded by stating, "I am marine, no one asks a marine if they have had too many because it's nobody's Goddamn business how much they have had to begin with."

Coswell thinks to himself, 'This guy is a good source but I can't let him go on breathing because he has seen me. Maybe the alcohol will take care of that for me.'

Hand keeps going, it seems to Coswell, he has wanted to get this story off his chest for years and a battalion couldn't stop him now.

Hand goes back to Roosevelt, "Corporal Roosevelt was the only living witness and I had recorded his complete statement but when I went back three days later to try and clear up the issue about how Captain Massengill's shoulder injury had been one that created such concussion and trauma to his shoulder I was informed by the ICU staff at Bethesda that he had succumbed to his wounds and died. When I asked how long he was in ICU they told me three weeks and he was scheduled for release in five days. I asked what he died of and the staff told me the autopsy was not done but should be available in three days. They assumed I would drop it and leave it at that, I didn't. When I spoke to the Medical Examiner he told me that the patient had died of cardiac arrest caused by asphyxiation. That was puzzling as that had nothing to do with his wounds. I checked the visitation log and twenty minutes before he went into cardiac arrest he was visited by his squad commander. That was Captain Leslie Massengill. No charges were ever filed but I have a sneaking suspicion he got rid of the one man who knew the truth about what really happened that night on the battlefield. My theory is that when he went to 'visit' Roosevelt he turned off his oxygen and since Roosevelt was unconscious went into cardiac arrest and succumbed to death in his weakened state. There is no way to prove that theory though. None of the Bethesda Hospital staff checked if the oxygen was on or off initially and it was assumed it was turned off after the dead body was removed. Either way this case just got more and more unclear the deeper I researched it."

"When I brought up the point to the commission for the Congressional Medal of Honor that the only eye witness had passed away, they only asked if I took a complete statement from him. When I told them 'Yes' they told me it was good enough and they fast tracked the award through."

The Colonel was now on his fourth double scotch and becoming even looser with facts that had been secret for too long. Next Colonel Hand delved into the personal side of Colonel Massengill.

"I questioned some of the other marines he was serving with and as long as they weren't in his chain of command they were forthcoming and frankly were painfully honest about what they thought. There was a Captain that I couldn't have used as a witness, because his black market connections made him easily impeachable. Massengill had caught him smoking a pipe full of hash, and rather than bring him up on charges, he had the Captain supply him with LSD and two Vietnamese hookers for a weekend furlough. Massengill knew how to get what he wanted and was a masterful blackmailer when he was in Vietnam."

"I don't know if he still has those skills but I would bet he brought those back stateside with him. I am sure they served him well even after the war. He was so rapidly promoted from Captain all the way to Colonel. There had to be ...." the Colonel was starting to drift off and his eyes were now bloodshot and drooping. After five double scotch whiskeys most men would have died of alcohol poisoning.

Coswell walks up to the bartender and asks if he can brew a pot of coffee. The bartender put on the coffee and tells Coswell, "It will be ready in five minutes."

After standing at the bar for the five minutes, the bartender pours a cup of black coffee in a thick white ceramic mug with a navy anchor on the side. He hands the cup to Coswell, and he walks back over to the Colonel and wakes him up. He hands him the coffee and he starts to drink it and perks up a little.

Hand continues, "As I was saying, Massengill always got what he wanted. The only time anything meant something to the Colonel, was when he profited personally. He served in the marines but didn't live by their code of unit, corps, God, and country. If he believed in Semper Fi it was only to be faithful to his own selfish pleasures."

The bartender walked over and set down a plate of chicken wings and onion rings and the Colonel asks Coswell "What's this?"

Coswell responded, "I wanted something to snack on and you looked like you could use a meal, other than scotch, which you have had a lot of tonight."

The Colonel tells Coswell thanks and starts to eat ravenously. Coswell thinks he is going to choke because he hasn't seen anyone eat that much, that quickly, in such a short period of time. He clears the plate of chicken wings and onion rings in moments and all that is left is just bones lying on the plate.

"Well I guess I was hungrier than I thought. Thanks for the meal and the scotch but I am done for the night. I can't think of anything else pertinent to the case and it is getting late."

Coswell looks at his watch and it reads 00:47. It was almost 01:00 and Coswell still has to drive back to Fayetteville that night. He has the dilemma that the Colonel can I.D. him if things with the target go bad and authorities start poking around into this case. He decides that Colonel Hand is a good source, he doesn't know his real name, and he is an apparent drunk that will be no problem to discredit so there is no reason to kill this man. Hand has enough demons and in the darkness one night they will all catch up to him and drag him down to his own personal hell, of this Coswell is sure.

Coswell thanks Colonel Hand, stands and lays $200.00 on the table, he tells Hand "This is the standard for what I pay for exclusive material and I think it is only fair after hearing such a story." The Colonel looks at him for a moment with a flash of rage, as if Coswell has insulted his honor, but then picks up the two bills folds them over and pushes them down in his pocket. Coswell walks by the bar and asks what the tab is and the barkeep tells him the total is 42.00. He gives him a fifty and tells him to keep the rest. Coswell is thinking to himself, 'What sort of cheap rot gut was the Colonel drinking?'

As he walks along the long bar towards the door he hears the bustle of the few patrons left in the bar and the screech of a chair on the wooden floor. Coswell pulls on the door, looks over his shoulder back in the direction of Colonel Hand and knows the demons have come for his soul. Colonel Hand is standing at attention, as if on a parade ground. When Coswell's eyes meet with Hand's he hears, "1st Lt. R. William

Hand reporting with my completed report sir! Forgive me sir, for not having the strength to stand up for the honor of the corp."

The patrons around him are all puzzled and bewildered by his behavior and his psychotic break from reality.

Just then Hand draws his 1911 Colt .45 service side arm from its holster beneath his long sleeve shirt, and places it to his right temple. The last thing Coswell sees is the body drop as the contents of Hand's skull are distributed across the full length mirror behind the bar. Coswell has a number of thoughts flash through his mind right then. The most prevalent thought being that the Colonel had not lied to him. Everyone who was a witness or knew the real truth about Colonel Leslie Massengill was dead, all except Coswell of course. He also thought that it was fitting Colonel Hand had a last meal but at least he is free now.

Chapter 5

Coswell climbs back into his explorer and reassumes the persona of John McNally, the sweet but strong industrial equipment salesman Brandy Potter finds irresistible.

After what seems like a long drive down the darkened hollows south of Fayetteville, John McNally arrives back in Cedar Creek at 0230 in the morning. After this long day he is exhausted. He parks the explorer around the corner of the building at the Shady Elms Motel, walks the short distance to the door, takes one quick look around, and steps inside for the evening. He bolts the door and wedges a wooden chair under the doorknob. The extra precaution is two fold. He knows he will sleep soundly and does not want any disturbances, and he wants to create a further obstacle for anyone that might try to enter unexpectedly. As he drowsily lays his Webley 45ACP revolver, which is his main firearm, on the nightstand beside him, he thinks 'You can never be too careful.' Then he kicks his boots off and crawls into bed. He sets his alarm for 10:30 and is asleep in moments. Tomorrow he will get a little later start, but this job may take longer than first anticipated. Things have become more complicated. They have begun to clear up from a consistency of muddy water to that of an opaque milk jug.

The morning comes soon enough and with the sunrise a new plan is born. McNally looks over what must be done and realizes this plan will take considerably more time. He calls the Holiday Inn in Columbia, where he is registered as James Winchester, and informs the desk there how much he is enjoying his vacation to Columbia. He asks if it is possible to keep his room for an extended stay beyond the seven days for which it is reserved. The courtesy desk tells him that the room has been reserved for another guest starting next week but luckily they have vacancies and can transfer the arriving guest to another room with equal or upgraded amenities. James Winchester thanks the desk personnel and requests that they reserve his room on an open ended status as he needs a place to stay and is considering house hunting in the area for a permanent move to South Carolina. The desk informs him that should not be a problem. James Winchester is taken care of, Coswell thinks to himself. Now just decide what John McNally will do.

McNally gets up and showers. He lets the steamy water roll down his neck and back and with it the tension this case has created flows away. So many facts swirl in McNally's head but all the pieces are beginning to make sense. McNally is getting ready to meet Brandy for lunch. He plans to pick her up at the Breakfast Nook restaurant around 12:30. As McNally steps out of the shower he looks at the clock hanging on the wall, it reads 11:15, this gives him plenty of time to get ready and drive over to the restaurant in Cedar Creek. McNally pulls on a pair of stonewashed jeans, a dark blue button down collar shirt, his riding boots, and a leather vest. It is a little cooler outside, but the vest is primarily to conceal his Webley .45ACP revolver he wears over his right hip. He steps outside, takes a quick look around and walks to the explorer. He climbs in the explorer, starts it up and drives toward the restaurant. He stops on the way to fuel up the SUV again. Last night he had burned ½ a tank of gas, but the facts uncovered by the trip were well worth the endeavor.

McNally parks in front of the diner, it is 12:15. He shuts off the engine gets out and walks in to wait at the counter. He can immediately tell when he sees Brandy something has upset her. The pink tracks of tears can be seen as they have run through her expertly applied make-up. McNally looks over at the corner and sees Colonel Massengill sitting there, basking in his own perceived greatness. He knows this bastard is the cause of Brandy's pain and he so much wants to kill him for that reason alone. McNally however holds back, he cannot unleash Coswell in such a public and open place. There will be a time and a reckoning McNally thinks to himself.

From the counter where McNally sits he can see Colonel Massengill. He distinctly hears a conversation but no one else is in the booth with him. McNally thinks maybe a phone call on one of those damn Bluetooth devices but upon a second look that also comes up empty.

Brandy walks out from behind the counter and over to McNally and smiles because he seems to be a genuinely caring man and she believes he truly cares for her.

McNally put his arms around Brandy and asks, "Have you been crying?"

She says, "Yes, I probably look awful don't I?"

"No Brandy, you look fine, why were you crying?"

"It is Colonel Massengill, it probably seems simple to everyone else but he was harassing my two best friends while I was serving him."

"I have been friends with these two sisters ever since we were in high school. They are twins, Cheryl and Madison Bridger. Both of them have blonde hair and grey-blue eyes and always turn the guy's heads, even today. They just left about ten minutes before you arrived. He was staring at them while they were eating and went over to their table. He spoke to them venomously and said, 'You girls shouldn't dress so cheaply. Apparently your clientele isn't upper class. Why don't you girls come to a party I am throwing and entertain my buddies. I am sure you will like how generous they are with their donations.' This upset me that he was treating my friends like a couple of hookers. He thinks since both of them have fabulous bodies they should be happy to perform at one of his stag parties. The sisters have normal lives and jobs, they are not sluts but he thinks all women are sluts."

"This upset the twins so much that they left immediately without paying and were both at the point of tears. When I told the manager what had happened he told me that Colonel Massengill is one of our VIP customers. Then he told me that the twin's breakfast would be coming out of my check."

McNally put his arms around Brandy and hugs her. She lays her head on his broad chest and listens to his powerful heart beating. She thinks at that moment, I hope this man is not like so many others. I hope he is genuine. She has a faint hope that he could possibly love her.

That thought is broken by Colonel Massengill's boisterous tone.

McNally asks Brandy, "Who is the Colonel talking to?"

Brandy responds, "Pastor Timothy Michaelson sitting in the booth behind him. I know it is weird, he doesn't even have the common courtesy to turn around and face the person he is talking to."

"That is weird." McNally exclaims. "What were they talking about?"

"The Pastor, he used to be a Marine Chaplain, invited him to a poker game down at the VFW post at the edge of town. They have one every Tuesday night and it starts about 8:00 pm and goes until…."

"Isn't that strange for the Chaplain to be organizing the poker game?"

"Well he's not only a Chaplain, but a former marine. He spends a lot of time down at the VFW with the other retired vets since his wife passed away. She died in an auto accident two years ago and the Chaplain was driving. Now the only part of her he has left is his fifteen year old daughter Chastity. Anyway Colonel Massengill told him he could make it but wouldn't be there until after 21:00. That's 9:00 pm right?"

McNally smiles and says, "Yes Brandy, now let's get you out of here so you can relax a little."

McNally thinks in the back of his mind that he can pick up the Colonel's trail at the VFW about 22:00, until then he can allow himself the pleasure of Brandy Potter's company. He has to make sure he is careful, he needs to keep his head clear. Falling in love with this girl could be so easy and of course an enjoyable adventure in itself, business first with just a sprinkling of pleasure.

He asks Brandy, "Would you like to get some lunch first or maybe go to a matinee?"

Brandy's eyes were swimming over the possibilities, "I would love to go to a movie; I haven't been to one in a couple of years."

"Could we go to the Valparaiso Theater that shows the old classic movies? It is only three dollars to get in and it is a classic old theater with the big red velvet stuffed seats and the big heavy curtain up front. It is really quite an experience and sometimes they show old Hitchcock films."

McNally tells her, "That sounds quite enjoyable, and we will have some dinner afterwards." The movie the theater is showing was a Hitchcock, McNally thought it is quite ironic the film being shown is North by Northwest. This is a film about a man who doesn't exist. The further McNally researched into the details of Colonel Massengill, the more and more the Congressional Medal of Honor award recipient he supposedly is did not seem to exist. The irony was amazing.

Everywhere McNally turns seems to be a reminder that he needs to get back on track and complete the job for which he was hired. Clearly this man deserves to die for the life he led before and the one he is currently forging now.

McNally needs to sit down, clear his head and get something to eat. He has not eaten all day and is drained from the lack of sleep and the day's events. In a gentlemanly fashion McNally had put his arm around Brandy in the movie and Brandy had clung to him like Velcro ever since. They walk from the theater to an upscale pizzeria and she holds his hand tightly. McNally, conflicted now, doesn't know whether to tie his watch or wind his shoes. He knows why he is, for the first time in a long time, indecisive. He is starting to fall for this woman and she already has for him.

They sit together in the restaurant and each table is lit with a small oil lamp. Even though it is a pizzeria the décor has a bit of a romantic allure to it. Much like the theater, the booths are large, comfortable, stuffed seats with gold tassel piping. Some booths are the wrap around type made in a U shape with a round table in the middle of it. The place is eclectic to say the least. In fact, McNally even spots an old Pac-man video game table over in the corner. Those haven't been around in years.

They are seated at one of the wrap around booths and she scoots around next to him, snuggling up to him as they both look at one menu. After studying it for several minutes he asks Brandy, "What looks good to you?"

She looks up at him for a moment and wants to tell him he does but she isn't so bold.

She responds, "The four cheese pizza with salami and Italian sausage here is great."

The waitress looks at Brandy and asks "what would you like to drink?"

Brandy replies, "Ginger Ale and if you don't have that 7UP."

The waitress smiles and rocks her gaze over to McNally who responds, "Blue Moon Belgian on draft."

She turns to take the order to the kitchen but just before asks McNally, "Orange slice?"

He smiles, "You know your beer."

As she leaves, McNally leans over and lightly kisses Brandy. When their lips part she audibly says "Ahh!" just like she has finished a deep drink from an ice cold coke bottle.

He smiles and almost laughs but restrains himself and she asks, "What took you so long? I have been waiting all day for that."

He smiles as he looks into her deep eyes and asks, "Those friends of yours, has Colonel Massengill given them any trouble before?"

Brandy replies, "He is such an awful man, he is so condescending and offensive to all the women that come in the restaurant."

"Let's not talk about him, what did you think of the movie?"

McNally smiles and responds, "That is one of my all time favorite Hitchcock films. The mystery and suspense surrounding George Kaplan is a woven fabric that appears seamless. I love how he is chased and put into so many close calls with danger only to blunder out of them and cause more havoc."

Brandy smiles while she looks up at his soft brown eyes. She squeezes his arm with her hand and lays her head upon his shoulder.

The waitress stops by the table and delivers McNally's Blue Moon Belgian Ale and a tall iced glass of Seagram's Ginger Ale to the lovely Brandy. The waitress tells Brandy and McNally their food is coming out momentarily.

When she steps away Brandy speaks.

"Yeah I really liked it too. The romance in those old films seems to be purer and not cheap and tawdry like newer movies today."

Just then the waitress returns with a pizza pie that smells wonderful. McNally can distinctly smell the spices in the sauce and the aroma of warm baked cheese fills the booth. The waitress sets the pizza down with two heavy white ceramic plates and a pizza server and tells the couple, "Bon Appétit."

McNally serves a piece to Brandy. As he pulls it away from the concentric circle of the rest of the pie long strings of gooey white cheese drip down and hang over the edge of the plate on which he sets it. He takes the server and cuts them and scoops the cheese strings over the top of the piece. This pizzeria was a fabulous choice for dinner. He in turn serves himself a slice and both of them eat the first slice quickly.

McNally is really beginning to like Brandy and how simple her outlook is on life. Just a few simple pleasures in life and she is gleeful like a schoolgirl. He wishes he could be that way but there are so many issues pressing on him now. There is so much turmoil from his past that makes McNally always vigilant for his own preservation.

They sit and eat for a little over an hour. He finds that just the simple fact of her presence relaxes him and eases his tension.

After paying the waitress, and telling her how much they enjoyed the meal, he looks down at his watch. It reads 19:45.

He asks Brandy "Would you like to go for a drive?"

She smiles, her smile is so electric when she is with McNally.

"Yes I would love to, but we can't be too late because I work early tomorrow."

"We should be back by about 21:00, is that ok?"

She thinks, "That's 9:00 right? That will be fine."

They drive out a country road, stop by a field and park. McNally parks up on a hill, opens the sunroof and they recline their seats staring at the stars.

"The sky is so clear tonight. Is it always like this?"

"Yes once you get out on these dark country roads the light from the city doesn't block out the stars."

McNally responds, "It looks like there are millions more stars than the ones you see in the city. This reminds me of when I was in the service there were nights I would look up in the desert sky and the stars were so vast you could see the milky way."

71

Brandy says, "I wish I could have seen that."

McNally smiles, "It was a beautiful sight in a sea of ugliness. I would have preferred to see it without the war….."

He asks, "Do you know astronomy, constellations and such?"

She looks down, "No."

"Nothing to be ashamed of, would you like me to point some out?"

"Yes, that would be nice."

McNally tells her about Ursa Major and Ursa Minor, the big dipper and the little dipper, points out Cassiopeia, the lady in the rocking chair, and then he pauses a moment. Finally, he looks up and tells her the next constellation has always had significance for him, he points out Orion, the hunter, this is his favorite constellation. He seems to identify with it for some reason.

Brandy looks at McNally and says, "I am having a great time, but I do need to get home soon."

McNally looks at his watch again, it is 20:45. He returns their seats to the upright position, closes the sunroof, and spins the motor to life. He then begins the drive back to the Breakfast Nook so he can drop her off.

When they arrive at Brandy's car she sheepishly asks, "You aren't tired of me yet are you?"

McNally says, "No. In fact I want to see a lot more of you as well."

"Well, I do not work on Thursday, why don't we skip lunch tomorrow and we can have a real date. How would you like to come to my house tomorrow night and I will make you dinner?"

McNally thinks for a moment, "Yes that sounds good. What is your address and what time should I be there?"

Brandy tells him, "How about 7:30 pm at my house? It is at 325 Saint Mary Street. It is only about ten minutes from here."

McNally smiles at her. He will follow up on Colonel Massengill during the day and chase down some leads before his dinner rendezvous.

Chapter 6

Brandy cannot seem to go to sleep once John has left her that night. The thought of him swims around her head and she is elated with this new man who is both mysterious and chivalrous. Where have men like this been her whole life? Is he too good to be true? She comes from a small town and is a bit naïve, but he seems to be a genuinely decent man. He is more worldly and well traveled, but does not seem condescending at all even know she is just a small town girl. This is a man that she believes could have true potential and maybe they could even fall in love. She has been hurt before but cannot live in fear. She knows that if she does not take a chance when she thinks the real thing has come along she will never find that true love that she believes exists for everyone. Then again she is getting way ahead of herself. She needs to proceed cautiously in this endeavor, but only if she can keep control of her feelings. Brandy lies back on her queen size pillow top bed and just lets the feeling of a wonderful night sink in. It is the first wonderful night she has had in as long as she can remember and she decides to just savor the moment. She thinks of this night and compares it in her mind to eating a ripe peach in early summer, and how she feels when she just lets the juices run down from the corners of her full lips. She feels like a teenager again just home from that first wonderful date. The beginning to a relationship is always so new and special, she needs to rein back these feelings, and not go headlong into something with a man she barely knows.

Soon enough, and from near emotional exhaustion, she fades away and the morning sun wakes her like it was all a dream. When she wakes up the next morning it is as if she spent last night in a different world. The first thing that comes to mind, after the thought of John McNally is the last scene from another old movie, The Wizard of Oz.

However while Brandy spent her night wildly dreaming about a fairytale relationship that is far from a consummated reality there were other dark realities at work. While McNally and Brandy enjoyed their after dinner moment the night before evil was lurking about in the shadows.

Chapter 7

At approximately 20:20 a black Chrysler 300 sedan drives down a quiet neighborhood street. The sedan makes a left turn onto Lourdes Avenue. The driver parks the dark sedan in the shadows under a large oak tree. The driver kills the engine and the lights go dark. In a moment, a thin man emerges from the driver's side and quickly moves along the dark empty street. He is wearing a dark black wind breaker jacket covering a black mock turtle neck, black slacks, black leather shoes, and full finger Italian leather driving gloves. He is carrying a small leather bag in his right hand. He slinks down the sidewalk from shadow to shadow. The faint light of a streetlight illuminates the name on the mailbox as he passes it. It reads Michaelson, 1140 Lourdes Avenue. This house is a single story brick home, not small but not too extravagant either. It is probably a three or four bedroom house, but one cannot tell from the street. The living room and kitchen face the street and the bedrooms are in the back of the floor plan as well as a den one would presume.

The thin man sneaks around the corner, slowly creeping down the brick side of the house to the one room that has light shining out the window. He slowly and quietly peers into the corner of the window. A young girl, on the brink of womanhood, lies on her stomach with her large stereo headphones over her ears. She is deeply entranced in the music, bobbing her head and kicking her feet back and forth in the air behind her in sort of a scissoring pattern. An evil and ever widening smile dances across the face of the thin man covered in black. He peers past the queen size bed she is laying on and over to the open door opposite the window he is peering through. The evil man thinks, 'Chastity no more.' This makes him almost gitty as he sneaks further around to the back corner of the brick home. He peers into the darkened room through the window and sees what seems to be an unused guest room. Just below the window and perhaps eighteen inches away is the outside A/C compressor unit. He sets his bag upon the unit, opens it and withdraws a flat steel putty knife. He slides it up between the window panes and easily jimmies the lock to the window and raises it slowly the full thirty inches of travel. He returns the putty knife to his kit withdraws a cotton ski mask and puts it on. He climbs up on the A/C unit and lowers the bag into the room, next he climbs through the window. Knowing he is so close to his prey he makes less noise than a spider weaving a web in the cotton. He quietly removes the chloroform and rag from his bag and moves towards the door. From the darkness of the guest room doorway he sees the lit bedroom one door down the hall. A tender, innocent, beautiful young woman lies on the bed with her back to him and completely unaware. She is still completely enveloped in the country CD that is playing on her stereo through the large headphones. In a swift, quick motion he moves into the room, pins her to the bed, and covers her mouth with the chloroform soaked rag. Moments later her supple body lies limp on the bed. He steps back into the other room and retrieves his bag. Quickly and quietly, with the efficiency of a Swiss watch maker, he returns and strips the young woman naked on her queen size bed. He reaches in the bag and produces a set of sex shackles. He shackles her hands above her, he attaches the shackles with a long chain to her ankles and loops the chain over the large wooden headboard of the bed so her ankles are up near her neck. He thinks, ' Isn't it nice how the young are so flexible.'

He blindfolds her and stuffs her panties embroidered with the name 'Chastity' in her mouth and covers her mouth with clear packing tape.

He is ready now; he dims the lights in the room, reaches in the bag and produces a vial of aromatic ammonia. He pops the smelling salts and puts it under her nose. She stirs but cannot begin to free herself.

Young Chastity's eyes are full of fear and rage. She wonders 'What is happening and is this man going to kill me?'

He tells her in a gruff voice, "I woke you for a reason; you need to remember your first time."

For the next half hour he sexually tortures her and culminates the experience which takes her innocence and makes him reach climax quickly too. He makes sure to use protection, and thoroughly clean her naked skin everywhere before leaving her chained in the precarious position.

He quietly leaves the same way he entered, leaving nothing but the restraints and destruction of a young soul behind. He gets in the dark sedan and without turning on the lights leaves the neighborhood. Once out on the main road he activates the lights, he makes a stop at the local good will thrift store to donate his clothes and deposit any proof of his presence in the outside donation box. He puts on his change of clothes, Brogans, jeans, a casual bowling shirt, and a fedora hat with a small red feather. He deposits the ski mask in a dumpster that will be picked up late that night, and calmly drives to the poker game at the VFW.

Colonel Leslie Massengill arrives at the VFW about 21:15 and sits down across from Chaplain Timothy Michaelson. Chaplain Michaelson says, "Leslie, what kept you?"

The Colonel responds, "One of my mares at the farm is in season and I was getting her ready for breeding."

"Is it Lady Jane that has come into season?"

"No. This is a new mare, first time in season, her name is Cherry Blossom."

Massengill sits looking at Chaplain Michaelson as they play 7-stud, nothing wild. Chaplain Michaelson is a shorter man, maybe five foot seven inches tall with a slight build and weighs about one hundred and forty pounds. He has a thin pale face short sandy blonde hair and wears the round wire rim glasses just like were issued to him when serving as an active marine.

Although he is a Chaplain he is also one hell of poker player.

It is the Colonel's deal and he calls a game of high Chicago. He is dealt pocket aces, one of which is the Ace of Spades worth half the pot. Chaplain Michaelson bets 3 dollars right out of the gate.

Massengill gives him a sardonic smile, as if he is the joker planning to kill batman. Michaelson bumps the bet, and Massengill smiles more intently, he thinks, 'Go ahead and bet big. You are just paying me for raping your daughter.'

Massengill then grunts, "Raise."

The Chaplain is the only one left in at this point and can't beat the Colonel's three aces and the ace of spades to boot.

The Chaplain is holding the king of spades.

Massengill says, "Close but this isn't horseshoes, hand grenades, or heavy artillery, better luck next time." as he smiles and drags the pot.

It is 22:00 and the poker game is taking a smoke break.

McNally walks through the door of the VFW and over to the bar. He sits so he can look one way at the door and the other at the entrance to the poker room. He orders a Bud Light on draft and sips his cold beer among the veterans, most of which are honorable men. He knows one in the VFW is truly a scum bag. He sits and drinks his beer over the course of the night. McNally looks around the old bar, dark mahogany paneling covers the walls with large wooden crown molding. The crown molding is the intricately carved type that was installed in buildings forty to fifty years ago. The rest of the décor matches that time period with high backed bar stools, brass rails around the edge of the bar and a rail near the floor to rest your feet. McNally is surprised there are not brass spittoon buckets at the corners of the bar and the room.

The game resumes and the players file back into the poker room. The next couple of hours are uneventful and McNally decides to head back to the hotel and get a fresh start in the morning.

Chapter 8

The next morning Coswell wakes up early, at 0600 and turns the television on while he gets ready for the day. Just as he is stepping into the shower the local Fayetteville news reports on a breaking story.

The newscaster says, "At 2 a.m. last night the police were called to Lourdes Avenue in the small town of Cedar Creek outside of Fayetteville. A local man and former marine arrived home from a social event at the local VFW to find a horrifying scene. His young fifteen year old daughter was chained to her bed and in a hysterical state. According to officers, the man was unable to free her, and she was still bound when police arrived. The local fire department had to be called to cut the stainless steel shackles off of the young woman."

The reporter continues, "She told the police that just before nine she was in her bedroom and an intruder came in and attacked her. The next thing she knew she woke up naked and chained. After some coaxing the police were able to obtain a full statement from her, in this statement she verified that she had been raped and sodomized.

There is one possible witness; an eighty-four year old woman living across the street thinks she may have seen a dark sedan. She described it as a black car like an undercover police car. The names of the victim and her family are currently being withheld."

The reporter closes with "This is Mason Knight reporting live in Cedar Creek."

The news anchors had some pandering comments of false empathy but media types are always like that.

Coswell's mind is a flash of red, could he have prevented this? If he would have been watching the Colonel, instead of indulging in his own pleasures, the fifteen year old victim may still have been an innocent girl today. He showers expeditiously and is ready to meet the day. He drives through Cedar Creek and runs through a local drive through for a biscuit and coffee, avoiding the Breakfast Nook this morning. Next he turns his vehicle toward the Colonel's small farm out on Cedar Village Way to find out more about this man.

Colonel Massengill is a man of routine. Once again he sits on his porch at his outdoor table and sips coffee in his robe. He sits there till just after 09:30

reading his morning paper and reveling in his victories of last night.

Coswell sits well out of view of the Colonel and watches him, taking photos with his Nikon camera. He watches Massengill through the big telephoto lens and wonders if he will be going to brunch at 11:30 as usual.

The Colonel goes into his house and emerges at 11:10, cleaned up, dressed and ready for his day. He climbs into the Jeep Wrangler and drives away. He drives in the opposite direction from Coswell. He then thinks, 'This is my chance.' He leaves the truck and sneaks down the quarter mile long driveway to the house. His heart is pounding and he can feel his pulse in his ears. He controls his breathing and his excitement too. He is calm when reaching the front steps and he walks up on the porch. He rings the doorbell and of course no one answers. He removes his lock pick set from his jacket then quickly and masterfully picks the lock to the front door. He looks around and thinks that such a depraved man should not have such a life of ease. This man is a coward, a pervert, a scoundrel and Coswell suspects him to also be a rapist. In the front of the house there is a nice den with all his military awards in shadowbox frames. The

Congressional Medal of Honor is the centerpiece in a lighted shadowbox frame with UV glass in it. The plaque below it that reads, 'For conspicuous gallantry above and beyond the call of duty the Congressional Medal of Honor is awarded to Captain Leslie D. Massengill on October 23rd 1972'. McNally thinks, 'Anniversary coming up real soon Colonel.'

Also in this room is the Colonel's gun collection. It ranges from his Vietnam service sidearm, a 1911 Colt Commander, to an old lever action Spencer Rifle that the union used as a cavalry gun. He of course had Colt and Smith & Wesson revolvers, a couple of Winchester bolt action model 70's, Benelli and Franchi shotguns, even a Holland and Holland English double rifle in .303 British. That one alone must have set him back fifteen thousand dollars or more. Coswell thinks this seems a little too extravagant even for a retired Marine Colonel. Something else is going on here; this Colonel has got to be into something sinister.

Coswell thinks back to what Louise Wilson, the Colonel's estranged wife, told him over the phone. He is an evil man, he needs killing, right then Coswell believes not only is that true, but Louise Wilson had no idea to what kind of man she had been married.

Coswell looks at his Seiko diver's watch, it's hands read 11:48, he needs to hurry up and plant the microwave bug so he can keep tabs on the Colonel from his phone and have ears inside as well as eyes on the outside of the house. He plants it on the bottom of a brass lamp by the phone in the den.

Before Coswell leaves he decides to take one quick look around, most of the house is fairly normal, but there is a room in the back that seems completely separated from all the others. He opens the heavy steel door, maybe this is a panic room. When the door is opens, Coswell immediately knows why the sight of this man sickens him so much. In the center of the room there is a bed with black satin sheets, around it on three sides are straight back leather English style chairs and in one of the corners an old church kneeler with restraints at the top edges, also hanging on a wooden rack against the back wall is a nice over/under shotgun with ammunition on a shelf. He knows right then why the twins were so offended by his invitation to one of his parties. This is his room for rough sex parties.

Coswell closes the door to the room, turns the latch back to lock, and quickly leaves the house exactly the way he found it making sure to lock the front door back. He works his way back up to the explorer and tests the bug frequency from the truck. It is working so he drives a little further away, he does not want Massengill to get suspicious of his vehicle.

Coswell moves about ½ mile further down the road and when he parks he looks at the clock on the radio, it reads 13:10. Just then he sees a cloud of dust coming down the road and pulling into Massengill's driveway. It is the Colonel in his Jeep.

Coswell brings up the app on his phone he has written for microwave reception. In the military one of Coswell's specialties had been microwave communication. He hears the gruff voice of the Colonel and the clinking of a scotch glass and a large crystal decanter. Coswell thinks, 'Little early for hard liquor isn't is Colonel?' He laughs to himself, thinking of Lt. Col. Hand and how he had told Coswell that it was nobody's business how much a marine drinks because he is a Goddamn marine. Coswell overhears a phone call between the Colonel and a man that answers the phone at Willis Hardware. When he answers the phone, "Jim Willis how may I help you?"

"Willie, how the hell are you, you damn Mick?"

"Who the hell, Mass, is that you?"

"Of Course, get the guys together we are having another one soon, you know when and where, right?"

"Yeah, but do you think we should right now?"

"Why not, this is my town…."

The vagueness does not help Coswell at all. Apparently, and unfortunately, Massengill and his "friends" are careful.

Coswell heads back into town to track down a couple of leads. He feels the need to visit the hardware store. When he drives back into town he quickly drives by the diner to make sure Brandy is safe, now that he knows the Colonel is not only a coward but a deviant as well.

Coswell parks in the lot of Willis Hardware and just as he is exiting his vehicle he hears the one thing that he dreads at this point in this case. His satellite phone and private number rings, only one person knows the number to that phone. He reaches in the console removes his Sat phone and answers with the one word, "Coswell…."

As he fears the one word response is returned, "Templar."

"I need your assistance old friend. I'll give you the details upon arrival. Arlington, VA, can you be here tomorrow by 18:00?"

"I will have to leave by 10:00 at the latest, it is the better part of 330 miles."

"See you then, regular place?"

"Yes, Arlington National Cemetery."

Templar had called at such an inconvenient time but they were there to take care of for one, what the other could not.

McNally starts to think about Brandy, should he cancel on her so he could prepare for the trip tomorrow? He thinks to himself, 'I will go back to the hotel and get the basics that are needed. Then I will still have a decent dinner before leaving in the morning.'

McNally returns back to the hotel and there is a notification on his doorknob. He reads it and it is a notice that his payment will run out on this room in another day. He enters his room, opens his luggage and packs a small essentials bag for the trip to Virginia. Next he removes his emergency money from the secret compartment in his luggage and gets out one thousand dollars. He places five hundred in the bag, and the other five hundred in his pocket. He also places a full box of hollow point .45ACP ammo in the bag, pulls out his Webley revolver and breaks open the top to check the ammo in it, the revolver is full up. After he has packed he walks down to the office and the same pale, thin, heroin addict of a clerk is taking care of everything at the Shady Elms Motel. He steps up to the counter and tells him he believes his stay might be a while longer and asks "What are your weekly rates?"

The clerk mumbles, "A hundred and twenty dollars a week, but that includes housekeeping."

"What if you don't want housekeeping?"

"I guess I could do it for ninety dollars, is that cool?"

"I'll give you three hundred and fifty dollars for the rest of this week and three more weeks as long as I am undisturbed."

The clerk stared at the crisp hundreds almost salivating. McNally knew that this money was going straight in his pocket but didn't care because that just means less evidence he was ever there.

The clerk grabbed the money and tells McNally, "Deal."

McNally thinks, 'Three fifty worth of smack is a lot for tonight.'

McNally goes back to his room and lies down for a couple of hours. He hopes this will recharge his body and his mind. When he wakes up at 17:20 he feels refreshed and goes to clean up for his date with Brandy. He takes a long, relaxing shower. Letting the hot water run over his neck and down his back relaxing every muscle in his body. He is looking forward to the evening so much. He needs to wipe the ugliness of that hidden room in the Colonel's house from his memory. He thinks of Brandy and how sweet and tender she is, he wonders if this relationship can have any hope. Is it possible for McNally to have some level of normalcy even if his life is far from it? Surprisingly, McNally vocalizes his thought with, "God I hope so."

He steps out of the shower, dries off, shaves, combs his thick hair, and splashes on some cologne. He walks over to the closet and gets out his boots, black slacks, dark green button down shirt and a camel hair coat. He retrieves his backup piece puts it in his essentials bag and zips it up. McNally sits down, slides his boots on, eases his slacks down over his boots, and for the first time in his long career seems to be dreading the drive to

Arlington in the morning. However, the duty filled soldier that still resides within him knows he will go and be happy to help another brother in arms.

Chapter 9

John McNally carries his bag with him as he walks out to the explorer. He opens up the back glass and drops the bag in the cargo area, and secures the glass. He opens the driver's door, slides in, spins the motor to life, then waits for the engine to warm up. Once warm he turns the cabin control system to heat and sets it at 78 degrees. The past couple of days have begun to have more of a nip in the air. McNally knows they are in October and the Colonel's Award Anniversary is coming. He thinks he will have to do something special for that.

McNally drives out past the Breakfast Nook to the neighborhood where Brandy Potter lives. He turns on Saint Mary Street and drives until he sees her car parked in front of a small wood sided house that is light blue with white trim and shutters. The mailbox has numbers on it and it reads 325 St. Mary Street. It is a quaint house that fits Brandy quite well. In front there is a small picket fence surrounding the front yard and at each end of the front porch there are large hanging plants. It is not a large house but there is nothing rundown or shabby about it either. McNally is impressed with her neatness and how everything is just so.

He parks his vehicle behind hers in the drive and walks up to the large natural oak door. He uses the knocker which is a large lion's head holding a ring in its mouth. He knocks three times and she quickly comes to the door. McNally is quite surprised when she opens it. He normally has seen her in her waitress outfit from the Breakfast Nook and didn't expect a great deal of difference. Her hair has always been up in some way but tonight it is long and straight. He did not know she had hair that long. Her make-up is flawless with the look of the women from the 1940's. She has applied soft alabaster base, ruby red lipstick a dot of rouge on her cheeks, and her eyes are expertly and tastefully done. McNally thinks, 'My, she is beautiful.'

She is wearing a knee length red satin dress and nice sandals that look both comfortable and elegant. She smiles tenderly and asks, "John would you like to come in?"

McNally responds, "Yes, very much so. You look stunning."

"Thank you I tried to dress up a little so I didn't look like I do at work."

"Well I think you look beautiful, although you look nice at work too."

"Thank you John, it is nice of you to say so."

John looked around the small living room and he could tell she was really looking forward to tonight. It was a nice room with a couch, loveseat, and a big stuffed chair. There was a large tube television on a wooden stand with decorative Hummel figurines below it. The flooring is covered with a thick white Berber carpet that has apparently never seen wine stains or grape juice. Everything is pristine but things are taken just one step further to set a certain mood. On the end tables and on the coffee table there are long taper candles with hurricane globes over them. These are the type that almost everyone associates with romance and a romantic dinner or evening. They are not lit yet, but McNally wonders if that is the plan or are they always part of the décor.

McNally asks, "What is that wonderful aroma?"

"That is one of my favorite dishes, Chicken provolone."

"It smells wonderful."

"I hope you like it. I didn't have time to ask you what your preference was when it came to dinner so I took a shot in the dark."

"I'm sure it will be delicious."

Just then, John steps forward, puts his muscular arms around her and looks down into her beautiful eyes. She is so innocent and beautiful. He says, "Thank you for inviting me to dinner. I don't get too many home cooked meals in my line of work."

She looks up at him, "You are welcome, I don't want to cook for many men, but you seem different John."

Just then he leans in and she closes her eyes and tilts her head to the left. He kisses her deeply for what seems like hours but only a minute has passed. When they break their deep kiss she hugs him and lays her head on his chest listening to his beating heart and knowing that John McNally is a good man.

John holds her the whole time thinking, 'This woman is too pure and innocent for a man with my past. Why does she only see the good in me?'

She asks, "Why don't we sit on the love seat for a few minutes while the chicken finishes broiling in the oven? It should take about ten minutes and dinner will be ready."

John tries to think, 'When was the last time he was in this position with a woman?'

He knows it has been years, there have been flings and one night stands but in the past eight years he has never allowed himself to be involved like he is now. He normally doesn't allow this sort of thing; he needs to be in control. It is one of the imperative axioms of his work.

He sits on the love seat and she snuggles up beside him. She puts her head on his right shoulder and runs her right hand across his chest. John, in turn, wraps his strong right arm around her and pulls her in close. They sit quietly and hold each other until the timer goes off for the chicken.

He asks, "Anything I can help with?"

Brandy replies, "Not right now, but I have something you can help with after dinner. By the way what would you like to drink?"

Remembering her order at the pizzeria he asks, "Do you have Ginger Ale?"

She says, "I always keep that handy, I will bring a bottle of Seagram's and two glasses of ice."

When she pulls away to go plate the food, John is compelled to follow her into the kitchen but he remains still.

As she gets up and pulls away from McNally to go to the kitchen he thinks, 'Am I losing my objectivity here? I shouldn't want her to stay, I shouldn't care, but I can't help it.'

She returns momentarily with two glasses filled with ice that look as though they have been chilling in the freezer. She then sets the tray down with the glasses and bottle of Seagram's Ginger Ale on it. She opens the bottle and pours the two tall, thin, cylindrical glasses full. The bubbles dance to the top, popping and fizzing with an almost gleeful excitement.

They sit and have a few sips of ginger ale and then she glides away to check on dinner.

Next to the living room, is a small but elegant dining room, with a dark, cherry, oval table and a dimly lit chandelier hanging above it. There are two taper candles surrounded by glass globes sitting on the table. The table is set for two, with place mats and a complete complement of silverware.

She smiles at John in the living room as she sets a chafing dish down on the table.

"John dinner is served. Would you mind bringing over the drinks?"

"Not at all Brandy."

She sits down and John does as well. Then she reaches over with the silver tongs and places a thin piece of chicken breaded in Italian bread crumbs and covered in provolone on his plate. She then ladles some sauce over the chicken, and finishes it off with a side of wild rice. She does the same on to her plate and then lights the candles on the table. Finally, she walks over to the doorway separating the kitchen from the dining room and turns off the chandelier.

"That isn't too dark is it John?"

McNally responds, "Not at all Brandy."

They eat quietly, not needing words. She stares at his soft brown eyes and he looks back into those sparkling, shimmering, green eyes of hers. The candlelight dances back and forth in the seas of emotion that are her eyes. McNally thinks, 'Control, I can feel my breathing quickening, my pulse becoming more rapid, my God this girl knows how to push the right buttons.'

They finish dinner and she asks, "Would you like for me to put on a record?"

McNally asks, "Record? You have records?"

"Yes my dad was military and brought a console stereo back from Europe."
She says, "I always like how much warmer vinyl sounds than today's digital music."

McNally responds, "I love it too, especially on the tube amps."

She walks into the living room and she goes over to a piece of furniture that McNally had thought was just a credenza. She opens the top and pushes a couple of buttons, as it warms up she reaches under the cabinet and asks, "What type of music?"

McNally responds, "You choose. I trust you."

What plays next sends chills up McNally's spine. One of the first albums he ever acquired, and his favorite song is playing.

He exclaims, "Not many people have the Buckingham Nicks album. I love your choice of album. Frozen Love is such a beautiful song and one of my absolute favorites."

She softly replies, "I wanted to play something so we could slow dance."

John wraps his arms around her and they smoothly sway across the thick Berber carpet in each other's arms. She looks at him in those soft brown eyes and kisses him. She dances with her head on his chest listening to his heart. She lifts her head and gently kisses his neck.

The record comes to an end and they realize they have been dancing for twenty minutes. Next Brandy asks if he will excuse her for a moment. He can make himself comfortable on the couch and she will be right back.

She disappears into the next room behind the living room. McNally politely sits on the couch awaiting her return.

While she is gone, he thinks over how he will have to leave by 10:00 to make the drive to Arlington by 18:00. It is only a shade less than 350 miles to Arlington but there is only about 100 miles that isn't congested with traffic because it is the only main artery from city to city through that area.

His concentration is broken when he hears Brandy's voice from the back room.
She calls, "John can you come help me with something?"

He gets up and walks toward the door leading to the hall. He walks down the short hall to the only room that is lit. It is dimly lit when he walks into the room, and there is a scent of rose and sandalwood in the air.

McNally turns into the doorway simultaneously saying, "How can I help……?"
His exclamation is cut off mid-sentence as he sees a room lit by candles. There is a queen size bed with fresh red linen sheets and a lacy comforter. The floor around the bed is covered with red rose petals and the fragrance of roses fills the room. That however, is not what stopped his speech. Brandy is leaning up against the bedpost with one arm wrapped around it. She is slightly biting her lower lip in a sexy, sultry way and those green eyes are gleaming like Columbian emeralds. She is wearing a long white silk robe with red trim and a red lace corset that has a plunging neckline showing off her cleavage.

She smiles, "Speechless? I hope that is a good thing."

McNally's Camel hair coat is on the floor before he knows it. Then he thinks, 'Don't lose your head.'
He tells Brandy, "Will you excuse me one moment?"

She responds, "Something wrong?"

He tells her, "Not at all. You look ravishing."

McNally steps into the attached rest room, unbuttons his shirt, removes his Webley revolver, and his boots. He stows his gun in one of his riding boots. He quickly opens the medicine cabinet behind the mirror and scans through all of her medications looking for narcotics and anti-psychotic drugs. When he discovers nothing of consequence he steps back into the bedroom.

They are standing next to the bed kissing and gently running their fingers all over each other's bodies. She unbuckles his belt and unbuttons his pants. Her robe drops to the floor and he runs his fingers gently over the back of her neck and then runs his fingers down to her soft cleavage as she finishes removing his shirt. In moments they are in the bed holding each other and staring into one another's eyes. They embrace and deeply kiss and fingers probe gently on perfumed skin. McNally reaches around, unties the corset, and one of Brandy's wishes is a reality. Ever since she met McNally she wanted to know the feeling of her breasts pressing against his broad chest. They make love for what seems like hours, nerve endings tingling and going wild. After her body is madly tingling, she reaches the point that she has been building up to ever since

McNally walked in the door at the Breakfast Nook and immediately treated her like a lady.

Both reach exhaustion and lie together in the queen sized bed holding one another late into the evening.

McNally knows this woman is something special, not just another fling or one night stand. Things have become exponentially more complicated now.

They fall asleep naked in one another's arms. She tells him as they fade off, "John, I don't know about love, but I know you are a caring man and you make my life better."

McNally thinks, 'Complicated to the power of ten. Dammit, I do care about her.'

He sets his phone at the bedside just before going to sleep, and sets the alarm for 09:15. He will have to get up then to be gone by 10:00.

The next morning Brandy wakes at 09:40 to the sound of McNally in the shower. He emerges from the washroom showered and ready for another day. He is dressing when she slides, still naked, from the linen sheets. She steps over to him and presses her naked body against him and deeply kisses him.

"Where do you think you are running off to?"

McNally responds, "I have to go to Nashville today, I will be gone for several days but should be back by the first of next week."

She steps back and immediately covers up. "So you are just going to dash off the next morning after we had such an intimate night?"

"I don't have a choice, I have to take care of some business there. I will be back next week. I enjoyed last night immensely but I travel for my work. I meant to tell you last night but there never seemed an appropriate time."

She sheepishly replies "Oh, so it isn't anything I did?"

McNally responds, "No, just life. I will call you when I get back. Don't know exactly what day I will be back, but should be the first of the week."

She responds, "Did I disappoint you? Are you really coming back?"

"Of course I will be back. Wild horses could not keep me away." With that McNally takes her in his arms, looks in her eyes and kisses her. Without another word he walks to his explorer and climbs in and starts it up. He stops at the truck stop north of town, gases up and has breakfast. He then settles in for the long hectic drive to Arlington. For the first time, in a long time, he feels remorse for lying to someone, especially her. He won't be anywhere near Nashville. He never liked Nashville much, but it feels wrong lying to someone so innocent.

Chapter 10

After John McNally has been gone for more than an hour, Brandy sits on the loveseat and stares blankly out the picture window wondering if the night before was a mistake. Was it too much too fast? Was it just a physical, lustful evening of passion? It seemed like so much more but how could she know for sure?

She sat in a melancholy mood for what seemed like days but was not much more than an hour. Every moment they had together and every small gesture she thought of as such a tender one swirled in her head for what seemed like an eternity. Maybe it was all real. Maybe he was being truthful and it was just another coincidence that he had to leave on the day after their first night of passion. Why did he have to do this now? Why could he not have told her last night and prepared her for this feeling of loss and emptiness? Was he just another man that wanted whatever he could take and then walk away? She had to have more faith and belief in true love and romance if she were ever to hope to one day have a relationship based on love and trust.

Every moment that day passed slowly and the fact it was the day she did not work made it even more unbearable because there was nothing to take her mind off of the fact that he was not there. All she wanted was to be held by the man she had so quickly fallen for, and the only thing she couldn't do that day was be in his arms.

Every record she put on simply brought memories rushing back of slow dancing in her living room. She warmed up lunch but food seemed to have no taste. This woman needed just a gesture, or a word from him to reassure herself. However, she did not hear from him and the sound of his low voice would have done so much to comfort her. The stretch of days from Thursday until the mysterious beginning of the week, whenever he might return, was an eternity that she hoped would pass quickly. She just had to have a little faith that John McNally was an honest, virtuous man, and would keep his word. Why couldn't he have stayed just one more day?

Chapter 11

Maybe Templar calls at the right times. Maybe Coswell needs some perspective on this whole situation and helping his old friend will supply just that. By 11:00 Coswell is just south of Dunn, North Carolina, he is making decent time but knows that will not last. Traffic will become much more congested once he crosses I-40. He is trying to clear his mind of all the cluttered issues that have been created as of late. The issues he has swirling in his head are a Lt. Colonel who killed himself, the Colonel who is the hometown hero and dark villain as well, and the woman who cares for him and is just ever so insecure about if he feels the same way. All of this fades from his mind as he drives down the sterile interstate. He thinks how he misses driving on the back roads of America and how much more pleasant the view always is. Coswell passes interstate forty and when he approaches Smithfield the traffic slows a bit. There are four cities around the area and this feeds the traffic on interstate forty and interstate ninety-five. Coswell cannot wait to see the Virginia state line, but after a little over 100 miles in Virginia this will start all over again.

It is early afternoon when Coswell reaches Virginia, he stops for a quick bite and some gas in Emporia. After recharging a little he gets back on the interstate and drives up I-95. He is just south of the little town of Stony Creek enjoying the wide open spaces and lack of population. While on this desolate section of highway he spots a single car accident on the side of the road. Coswell pulls the Explorer over and sees a young couple driving a Ford Mustang trapped in the car. Coswell leaps to action. He runs up to the now burning vehicle and jerks open the passenger's door. A petite, attractive, blonde girl who couldn't be more than twenty-two is dazed from the crash. It seems to Coswell that this accident was caused by the zealousness of youth and the love for speed. The driver, he assumes her boyfriend, must have lost control of the car in the turn and spun into the guard rail. Coswell believes this because the vehicle is facing traffic and the driver's door is slammed against the guardrail. Coswell pulls her from the burning wreck and carries her about fifty yards from the car. She is unconscious but only has bruises, abrasions, and light burns. Coswell races back to the burning vehicle but cannot access the driver's door because of the car's position. He tries to pull the driver from his seat from the passenger's side.

Coswell is pulling with all of his strength and feels a pop in his shoulder. Damn, he re-aggravates his old shoulder injury from jump school. He pulls one last time and the driver comes free. His leg had been pinned by the steering column. Coswell looks and knows all of his efforts here are for naught because the left side of the driver's skull is split open like a smashed pumpkin.

Coswell runs from the burning car to the surviving girl. He finds her cell phone in her pocket, calls 911, and after making sure she is well, quickly dashes to his vehicle and is away.

As Coswell drives again north on interstate ninety-five he sees Sussex County fire, rescue, and sheriff tearing south down ninety-five. He thinks they must have been dispatched from the city of Sussex north of Stony Creek. He continues his trek northward as he cannot afford any delays.

Back at the scene, fire fighters put out what remains of the now exploded car, rescue EMT's work on the young woman and the police take her statement. The Sheriff is quite sure that these youngsters had to be on something. One is of course dead, and the other is swearing that she was delivered from the car by an angel of mercy. The sheriff asks for a description and she said, "He just appeared from nowhere, he had blonde hair and a beard and wore all white. He carried me through the air away from the car and then went back for Jimmy. When Jimmy died the angel disappeared into thin air."

If Coswell knew that was her description he would have nothing to worry about but he was not privy to that information and would not know unless the news reported on it.

Coswell listens to smooth jazz on the CD player in his explorer as he drives north. He takes the I-295 bypass around Richmond. This way he will not get caught in any city accidents or traffic. Once he emerges back onto ninety-five there is a long open section of road until he hits the next congested city of Fredericksburg.

Fredericksburg comes and goes and Coswell is going over all the events of late in his mind. He has time for this because the traffic is quite congested from Fredericksburg to Arlington. He keeps thinking of Brandy and is it too harsh how he left things. Does she know that he really had to go and she need not be insecure? She has no reason to be insecure because she gave him the most enjoyable night of love making in the past eight years. He begins to think that he really should be open to the possibility of having her as a part of his life. Give things a chance to blossom naturally.

Just then he is approaching the intersection of ninety-five and the Capital Beltway. He crosses over the four ninety-five beltway and proceeds up three ninety-five heading past Alexandria and into Arlington, Virginia. As he comes into the city limits of Arlington he thinks to himself, 'This is not Nashville. You damn liar.'

He begins to brush all of those thoughts away and concentrate on the issue at hand. He is there to help Templar with this issue of his no matter what. He pulls into the Arlington National Cemetery and makes a quick stop by his grandfather's grave. His grandfather Kenneth Ripley had been a carrier pilot, flying off the Yorktown in World War II. He was one of the unlucky ones not to have returned alive. He was however buried with full military honors at Arlington. Coswell drives up Memorial drive and takes a right on Schley Drive, shortly it curves left and merges into Sherman Drive.

One last turn and he parks. He exits the vehicle and walks a few hundred yards to the burial sight of Oliver Wendell Holmes Jr., the famous Chief Justice of the United States Supreme Court. He sits on one of the park benches and watches the people pass as almost all of them go to the sight of John F. Kennedy's grave, a stone's throw from the great Dissenter's, but no one seems to give Oliver Wendell Holmes the respect he deserves.

In moments, and what seems like out of nowhere, Templar appears carrying a bag of donut holes and two coffees from the same doughnut shop. They both sit silently for a few moments sipping coffee and paying homage to a man whose life was all about justice.

Templar speaks first, "How was the drive up? Anything eventful happen?"

"Not a whole lot, I did drive by a bad wreck down by Stony Creek. So what is our pressing engagement?"

Templar smiles his thin devious smile, "I was contacted by a local Georgetown lawyer, Charles Alexander Thomas. He gave a reference from one of my former clients and I knew he was legitimate. I set up a meet with him, but as you know we do not meet our employer's face to face, unless it absolutely cannot be avoided, and you were busy with your own job. When he showed to the late night meet downtown in his Armani suit, Gucci shoes, and Stefano Ricci tie I knew he was serious, he would not of shown up if his claim was a farce or an attempt at entrapment. While he was standing next to his Mercedes S500 in the abandoned parking lot waiting on me I phoned him. I told him to leave the dossier under the entrance to the footbridge that spanned the street and leave promptly. An hour later I retrieved it and this is what was in it.

His fiancée is a doctorial candidate at Georgetown University. The issue is a simple one. She is a victim of sexual harassment by her doctorial advisor.

Coswell looks at a picture of her, "She is quite beautiful, she is a little young to be in the PHD program isn't she?"

"Yes, she is quite gifted. She graduated with a bachelor's degree at the age of 19, Masters Degree just before her 21st birthday and writing her doctorial thesis at 23. Her name is Catherine Louise Parker. She is studying for a doctorate in Business Law."

"That is impressive. Are we supposed to kill a college professor?"

"No, it is a simple issue, but not as simple as we would hope. The doctorial advisor is the Chair of the department and a well known and respected author in the field, the Dr. Susan Stock."

"The advisor is a woman? I thought you said this is a sexual harassment problem."

"It is before Miss Parker dated her current fiancé. She was quite free and had a semester of sexual experimentation. She had a one night stand with Dr. Stock when she was in the bachelor's program. A few years later she has 'straightened out so to say' and ends up in the doctorial program. Then who ends up being her advisor but the one woman that knows her 'in a very intimate fashion' we will say."

"According to Miss Parker, Doctor Stock told her 'If you want to ever be known as doctor you will do things my way. I will have your body as my playground.' Miss Parker had to come clean to Charles Thomas but he understood. He just wants the advances to go away. He doesn't want anyone killed just scared 'straight' so to say."

117

"Well that is a more complicated issue. Killing is always easier than instilling fear to the point of righteousness. So why did you need me Templar?"

"Even know I was careful when I made the exchange for the dossier, I cannot be certain that he does not know what I look like. He may have been foolish enough to put the drop under surveillance. If he is so foolish Charles Thomas only endangers his own life."

Coswell responds, "Some people think this is a game and do not show it the seriousness it deserves."

"So what do we know about Dr. Susan Stock that we can use?"

"She is highly regarded in her field, and although academic types are very much more liberal than most, the fact that she is sexually pressuring a student will not be well received. The fact that she is a well concealed lesbian, or at least bisexual, would not really matter in university circles."

"How are we to approach this? Any ideas how we proceed scaring her into compliance?"

"She is still a woman that is taught to be on high alert when walking across a dark parking lot on a downtown street. We take advantage of that and exploit it. She teaches some classes in the evening and usually stays an hour or so after the classes are over so she is leaving the university a couple of nights a week at or just after 21:00"

"That is perfect if we can exploit it, and there will be a much higher chance we will not be noticed by someone on the street."

"Did you already visit grandpa's grave?"

"Yes on the way in to meet you."

"I think he would have been proud of us, patriots to the bone."

The two head back to Templar's home in Ravenwood, out on the edge of Lake Barcroft. Templar lives in a rustic style log cabin, on the edge of the lake, and it is a nice home with most of the living space on the main floor and a small upper floor consisting of two bedrooms and a shared bath. The main floor has a living room, kitchen, den, dining room, and another spare room. Across the front of the house is a full length porch that has a view of the lake. It is a wonderful view in the morning because one can sit on the porch sipping coffee and watch the sun rise over the water of Lake Barcroft.

They sit on the porch that evening and Templar tells Coswell that Dr. Stock teaches a Sunday night class that may be perfect. The class is Ethics in Interpersonal Business Law, ironically enough. It is a class that starts at 19:00 and concludes by 20:35. This should put her leaving her office at 21:15-21:30. This gives them two days to recon, Friday and Saturday, and then they make their move. If everything goes well, by Tuesday Coswell can be back at his other job. It seems to be a sound plan so the two turn in for the evening and prepare for a full day the next day.

Chapter 12

First thing the next morning, after finishing his coffee, Templar makes a call to the law offices of Charles Alexander Thomas. He is put on hold by the secretary when he asks to speak to Mr. Thomas. She returns to the line and inquires to Templar, "Who should I say is calling?"

Templar responds to the secretary, "Tell him it is Oliver Holmes."

The line is silent for a moment, and within thirty seconds Charles Alexander Thomas, one of the hardest men in D.C. to see, is on the phone and says, "What can you do? Can you help me?"

Templar tells him, "The job is a go, transfer twelve thousand five hundred dollars to the agreed upon account before end of business today. The other half will be payable upon completion. If you tell anyone, the job is off. The first half is mine to keep regardless, but this will be a problem and it will be taken care of if you understand me."

Mr. Thomas responds, "Yes sir. It will be done exactly to your specification."

Templar tells him, "You will hear from me again within 5-7 days and this will no longer be an issue for you." Before Mr. Thomas says thank you, the line is dead.

Coswell leaves and drives into the Arlington area, near Georgetown. He parks his truck, and carries his touristy camera, walking around the city taking pictures of the buildings at the university and waiting for Dr. Susan Stock to emerge from her first class. He walks around the campus of Georgetown sight seeing or so it seems. Recon has always been something Coswell is quite good at. He is quite good at being seen, but not seen. He fades into the scenery like a picture on a wall. Something that someone knows is there but could not describe to save their lives.

He follows Dr. Stock from her first class that lets out at 10:00, and she heads over to the cafeteria building for coffee, she sits and reads the New York Times until it time for her second class to begin at 12:30. She has two classes that take up most of the remainder of her day. Coswell constantly takes photos and makes sure to document the times the standard police patrol come by the buildings. He follows her the short distance to her office from the classroom building then she finishes up her day about 17:50. He watches as she walks from the building her office is in to an adjoining parking lot where her 1966 British Racing Green Jaguar XK E-type is parked. Coswell is impressed and wishes he could drive around in something so extravagant but the fact that he does not want to be noticed precludes that. He does think he might buy that 1967 Corvette he has been looking at back home when this is over.

After she leaves Coswell walks back to his vehicle and drives to the street where her parking lot is located. He stops on the way and gets some coffee from a local all night diner. He is reminded of Brandy, he hopes this job will go well and without a hitch, he so wants to keep his promise of returning soon. He parallel parks the explorer on the street and watches all of the surrounding areas of the parking lot and the office building. The standard police patrol comes by at 19:25, 20:45, and 22:00. He watches until 23:15 and no other patrol comes by. If all goes as planned he will be able to take care of this at about 21:30 and disappear into the night without any viable witnesses. He drives back to the cabin that night in Ravenwood to inform Templar of his day's recon. Templar should also have some interesting information concerning the end of the job he took care of today. By the time he gets back to Ravenwood, Templar should already have the payment in the Cayman Islands bank and the plan worked out. However, this recon will help fine tune some of the details. He drives back and is famished; he hopes Templar has cooked something because he does not like going all day on coffee and a biscuit from this morning. He arrives at the cabin, and when he walks in, the familiar smell coming from the kitchen brings back memories.

Coswell yells, "Is that chipped beef on toast I smell?"

Templar tells him come on in the den, "Tonight we are having shit on a shingle, mashed potatoes, and coffee. Remind you of those days in basic?"

They sit and enjoy the simple, but wonderful, dinner in front of a warm fire. While they eat Coswell informs Templar of his day's events and when the police standard patrols come by her office building. Templar tells him to check that again tomorrow and make sure the intervals do not fluctuate by more than 5 or 10 minutes. After their simple dinner, they each have a shot of cognac.

Templar tells him, "If this all goes by the plan, when it is finished, we will celebrate with a small snifter of L'Esprit de Courvoisier."

Templar is fortunate enough to have one of the finest cognacs in the world. This particular cognac was first used at the coronation of Napoleon in 1802 and Templar's bottle dates back to that year so it should be quite smooth.

They turn in before too long, and in the morning Templar makes a call contacting Charles Thomas. He tells him, "This is Oliver Holmes and I will be sending a courier over today to meet you."

Mr. Thomas becomes quite nervous, "Is that necessary? No one else knows of this I assure you!"

"Yes, but my employer just needs to go over a couple of details with you, there is no reason to be alarmed."

Charles Thomas has no choice but to accept.

Coswell asks Templar, "You want me to go see him today?"

"No. I am going to see him to test his response upon seeing my face. This way I will be sure if he knows who I am or not."

"Ok, sounds good. Should I continue to follow our target and plan for Sunday night as our time to strike?"

"If all goes as planned you should be away from here by Tuesday at the latest."

Coswell starts to think about the small town of Cedar Creek and the evil man that has been left unchecked there for now. He hopes that Brandy is alright and knows that he is thinking about her too much. He wishes he could see her sooner but business before pleasure.

He drives into Georgetown and continues his 'sightseeing'. While Dr. Susan Stock is in her second class he runs by an all night diner on campus, the type that serves cheap breakfast anytime of day. He goes in, sits down at the counter, and orders a breakfast of sausage, scrambled eggs, and toast. One thing he notices is even know there are many beautiful women on campus, none of them work in this greasy spoon. This is what truckers refer to as a choke and puke. He eats quickly and gets back to his post watching for another beautiful, but sadistic woman, Dr. Stock. She is in her very late 40's, or early 50's, but is still quite stunning, and although Coswell does not subscribe to her lifestyle, he is sure she could have attracted another beautiful woman. She is successful and cultured but also apparently must be domineering. She, like the Colonel, has to be in control and would rather have a sexual slave than a partner. Coswell wonders if she is as much of a perverse coward as the Colonel, or has she not reached that level of perversion yet. Just then he watches the doctor make the short walk to her office and in twenty minutes something happens that highly surprises Coswell. This is not what he expects as one of the events of the day. He notices a woman that he recognizes but one he has never seen in person before. He looks over to his file and looks at the picture of Catherine Louise Parker. He reaches down for his camera and begins snapping pictures, knowing that the pictures could be useful at a later date. She is ringing the bell of the rear entrance to Dr. Stock's office. Dr. Susan Stock soon comes to the door and the two speak for a moment. The next moment the tone changes completely. Dr. Stock slaps Catherine and then pulls her up close and kisses her. They go back into the building and Catherine is in tow behind her holding her hand. Coswell has to investigate further; he thinks 'best way to do something is in broad daylight.' He sneaks up to the building and enters through the front. He looks at the directory and sees that the Chair's office, Dr. Stock's, is the only one on the third floor and the only other rooms up on that floor are empty class rooms as there are no mid-afternoon classes on Saturdays. He opens the stairwell door and slowly, quietly, scales the stairs to the third floor. He is in the stairwell at the opposite end of the corridor from Susan Stock's office. There is a maintenance room between the other stairwell and Dr. Stock's office. He sneaks down the hall and opens the maintenance room with his lock picks. Once inside the large heavy doors leading to the halls are unable to muffle the sounds from the inner office. Coswell hears something that complicates things here as well, something that may cause Templar to drop the job.

He hears a voice he knows is from Dr. Stock, it just seems to be one of authority and context gives it away. Dr. Stock says, "Who am I?"
Catherine Parker responds, "You are the mistress who controls all."

"Right, and who are you?"

"I am your slave and my naked body is yours."

"Correct again. What can I do with your naked body?"

"Anything you desire, it is your playground and I am your toy. I live to serve you and pleasure you."

Coswell knows where this is going and quietly exits into the hall. Just before going back down the stairwell he purposely dumps over a metal desk and this makes a loud crashing noise. He bolts down two flights of stairs and hugs the wall so he cannot be seen from above. He hears the door to the stairwell open moments later. He has successfully disrupted whatever sick twisted game being played, and he doubts they will continue for fear of being discovered by someone connected to the administration. Hopefully, Catherine Parker will either tell the truth to her fiancé that she is a lesbian or bi-sexual or stop this self destructive practice. If she is not willing to stop, there is no way she is willing to live faithfully with Charles Thomas. She cannot have it both ways; it will only destroy them both. However, that is not for Coswell to decide. He makes his way back out to the explorer and waits to see if Miss Parker leaves so he can continue his recon of Dr. Stock. He photographs Catherine Parker as she hurriedly leaves the doctor's office building and races to her vehicle. Dr. Susan Stock remains in her office. She is a cool customer that does not panic easily.

Coswell does now know that the story they were told about the harassment was highly biased and will need to be taken into account before continuing on the current path. Coswell races to the local office supply store to use their computer and email Templar the photos. He sends them as an attachment to an email and in the email explains to Templar that consequences are completely different.

He types, 'Situation changed. Attached file explains all. This will have severe consequences. Please review before courier sent. Delete afterwards.' Coswell.

He drives back to the location of her office and parks watching the parking lot with her classic Jaguar XKE in it. By the time he arrives at his destination there is a buzzing notification on his phone. He looks and sees a short concise email from Templar. When he opens it the email simply reads, 'Message received. 10-4'. Coswell is relieved that the information has been relayed successfully before the courier meeting.

Chapter 13

Oliver Holmes' courier arrives at the law offices of Charles Alexander Thomas at 14:30 and the only one in the office on this particular Saturday is Charles Thomas. Templar expects this is by design. If Charles Thomas recognizes Templar, he will quickly dispatch him by the application of 66 lbs of torque to his neck and swivel his eyes so they will be looking out from the other side. If Mr. Thomas was a wise man at the drop off point, he should survive meeting with Oliver Holmes' emissary.

Thomas opens the heavy wooden door to the law office and asks the man his name. Speaking with a Cockney accent, Templar responds, "Liam, Liam McGregor."

Thomas tells him, "Right this way."

McGregor responds, "Aye. Lead the way."

They sit in the large conference room with a long oak table and expensive carved oak chairs surrounding it. The chair at the end is a large stuffed leather chair with brass tacks along the piping of the chair. This is obviously Charles Thomas' chair. He walks to the chair and sits down, he motions

131

for McGregor to sit at the fine carved chair just around the end corner of the large table.

Thomas asks, "What is the need of this meeting?"

McGregor responds plainly, "They say a picture tells a thousand words. I have three pictures you may not like, but need to see."

McGregor withdraws a tablet computer from its' leather carrying case and loads the pictures. McGregor slides the tablet over in front of Charles Alexander Thomas. He tells him to swipe to move to the next photo. The first photo shows his fiancée at the back entrance to Dr. Stock's office building. McGregor narrates for him, "The first photo was taken today about 11:00 when on recon for the doctorial advisor."

Thomas tells him, "This could be anything, Even know she is being harassed she is still having to meet with her advisor because she is a doctorial candidate."

McGregor tells him, "Swipe to the next picture."

Thomas slides the picture forward and sees the picture of Dr. Stock slapping Miss Parker across the face. Thomas is enraged, "She struck her, damn her. I want this taken care of, this is enough. Catherine should not have to take this punishment for a moment of indiscretion in her past."

McGregor tells him, "There is one last picture, swipe forward on the screen."

The next picture is the one of the two in an embrace, deeply and passionately kissing.

Thomas sees this picture and his face turns grey. He can only manage one word over and over, "How, how, how......"

McGregor tells him he will give him a moment to absorb this. He takes the computer tablet and walks from the room, waiting for Charles Thomas to compose himself.

Five minutes later he re-enters the room and walks back over to Mr. Thomas.

McGregor says, "We have a couple of ways this can proceed. Either way we need you to make a decision. You may want to speak with your fiancée and let her know you are not in the dark about her actions. I understand she was the one that came to you and asked for help. You may have to confront her but that is your decision."

Thomas responds, "I guess, I just don't know."

McGregor hands him a card and tells him, "Contact me at this number at 12:00 sharp tomorrow. Tell me Yes or No. Yes we continue, No, this never happened and you got your money's worth investigating your fiancée before you married her."

McGregor lays an SD card on the table and tells Thomas, "Here is a copy of the pictures."

"You are a rich, powerful man of presumably strong character. If I do not hear from you at 12:00, my employers which you contracted with will be greatly disappointed. If you do not make a decision you are wasting their time. That is not only expensive but potentially lethal. Remember 12:00 tomorrow, Sunday."

With that Liam McGregor turns and shows himself out leaving a despondent and rejected Charles Alexander Thomas slumped in his conference room chair.

Templar thinks, 'He did not know me, that much is for sure. However, he needs to collect himself and get it together or he will find out who I truly am.'

He exits the law office and starts the drive back to Ravenwood to meet up with Coswell and wait, at least for now.

Charles Alexander Thomas makes a call and asks Catherine Louise Parker to meet him for dinner at his loft in Georgetown near the national mall. He says to her that he wants them to have a nice candlelit dinner that night. He is having Naomi Sanchez, his Argentinean housekeeper, prepare Chicken enchiladas and tapas for them. Catherine Parker of course accepts. He picks up the SD card off the large wooden table, puts it in his jacket pocket, and heads for his loft. He drives across the river into Washington D.C. and to Georgetown. He pulls his car into the large stone parking deck attached to the building where his in-town loft resides. He sits for a long time at the wheel of his Mercedes S500, silently surrounded by the smell of rich leather and finally when what he must do dawns on him he loudly exclaims, "DAMN!"

His Hispanic maid is working away in the kitchen making what could be the couple's last supper. At the same time Charles Thomas is in his study working on his computer. He has the SD card plugged into the computer and is looking at the pictures again. He reaches into the heavy wooden desk drawer and withdraws a few sheets of glossy photo paper from it. He loads the paper into his color laser printer and reluctantly presses print. Moments later perfect facsimiles of the digital pictures are sitting on his desk and he slides them into a heavy brown manila envelope. He looks at the clock, 5:41 pm, Catherine is not scheduled to arrive until 7:00 pm and she has always been fashionably late to everything. Thomas powers down his computer and sits in his dark study and library. He walks over to his large chair, similar to the one he has in his conference room at the law office, and sinks into it. He reaches over and grabs a tumbler and crystal decanter and pours himself a nice drink of single malt scotch. He drops in a couple of ice cubes for good measure and quietly sits drinking alone in the dark awaiting the reckoning.

Seven o'clock comes and goes, at 7:21 pm the buzzer to Mr. Thomas' large condominium loft apartment goes off. He buzzes Catherine Parker in and she bounces into the living room and throws her arms around Charles Thomas' neck and kisses him. She playfully asks, "You miss me babe?"

He responds, "You certainly are joyous today, anything special happen?"

"No not really just had a good day I guess."

"Would you like a drink or are you starving as much as I am?"

"Famished, let's eat."

They walk to the formal dining room where Naomi Sanchez has everything laid out and is pouring the white wine to go with the chicken. She pulls out Catherine's chair and then helps her into it. Next she goes over and helps Mr. Thomas off with his sport coat and then pulls his chair out. If she were not around all the time someone would think that there is almost a sensual vibe between Naomi and Charles Thomas but it is just the familiarity between them.

Naomi departs and the couple begins their meal with the standard small talk of dinner. When they are almost finished Charles asks again, "Why were you so ecstatic earlier?"

"I went to see my doctorial advisor today and you know the problems I have had with her. However, we talked about the issue and I think she has agreed to leave me alone and treat me as any other doctorial candidate."

"That's wonderful what did you have to tell her to get her to agree?"

"Well I just told her that I don't have those types of feelings for women and I am engaged to be married to you. She said that she understands and it was inappropriate for her to make advances before. She even agreed to, if necessary; change my doctorial advisor this semester and I will not lose a semester in the program."

"That is great! What did you say?"

"I told her it is very adult of her to see things from my point of view and if she can view things in a non-biased fashion I see no reason to change doctorial advisors."

Charles Thomas looks at his fiancée and asks, "Why are you such a Goddamn liar and a money grubbing whore? Dammit, I loved you."

She almost falls out of her chair, "What are you talking about? I am not lying to you, and I am most certainly NOT a whore."

Just then Charles reaches under his chair and produces a brown manila envelope. Next three photos spread across the table like time lapse photography. "So this isn't you being her little toy. Slapping you, kissing you and leading you inside to do who knows what else?"

She gasps at the sight of the photos, "I can explain it isn't like that."

"How is it then? Do you like the touch of a woman or a man?"

"It isn't that simple, I don't have a choice."

"What do you mean don't have a choice?"

"I belong to her, I love you and want to be your wife but she is my mistress. Maybe you could come along with me?"

"No. I am a respected D.C. lawyer, one of the most powerful men on the eastern seaboard. You expect me to let a glorified high school teacher have power over me? I don't think so. You are much sicker than I thought. Right now make your choice, her and the perversion or me and the normalcy of living in the lap of luxury."

"Charles, I love you but I can't she won't let me."

He stands up and walks to her side of the table and takes her by the elbow. He leads her to the private elevator door as she stumbles beside him. He opens the door to the private elevator that leads to the parking garage and pushes Miss Parker into the elevator car. She slides down against the back wall on her butt. He reaches in removes her engagement ring, takes out his key and activates the elevator and steps out as the doors close. He can hear the humming of the lift taking her on the one way trip to the cold parking garage. He thinks to himself, 'I guess love isn't strong enough for some things.' He looks at the 1.25 carat solitaire diamond ring in his palm. He walks back to the dining room and Naomi Sanchez is finishing clearing the table. She asks, "Is Miss Parker gone? Is she feeling ill?"

He says to her, "No we have irreconcilable differences." Then he smiles and says, "Naomi when was the last time I gave you a raise?"

Naomi responds, "Last year but you pay me well sir."

He smiles a wide smile and flips the ring to her, "This should help. However, I do need you to come clean in the bedroom."

Charles thinks, 'Always thought Hispanic maids were so sexy.'

He goes in the bedroom, sets his alarm for 11:00 A.M. so he will be up to make his important call. He then starts getting ready for bed.

Naomi comes in and asks where she needs to clean.

He says, "I don't care as long as you are naked and in this bed."

Naomi simply responds, "Yes sir."

<u>Chapter 14</u>

Templar and Coswell sit on the porch on Sunday morning eating and drinking coffee. They are awaiting the call at 12:00; Charles Thomas should be calling with his decision in the next twenty minutes.

Coswell asks, "What do you think he will decide?"

Templar tells him, "If his character holds, he should call this off. However, love will make a man do stupid things sometimes."

Coswell thinks quietly to himself, 'I wonder if I am a man that is being led astray stupidly by love?'

Coswell then responds, "Yes sometimes it can. If he is wise he will step away from her. She may like him as a man, and love his money, but her true desire lies with the twisted relationship she is in."

Templar smiles and says, "It may be quite different but in every relationship, whether it is traditional or not, one person has the powerful position and the other the submissive. That is Biblical."

Coswell and Templar are silent for a few moments and at 11:58 the phone rings, Templar lets it ring three times and slowly, calmly, picks up the receiver.

His stoic voice is heard and he speaks, "What is your decision?"

Charles Alexander Thomas is on the line, he speaks, "No, but I ......"

By the time Mr. Thomas got to his second word Templar had hung up.

Templar did not care to be Mr. Thomas' analyst, he is simply there to either take care of a problem or not. Mr. Thomas has gotten his money's worth, for twelve thousand five hundred dollars he found out before the nuptials that his fiancée is not the woman he thought she was.

It would have been well worth that dollar amount. It would have cost him much more in divorce, and the fact of the embarrassment, if it had ever come to light that a high end D.C. lawyer was married to a promiscuous bi-sexual woman.

Coswell looks at Templar. Even with Templar's deadpan look, Coswell knows,

"That is a No. I'll pack after dinner tonight."

Templar tells him, "I'll transfer your $6250.00 to your Cayman Account tomorrow morning when the banks open."

"I trust it will be there by end of business." Coswell responds.

"Should we still have a drink of L'Esprit de Courvoisier tonight?"

Coswell smiles, "I would love to, but it is your cognac and your decision."

Templar says, "Yes, we did our job. We will toast before you leave this evening."

Coswell thinks, 'He will leave after dinner and begin the southerly drive back to Fayetteville, NC but he might split up the trip. He hasn't been to the Canal Club in Richmond in years. The Canal Club is a live music blues and jazz club, and restaurant with a myriad of beers on tap. However, before he leaves the Arlington area he will make a quick stop at Nick's Nightclub in Arlington and pick up a country themed gift for Brandy. Maybe he can get her a Grand Ole Opry snow globe to go in her living room. That should look very much like something from Nashville.

That evening the two eat beef tips and rice and then retire to the den for a drink. Templar opens up a case that stores his cognac, snifters and everything he needs for a proper toast. Templar removes the crystal decanter, sets it on the cherry side table, then removes two small snifters and a large ornamental lighter. He pours about an ounce and a half of L'Esprit de Courvoisier in the first snifter, and puts the open flame of the lighter under the ball of the glass as he rolls the cognac around in the glass. He hands the snifter to Coswell and repeats the process for himself.

Templar holds up his glass and speaks, "A toast, to a job well done, or at least one where we kept the faith."

Coswell raises his glass and deeply inhales the aroma of the smooth cognac. After taking in the oaky scent, he quietly sits and sips his cognac until it is gone. All the while he is thinking of getting on the road, he needs to finish his job too. Will finishing his job mean an end to this new found relationship with Brandy? Does that really matter? She doesn't know who he really is anyway, and she is falling for John McNally. Would she love Jefferson Ripley or is that beyond his wildest dreams.

Coswell rises, shakes Templar's hand and walks to the front door where his bag is sitting. He picks up his bag, carries it to the explorer and throws it in the back, and then he rolls southward out of town stealing away like a thief in the night.

Now Coswell makes his first stop, Nick's Nightclub in Arlington before taking off down I-395. He stops there and looks around in the area where they have keepsakes for tourists to buy, and picks out a nice country western themed gift. He finds a small statue of Alan Jackson that was modeled after one of his album covers. He would have liked to find a Grand Ole Opry snow globe, but that wasn't one of the choices.

Coswell drives down the dark interstate, he is heading in the opposite direction of most traffic, since traffic in that area is almost always heading into the D.C. beltway. He drives south past the exits for Alexandria and Manassas. He drives along I-95 with the Potomac River to the east and comes up on Fredericksburg. He pulls off and exits the interstate at Fredericksburg to stop for some fuel and coffee.

Within minutes he is heading south again and in just over an hour he is pulling into Richmond, Va. He gets off the interstate right in the heart of Richmond and drives down Main Street until he finds a small motel for the night. He checks in, pays cash for one night, stores his things in the room, and takes a long hot shower.

It is 21:00 when Coswell emerges from the well deserved and relaxing shower. He puts on a fresh oxford shirt, British khakis pants, his oxblood wingtips and his camel hair coat. He slides the Webley revolver over his right hip and locks the door as he leaves and heads to the Canal Club over on Cary Street. He pulls into the dark parking lot and can feel electricity in the air as he casually strolls into the jazz club. He takes a small table that is supposedly for two, about 10 feet away from the stage. He orders a Blue Moon Belgian Ale and the waitress brings it promptly. He listens to the saxophone player as he wails away on his alto. He is playing 'Just to be next to you' an excerpt from Dave Koz' Saxophonic album. It is more adventurous fusion jazz than Coswell normally likes but he knows the piece and the title gets him thinking about Brandy. Later that night, a lovely jazz singer named Daphne Ambrose takes the stage. She is probably in her early to mid thirties, has long wavy dark blonde hair, those ruby lips like Brandy's, and is wearing a slinky sequined gown. She stands singing and swaying holding the microphone stand. Her voice is so melodic; the notes just seem to flow like honey from her throat. She is singing some original material, but also a lot of jazz standards.

146

Coswell looks around and the thing he notices the most is there seem to be couples together staring into each other's eyes, and the music is just background to them. The jazz to them is just the soundtrack for their date, something to refer to while describing a great date to a friend. To Coswell the music is deeply spiritual. He sits enthralled by the beautiful woman while she sings. He sits back closes his eyes and just lets the experience wash over him like waves crashing onto the beach. In this case, it is waves of soft, sweet, jazz consoling Coswell's soul.

He sits all night sipping beer, watching and listening to this amazing singer, and observing the people at the other tables. He knows he needs this cleansing of the soul. She sings so many beautiful old songs; she sings Minnie the moocher, then almost every song after that only reminds him more and more of Brandy. She sings I'm in the Mood for love, Begin the Beguine, late in the evening she digs deep into the past and sings Etta James 'At Last'. This is a beautiful song and makes Coswell think of nothing but Brandy. To close her set and the live music for the night, she sings one of Coswell's most favorite standards by the Jazz

Singer herself, Billie Holiday. The song is 'One more for the Road'.

After Daphne Ambrose steps off stage, Coswell just wants more. She walks over to his table and speaks, "I couldn't help but notice how much you seemed to enjoy the show."

Her speaking voice had a different lilt to it. Coswell knew from his time in the service, and the time he was stationed overseas, that it is a Liverpool England accent. This just isn't fair. He tells her, "Yes you have such a wonderful voice and a wide selection of songs in your set. You cover almost every era of jazz."

Daphne asks, "Do you mind if I sit down?"

"I am sorry. I didn't mean to be rude, please join me. I should have also introduced myself, my name is John McNally. Please let me have the honor of buying you a drink."

She responds, "Just tea with honey and lemon, I have to take care of my voice. My name is Daphne Ambrose. It is very nice to meet you Mr. McNally."

"Please, call me John."

McNally calls the waitress over and she takes Daphne's order, and McNally asks if they have any coffee.

"I haven't seen you in here before I don't think. What brings you in tonight?"

"I come through this area every couple of years and I always stop here because it has always been the best place for good jazz in Richmond, in my opinion."

The waitress brings her hot tea and McNally a cup of coffee.

She sips her tea and says, "You know I think you were the only one in here tonight that was actually listening to me sing. You looked like it was quite an experience, you took in ever note I sang like it was the last music you would ever hear. I had the feeling you were feeding off of it."

McNally tells her, "A little jazz is always good for the soul. There are so many different types but you just struck a chord with what I needed."

She gingerly smiles, "I normally end with the Etta James, 'At Last.' I don't normally sing Billie Holiday but I did that last one for you."

McNally didn't realize it because he has been thinking of Brandy while they talked but Daphne is holding his hand. Then he notices that she is rubbing her bare leg against his through the split that goes up the side of her dress.

His eyes are immediately the size of half dollars.

She asks, "You don't like a woman who is forward, or goes after what she wants? What do you say we get out of here and go back to my place for a nightcap?"

McNally tells her, "I would love to but….."

She interrupts, "Let me guess you're married."

"No it is not that, I am however, 'involved' and when you sang tonight it reminded me of her and the fact I am on my way back to her tomorrow. Every one of your songs was beautiful but just made me think of her more."

She smiles a wide glowing smile, "I am glad to hear that there are some good men left in this world. Maybe that means there is someone as chivalrous as you for me too."

"Glad you understand. You are the most beautiful singer I have seen in a long time and your voice is absolutely angelic. It really made my night but I need to be going. I have got to catch a little sleep before I take off in the morning."

McNally gets up, kisses her hand and tells her, "It was charming to have met you."

She responds, "Thank you, and I hope your woman knows what a good man you are."

McNally walks out of the club and thinks to himself, 'If she only knew, when most people think of me, they do not think he is such a good man.'

He thinks of Brandy even more that night and decides that he will run by Deep Groove in the morning before he leaves and get a more meaningful gift for Brandy. He thinks 'I wonder if I can find Billie Holiday, Lady sings the Blues."

Chapter 15

McNally arises the next morning refreshed and rejuvenated. He feels like a new man and is prepared to take on the original job with a renewed vigor. At 09:00 he is finishing his shower and gets dressed in some comfortable jeans and a long sleeve chamois shirt. He wants to make sure he will be comfortable for the remainder of the drive to Fayetteville, NC.

McNally checks out of the small motel and loads up in the Ford Explorer to drive to Deep Groove Records. He looks around for a few minutes searching for a special album for Brandy. He is unsuccessful in finding something particularly special so he asks the clerk specifically for the Billie Holiday album Lady Sings the Blues. They do have it, in near mint shape and it is even a first pressing.

The clerk asks McNally, "Are you sure you want this album? You do know this album is $185.00 right?"

McNally tells her, "Have you heard it? The silky smooth voice of Billie Holiday is an almost religious experience. I'm underpaying if anything."

He thanks her and walks out with the album wrapped in bubble wrap.

He stops at a truck stop just before he gets to the interstate entrance, and as soon as he has a chance to fuel up, he is on his way. Within an hour he covers the ground between Richmond and the small town of Stony Creek where one young soul had been saved and another had faded away. He wishes that he could enjoy the euphoria of living in a little out of the way place like Emporia or maybe Roanoke Rapids. He loves the life in a small town. Maybe that is why he is so strongly drawn back to Cedar Creek. Maybe that could explain it, but he knows that is not the reason at all. McNally likes the little town of Cedar Creek because some of the people, mainly Brandy, who are so innocent at heart, and look at life like a naïve child, are there. Years of hard living in the Army, and his chosen profession beyond his time in the service, would never allow McNally to have such a pure, simple outlook again. However, he would not be so good at self preservation without the skills of his unique background.

In another hour he is crossing I-40 and in his mind he starts to think, 'I'm on the homestretch, it won't be long now.'

About the same time McNally left the city of Richmond, Cheryl and Madison Bridger, were getting off work in the town of Cedar Creek. They both work at the local AT&T call center as customer service operators and work the late shift from twelve midnight to eight in the morning. The call center office is about three blocks from the Breakfast Nook and they go there in the mornings for breakfast to enjoy a good meal and chat with their friend Brandy most of the time after finishing their shift. When they walk out that Monday morning there is a figure in a black sedan, a Chrysler 300, parked just down the block. It is Lt. Colonel Leslie Massengill and he gets out of his car and strolls along the sidewalk leading to the Breakfast Nook from the AT&T call center. He is walking in the direction of the telephone call center when he comes face to face with the twins.

Colonel Massengill smiles his thin evil smile, "Have you two whores smartened up? I know you girls would like to come and entertain at a party for me. If you were our entertainment I know you could make eight hundred to a thousand dollars apiece that night. Tips are so much better at private parties than clubs. You girls do strip with bodies like those don't you?"

Madison starts to cry and yells through the sobs, "Damn you, we are not whores. We work hard and long and don't want your sleazy money."

He responds, "My dear, money is money and I would spend two hundred dollars to have a few minutes with you two, I have always wanted a threesome with twins."

Cheryl took a step at him like she is going to hit him, "You bastard you cannot have a woman just for your sick carnal pleasure at your whim. WE are not for sale, leave my sister and I alone."

The Colonel, still smiling says, "Powerful aren't we. Were you going to strike a helpless old man and a pillar of this community? I will show you what real power is, soon enough you will be begging me to let you 'entertain' for me my little sluts."

Cheryl grabs Madison's arm and shoves by him, although they are both troubled by this, they continue on to the Breakfast Nook. Maybe a nice meal, and seeing their friend Brandy, will make this memory fade quickly.

As they rush away the Colonel turns and watches their tight curvaceous asses on top of those long sexy legs. Their hips move in synchronicity like the perfect time of a metronome.

He then quietly sneers, "I will have you both."

The twins arrive at the Breakfast Nook emotionally drained and Madison is still crying. Brandy comes over to them at their booth and in her cheery way asks, "What will you two have....What is wrong? Madison, why are you crying?"

Madison responds through the gasps, "Colonel Massengill" that is all she can get out as she leans against her sister and slowly calms down.

Brandy rushes away and returns to both of them with some hot cocoa and slides two cups in front of her friends. She says, "We will talk about this but not here, I get off at noon can we meet for lunch? We can go down to the barbeque place."

Just then Colonel Massengill slithers in the door and over to the corner booth he always occupies. He waves down Brandy, his server, and demands his standard order of coffee, limp bacon, and runny eggs over easy. He runs his fingers up the side of Brandy's soft legs and she jumps like she has been bitten by a rattlesnake.

She tells him, "Do not touch me, I am your waitress nothing more."

He smiles, "You don't know it but you are so much more."

She feels sick to her stomach. She tells her boss that she doesn't feel well and leaves work early and goes to the barbeque restaurant down the street, it is aptly named, Pig on a Spit. Within twenty minutes the twins, having only had cocoa that morning, walk in to the barbeque place and join their friend.

The three sit and console each other and have a meal free of sexual harassment. The only man there is Bishop, the cook that smokes the ribs and meat.

Brandy finally states what all three are thinking, "What are we going to do about this man. The whole town reveres him as a hero, but he is just a creepy, sleazy, perverted man."

The girls all sit silently together contemplating how they can get him to leave them alone.

At the same moment, McNally is rolling down I-95 into Fayetteville and making the turn to head out towards Cedar Creek. His first stop is the dry cleaners. He drops off all his clothing from the trip to be laundered or dry cleaned and they tell him it will be ready the next morning. He looks at his watch, it reads 13:00, the first thing that crosses his mind is, 'I wonder

157

where Brandy is right now?' He knows that she normally is off work by this time and doesn't know if she goes straight home after work or not. He thinks she probably goes to eat before going home. He has such a compulsion to see her, but doesn't want to seem eager when he does. He decides he will be disciplined and wait. He will get a fresh start tomorrow after he picks up his clothes from the cleaners. Then he can head over to the Breakfast Nook for Brandy. He will have time to rest, and put himself back into the proper mindset.

He can kill two birds with one stone. He will pick up the Colonel's trail at the same time he shows up for his breakfast.

He showers that night, and for a first time in a long time, relaxes on the bed and watches a little television. That evening there is a news update on an ongoing police investigation in the Cedar Creek area. The story the news is updating is the one about the young girl who was raped just before McNally had left town for D.C. McNally knew that the girl who was violated is none other than the daughter of Chaplain Timothy Michaelson. The news does not reveal this, but McNally had put this together the morning after it happened. Dammit, why didn't he pick up the Colonel's trail that night instead of stargazing with Brandy? He was selfish that night and it cost a young girl her innocence. Would she ever be able to connect the act of sex with love and tenderness between people that care for each other, or is she destined to a life where she searches for men to dominate her and use her?

McNally listens and the news has some new facts that the police have uncovered and released. There was a partial smudged print found on the stainless steel shackles used to restrain the girl. It isn't much to go on because the print only has two definable points but when the police ran the print against the national database they came up with 25 possible suspects within a 100 mile radius of Fayetteville. McNally knows that if the police in this town are any good at all they should at least have Massengill as a suspect. His fingerprints are on file as a former marine and maybe they will question him. McNally only wonders will it be at the Colonel's house with the dungeon in it or will the Colonel come down to the station. McNally knows the Colonel is arrogant enough to march into the police precinct knowing there is no way he can be connected to anything. The news also reports that the girl has just been released from the hospital after treatment of her wounds and illness. McNally knows what that means; he knows she has been in the psycho ward for observation and treatment for a few days now. She probably was sedated for the first 72 hours. He must take care of this cancer to the world. At that moment, McNally knows that soon Coswell will be called upon to finish this. October 23rd is the anniversary date when Massengill was awarded the Congressional Medal of Honor. McNally decides it is a fitting time to unleash Coswell and remove the tarnish from this highly regarded award.

Chapter 16

The next morning Coswell arises very early, at that time it dawns on him that much more needs to be known about the Colonel and the intricacies of his life. He is still too mysterious. At this point, Coswell has no proof that he raped the girl, but he does know about the sex dungeon in the back of the Colonel's otherwise normal ranch home. Coswell's instincts however, have always been dead on and he knows that further, more in depth investigation into the Colonel's daily routine is a must to learn what makes him tick.

Coswell is half a mile down the road from Colonel Massengill's farm on Cedar Village Way. He listens in, using the bug he planted in the den, to see if he can pick up any conversation but the house is quiet for now. Like clockwork at 0730 Massengill is sitting out on his porch, sipping his coffee, and reading the morning paper. Coswell wishes he had some coffee but he didn't have time to stop and get any this morning before making the drive out to the Colonel's place. He will have some soon enough at the Breakfast Nook, if Massengill's routine holds true. Massengill reads the paper and drinks his hot coffee in his robe until 0930 when he goes inside, regimented as clockwork.

Next Coswell overhears a conversation between James Willis and Massengill again.

"Hey Willis can you have things ready by Saturday the 25th?"

"Yeah but I don't think it is a good idea, you were named as a possible suspect for the rape of Michaelson's daughter."

"They've got nothing; I cannot be touched in this town."

Willis says, "Okay, it's your ass if you get caught but I am going to be very careful. Should we just get some Latina prostitutes from Fayetteville?"

"I have another idea for the entertainment, but look around in case we have to purchase other entertainment as a backup plan."

Coswell listens intently but the content of the conversation makes his blood boil and stomach turn. He only wishes they had gone into more detail. What is this other deranged plan Colonel Massengill has come up with? Where is he going to get his 'entertainment' if not from east Fayetteville? Where else is that sort of entertainment available in such a small town? Coswell is still missing pieces, and is waiting to discover if the right ones will fall into place. Once more is revealed the picture will become clearer.

At 11:00 the Colonel emerges from the house, climbs into the Jeep Wrangler, and drives into town. Coswell follows him, knowing just where he is going. As Coswell suspects, he drives straight to the Breakfast Nook. As always, he walks in and straight over to his reserved corner booth.

Once again Coswell assumes the persona of John McNally and pushes open the wood frame door to the Breakfast Nook. When he does it rattles against the brass bell, ringing and indicating someone has just come in. Brandy is taking the Colonel's order of coffee, limp bacon and runny eggs sunny side up when she looks over to the door.

Even know she is standing at the Colonel's table a smile crosses her face. This smile is like that first glimmer of sunlight after a long cold night that seems to flood the sky and beat the darkness away.

She quickly finishes up with the Colonel and bounces behind the counter. McNally sits down at the high top stools and says, "Hi Brandy, did you miss me?"

"More than you could know John. I wasn't sure you were coming back."

"I said it would be the first part of this week and I am here. I couldn't possibly lie to you, you know that."

He orders coffee and a cinnamon roll and Brandy retrieves it for him. The kitchen then yells at her, "Orders up!" She walks over to the window and it is Colonel Massengill's food. She takes it over and tries to drop it off with as little contact as possible. She returns to John to give him a warm up, "John can we go somewhere after I get off here at 12:30? I need to talk to you about something?"

McNally responds, "I am sorry but I can't today Brandy. I have got some errands to run and business leads to follow up on. Are you still off on Thursdays?"

She gently pouts, "Yeah but it's only Tuesday."

"I know but how about I pick you up tomorrow after work and take you to a movie. Then, if you trust me, I'll take you back to your place and this time I'll cook a nice dinner for you. Oh, I also got you a present on my trip. That's worth waiting for right?"

"I suppose I can wait John, I have waited this long what is one more day." she slides him a piece of paper and says, "I know how we did this is a little backward, but here is my number just in case."

McNally smiles, and as he is finishing his coffee, he notices the Colonel finishing his breakfast and leaving a fifty cent tip. He walks by McNally and out the door. McNally gives him a twenty count, drops ten dollars on the counter, and walks out to his vehicle.

Colonel Massengill drives to the local mall, parks his Jeep and enters at the food court entrance at the center of the building. McNally smiles, he knows it will be easy to track the Colonel while remaining unseen in a mall on a weekday afternoon.

McNally enters the same location of the mall about one hundred and fifty yards behind the Colonel. He knows the easiest time to lose track of someone in this situation is when they enter, or are leaving the building, so he needs to keep eyes on the Colonel until they are in the mall.

Colonel Massengill walks efficiently from one store to the other. He first shops in the cigar and tobacco store and picks up a new pipe, pipe cleaners, and a pouch of cherry tobacco. He walks in a men's clothing store, and buys a new pair of dark blue jeans and another flannel shirt. Apparently the Colonel is convinced he is a lumberjack. Finally, he walks to the sporting goods store named Maple's sports. He walks around in the sporting goods store for a long time so McNally moves in a little closer to see what is preoccupying him so much. McNally acts as if he is shopping for a sports jersey, but is intently listening to the Colonel's conversation with the assistant manager who is standing behind the customer service desk.

The Colonel says, "I sure am glad you guys finally fired Rich O'Donnell. I complained about him for almost a month. You guys did know he was stealing didn't you? I told your store manager, more than once, and I know about people. I could have told you he was a no good thief, in fact I did. How long has he been gone, a couple months now?"

The assistant manager responds, "I cannot really comment on that sir, there are privacy issues."

"That doesn't apply to me, I am the one that pointed it out, and did your job for you. In fact with an attitude like yours I am sure you should probably be fired too. I do like the sexy little thing that replaced Rich. She is what, nineteen, blonde and blossoming we shall say."

"That is not appropriate Colonel. She is an employee and I cannot allow you to harass her like that. Are you buying anything or should I ask you to leave?"

"If you don't know already, you aren't a very good manager, excuse me, <u>assistant</u> manager. Maybe Chuck Maple should get rid of you, and replace you with a woman that looks like your new employee's older sister."

"I am going to have to ask you to leave now sir."

"Kiss my ass, me and Chuck Maple go back a long way. He served at the Pentagon with me. That was a long time before you were even a glint in the milkman's eye."

"Am I going to have to call security?"

"I doubt rent-a-cop could do anything, but you don't have what I am looking for anyway. Doesn't anyone carry good baseball socks anymore?"

With that the Colonel turned on his heel and marched proudly from the store like a conquering hero.

McNally shops for a moment, lingering behind, and then follows the Colonel to his next and final stop before leaving the mall, the Remington store.

McNally walks out to his explorer, keeps an eye on the Jeep Wrangler, and continues to wait for Massengill to emerge so he can follow him wherever else he may go today. McNally looks at his watch, it reads 15:30. Within ten minutes Colonel Massengill is walking out and climbs into his Jeep storing all his purchases in the backseat of the Wrangler. The Colonel drives directly back out to Cedar Village Way, to his farm. When McNally realizes this is where he is going, he decides to fall back so as not to be spotted while following him. McNally runs into a restaurant and gets a roast beef sandwich and a nice cold coke. McNally thinks about everything that has happened since he took on this job, he decides maybe he should make a call to his employer to see if she is still 'all in' on this job. After he finishes his meal he begins the drive out to Cedar Village Way and on the way calls the burn phone that Templar had delivered to Louise Wilson.

A nervous voice timidly answers, "Hello?"

"This is Coswell, and I am calling because I am sending a courier to meet you this Thursday in Wrightsville Beach outside of Wilmington. There are a couple of issues that need to be discussed and clarified, and the man I am sending will contact me with your response about them."

"Yes sir. When on Thursday and where?"

"He will meet you at the Dockside Waterfront Restaurant and Bar in Wrightsville Beach at 18:00. Do not be late!"

Louise Wilson sat hyperventilating on the other end of the dead line. Coswell had already hung up and all she could think is, "Why is he sending someone to see me? Is it more money he wants? Did Leslie get to him because they are both military? Oh God why did I do this? Should I have just left it alone?" She had so many questions but has no one to ask, at least not until Thursday when all will be answered, hopefully.

McNally sits listening to the bug he planted and watches the home of Colonel Leslie D. Massengill. He hears nothing, sees nothing, all he can do at this point is quietly and patiently wait for the Colonel to make his next move in this game of chess between them. A game the Colonel doesn't even know he is playing.

McNally sits and waits for what seems like a long time. He arrived outside the Colonel's home at about 16:30; it is now 19:00. Dusk has fallen and the last glimmering light is fading from the sky over Cedar

169

Creek. Just then McNally hears the bug he has planted in the Colonel's den. Massengill is making a phone call. It rings several times then a woman's voice answers on the other end.

"Grace Greathouse Attorney at Law, how may I help you?"

"I know it is late to call for legal advice. Is the Madam in to advise me?"

You could hear her voice switch from business, to pleasure. "The Madam will be happy to advise you, but it won't be free."

"I know you run most of the quality prostitution in this town. Do you run the Bridger twins?"

"Who? Do you mean Cheryl and Madison Bridger?"

"Yes, I need them to be persuaded to work a party, and they will be well compensated. Can you set that up for me?"

"I could but they don't work the escort scene, as far as I know they just work for the phone company, they aren't whores that I am aware of, and I would be aware!"

Massengill says, "I would really like them for the party, do you know anything I might be able to leverage them with? I can make it worth your while."

"You <u>will</u> make it worth my while anyway you slime. Without me you will have a sausage party, remember I control the whores in this town."

Massengill responds, "Yes madam." Then suddenly the line goes dead.

McNally continues to watch the house and at 21:15 the Colonel, dressed completely in black, steps out of his house and walks to the black Chrysler 300.

He gets inside, spins the engine to life, and lights come on at the perimeter of the sedan. Nothing can be seen but the taillights and headlights in the darkness. The Chrysler is like a black cat slinking down the road, stalking its prey. McNally starts his vehicle and follows at a distance. Following a car on a lonely country road in complete darkness is easier and can be accomplished from a further distance. He follows the Colonel's car for a long while, all the way through Cedar Creek and heading up the two lane highway towards interstate ninety-five and Fayetteville, North Carolina. Once they cross interstate ninety-five, they are in the east section of Fayetteville, which is a seedy area full of adult bookstores, blue theaters, drug addled street walker hookers, liquor stores, check advance places, and of course sleazy by the hour motels.

The Colonel parks his Chrysler at the parking lot of the Bushy Hills Motel and steps inside. McNally watches from the parking lot as he goes in and secures a room for the evening. Massengill leaves the motel office, and then walks down the side walk towards a theater named the Blue Danube. McNally parks out away from the motel building and follows on foot. McNally is keeping watch from a couple hundred yards away. The Colonel seems more in his own element here as he walks by the hookers and looks them up and down, salivating like an animal about to devour its prey, but that will be for later. He continues on to the theater, and when he arrives, McNally has moved up about a hundred yards away. Massengill leisurely strolls inside and after thirty seconds McNally follows him.

McNally is milling around, looking at the adult material that is for sale in the lobby of this theater, while the Colonel is talking with the ticket taker. They seem to know one another, but the ticket taker is uncomfortable and the Colonel is very condescending in their conversation.

Massengill says, "I see you finally found a new, more fitting job you pathetic excuse for a man."

The ticket taker responds, "I wouldn't have had to if you wouldn't have gotten me fired from the sporting goods store. I loved that job, was good at it, and didn't have to lie to people about where I work. You're a bastard Colonel Massengill."

McNally realizes this is Rich O'Donnell, the man that the Colonel had accused of stealing and gotten fired from Maple's Sports.

The Colonel responds, "Maybe, but I am still the hometown hero and you are a lying thief who works in a porno theater because no one in your hometown will hire you. That should teach you never to cross Leslie D. Massengill."

"Why did you do that, I did not steal anything. What have you got against me?"

"Didn't you date Madison Bridger?"

O'Donnell responds, "Yes I did, what has that got to do with anything?"

"Why don't you tell me about fucking her and how it felt to use her for your dirty pleasure? Did you degrade her and make her beg you for the honor of worshiping at the altar of your loins?"

"You sick bastard, don't talk about Madison like that, I loved her, and I still do. Now she won't talk to me because everyone in town thinks that I stole from an injured war veteran. Mr. Maples was always so nice and made me feel like I was worth something. Now he won't speak to me because I represent all that is wrong with the world. Easy money, easy living, and now that I work here, easy morals."

"Give me the ticket to Behind the Green Door and shut up you sniveling little worm."

The Colonel walks away and goes into the first theater, there are three in the building. Most adult theaters are not like this one, this one actually is a converted movie theater that, in its glory days, and better times for Fayetteville, was an old Cineplex with the marquee and tubular neon lights. Of course, the pomp and circumstance of those days are gone, and the lights no longer function outside. It is a shell of a once beautiful place. It, like most of the eastside of Fayetteville, has fallen into disrepair and dropped in status from an elegant place of youth and romance to a place where dirty old men and perverts go to get worked up before picking up a twenty dollar hooker for the evening.

174

McNally thinks how this place is such an editorial on how things in society have changed. He walks over to O'Donnell and asks for at ticket.

O'Donnell asks, "Which show?"

"Which one did the asshole you were arguing with go in?"

"Behind the Green Door, that is the first theater where the classic porno movies are shown, the other two are hardcore and lesbian shows."

McNally says, "That will do. Thanks."

McNally thinks, 'This kid even takes pride in his work at a skin flick theater. McNally would love to help him out because this kid got dealt a raw deal.'

McNally's eyes adjust to the darkness and he sees the theater is sparsely populated. He spots Massengill sitting in the back, three rows from the last one in the middle section of seats. McNally goes all the way to the back row of seats on the far right of the section the Colonel is seated in and takes a seat. Massengill is enthralled in the movie on the screen. Most of the other patrons are casually watching, or sleeping off a drunk, but Massengill watches the screen with anticipation. He wouldn't know if there is anyone in a hundred miles. McNally reaches in his pocket and removes a micro camera made to take short videos or still pictures without the assistance of light. He films the Colonel for about two minutes, and he makes sure to get the screen in part of the shot for context. In about an hour the Colonel gets up and leaves, McNally waits until he is gone for about a minute and then he gets up and follows the Colonel out of the theater. McNally walks through the doors made of glass and brass, and begins his search to pick up Massengill on the street. McNally crosses to the other side of the street outside the theater. He spots Massengill, who is still on the same side of the street as the theater, he is strolling down the road towards the motel, when he stops and finds a curvy Latina girl among the prostitutes on the street. Massengill asks, "Cuánto cuesta la puta?"

She responds, "Cincuenta dollares a hora papí."

Massengill says, "Fifty is way too much for your chubby little ass. I'll give you thirty-five and you'll be happy to get it."

"Ok papí where are we going?"

"Bushy Hills Motel, be there in thirty minutes, room 169. If you still want fifty, bring a friend."

McNally continues on to the motel, and is in his truck when the Colonel comes strolling across the parking lot, he walks past his Chrysler and into his room. In about twenty minutes the hooker he spoke to just outside theater arrives at the motel with another thinner pale looking crack whore. They walk directly to room 169 and just as they arrive there the door opens and the Colonel pulls them both inside.

After about an hour and a half there is no further activity and McNally looks at his watch, 01:30. It is Wednesday morning now and McNally thinks about Brandy as his mind wanders from the indecency of the man he is following and where he is now. He is thinking of her and how open and honest she is. How he wishes he could be the same with her. He does know that John McNally may not be real, but the man behind him is the man she is falling in love with.

Just then he sees the Colonel exit the motel room; he quickly makes his way to his Chrysler and is gone. McNally is confused for a moment, most whores work as fast as they can to do as many johns as they can in an evening. It is a volume business although the thought is disturbing to McNally. Even if a whore tells you fifty dollars an hour it is really till you get off and then she is gone. It is up to the john to last the hour.

He realizes the two hookers haven't come out, so he dismounts the vehicle, and walks over to the door of room 169. He pulls out his lock picks, this motel hasn't upgraded to electronic cards and probably never will, in a moment the door is open and the scene in the room is extremely disturbing. The chubby Latina girl is tied up on the bed at all four corners and is unconscious, and the pale white crack whore is tied to the chair in the room. McNally walks over to her, and a syringe is hanging out of her arm, he puts his finger on her neck and finds no pulse. He reaches inside his coat, retrieves an alcohol wipe he normally uses to clean prints off of a gun and wipes her neck where he touched it. He looks at the Latina girl, and the thought of Chastity Michaelson swirls through his mind, although this girl's innocence has been gone for ages. He walks over to her and puts his watch in front of her mouth, the face of the watch fogs with moisture, she is breathing.

McNally immediately leaves and wipes down the door where he had touched it while picking the lock. He locks the door behind him and makes his way back to his vehicle. As he leaves the parking lot he calls the phone number of the motel. It rings several times, and

McNally is down the road when a disinterested voice answers with, "What do you want?"

He says, "Who is registered in room 169?"

The clerk responds, "Why should I tell you? What's in it for me buddy?"

"Tell me and maybe they won't charge you with the murder of the dead girl in that room."

"What?!! Dead girl, what dead girl are you talking about?"
"Does it matter? Who is registered?"

"He paid cash, didn't get an I.D. He signed the register Alex Hidel."

McNally tells him, "I would recommend calling the police immediately."
McNally pushes the end button on his phone, pulls over into the parking lot of a dry cleaning business, wipes the phone with an alcohol swab, removes the simm card from the phone and tosses the phone into the dumpster. While making the drive back to Cedar Creek, he snaps the simm card into four pieces and throws them, one by one, out the window over a ten mile stretch. He gets back to the Shady Elms Motel and collapses in the bed. He sleeps until 10:30 the next morning, and when he awakens late in the morning, he knows that he has to

kill this man, not just for the money or for Louise Wilson's reasons, but to protect Brandy and the rest of the world from this eminent danger.

Chapter 17

In the early morning hours, on Wednesday while McNally is sleeping, the Fayetteville police are hard at work. Three black and white patrol cars and a detective's unmarked car are in the parking lot of the Bushy Hills Motel, and the blue strobe lights of the cars fill the darkness of the night. A forensic team has the room taped off, is dusting every surface possible for prints, and collecting any hair and skin samples they can find. Meanwhile, the body of the nameless pale hooker, who has been overdosed with heroin, is being carried out to the meat wagon. A drugged and confused Latina prostitute sits on the back of an EMT truck wrapped in a blanket, and she is thankful to be alive. The police have freed her from her bondage, and are interviewing her, to try and get an idea of who the killer might be.

Her name is Lupe Gonzalez, but everyone knows her on the street by the name Amber Rose. A police sergeant questions her, trying to get a clear idea what the assailant looks like. She is little help because the drugs given to her during the ordeal have clouded her mind. She does remember that when she showed up she was immediately pulled into the room and chloroformed. The other girl, who did not survive, was apparently hit in the head with a heavy object to render her unconscious, a shattered lamp had been found near the door to the room. Amber Rose woke up blindfolded and tied to the bed naked. The only recollection she has of the attacker was of a man that propositioned her down the street and instructed her to come to this room. She cannot be certain if the same man is the one who was in the room when she was assaulted. She remembers being violently raped, and a gravelly voice telling her he is in control and she is his play thing. If she gives him enough pleasure she may survive. Amber Rose begins to cry uncontrollably while speaking with the sergeant. Knowing how close she came to dying is disturbing, and the fact that her friend is now just a memory and all that remains is a cold corpse makes that all too real.

At the same time a detective, Lt. Dallas Bird, is interviewing the mostly useless clerk who is the only person that laid eyes on the suspected killer. He asks the scruffy, fat, man who reeks of cigar smoke, "What did the man who checked into room 169 look like?"

"He was about 6 feet tall, slender, older, looked pretty average."

Dallas Bird asks, "Any distinguishing features? What color was his hair or his eyes?"

"I don't think he has any scars or anything you could see, hair was gray, don't know about his eyes. He was an old guy and an asshole too. He did sign in though."

Dallas may have a lead, "He signed in? What was his name? Did you check his I.D.?"

The clerk tells Lt. Bird, "He signed in as, um, Alex Hidel. I did not get an I.D. to verify it, he was paying cash."

Lt. Bird says, "Ok this should be easy we are looking for a tall, old, gray headed, asshole, probably using a false name. I'll put the APB out right now. I'm sure we'll find <u>him</u> by morning. You know this description is useless don't you buster?"

The clerk responds, "Man I just don't remember so good. If I do is there any reward in it for me?"

"Yeah, if I find out you are holding out on me I will beat your ass, then charge you with obstruction of justice, and throw you in a cell overnight with a big hairy guy being held for molesting farm animals. Also you don't remember so <u>well</u> not <u>good</u>."

The clerk tells Dallas Bird in a panic, "That's all I know man, if anything comes to me I'll call you immediately. Oh one thing I did forget, when he checked in he left immediately and walked down the road in the direction of the theater."

"Thanks for your help."

Lt. Bird walks back out to his unmarked car, and as he sits behind the wheel knowing this case is going nowhere, he thinks, 'We never would have had this problem in the Corp. I really miss the Marine way of doing things sometimes.'

The other police, and forensic team, have just finished printing the room, and the body of the deceased victim has been removed from room 169. Now comes the hard part, putting all the evidence, or the lack of evidence, together to try and find this sicko, rapist and killer.

Before heading back to the station, Lt. Bird drives to the Blue Danube Theater. He goes in, and the only person he sees, is Rich O'Donnell.

He thinks, 'Sure is funny how, these places are legal, but when police are in the area they clear out like a plague has been released.'

Lt. Bird walks up to the ticket taker, flashes his badge, and asks, "Do you mind if I ask you a few questions?"

The ticket taker responds, "Not at all. I would love to help."

"What is your name?"

"Rich O'Donnell."

"Have you been working all night?"

"Yes, I work the 8 pm to 6am shift."

"Was there anyone suspicious in here tonight?"

"Only everyone who comes in here is suspicious, can you be more specific?"

"I know this is a bad description, but my only eye witness told me an older man, about six feet tall or so, who is slender with gray hair."

"There were several in here tonight, and every night, that fit that description. A lot of the older guys come here to get worked up before picking up a hooker."

"Well the only other clue I got from the eye witness is that he is an asshole. Does that help?"

"Not a lot but, the guy who is the biggest asshole, matches that description, and came in tonight is Lt. Colonel Leslie Massengill, USMC Retired. He came in and watched the classic porno movie for about an hour, and left about 11:00 or so, maybe a little after." Lt. Dallas Bird hands Rich O'Donnell a business card and tells him, "Call me if you remember anything at all, no matter how trivial, small details are what solve these cases."

After that visit, Bird goes back to the station, and fills out all the paperwork. Just as McNally is waking up that morning, the Lieutenant is finishing up his police report and beginning his drive home. On the drive home Lt. Bird thinks, 'I can't accuse a Marine Colonel, especially such a highly decorated one, of such a heinous crime without more proof. Even the indictment of something like that could tarnish a fine and honorable career.'

He did not know Lt. Colonel Massengill the way McNally did, but maybe he would be an impartial cop and find the truth. Even if he did go by the book, it probably would not be in time to save Massengill from the reckoning that is quickly approaching. Coswell will be called on soon enough to finish this.

Chapter 18

After cleaning up late the next morning, McNally drives into Cedar Creek to visit Brandy before her morning shift is over at the Breakfast Nook. He sees her and his angst is set at ease because she seems happy and unafraid. McNally also notices that the Colonel is not in the restaurant, apparently he overexerted himself with his activities the night before, rape and murder can be so tiring.

McNally walks to the counter and Brandy is leaning on her elbows with her chin perched on the palm of her hand. She bats her long eyelashes at John McNally and says, "Hello, sweetie. What can I do you for?"

McNally smiles, "Glad to see you are in such high spirits, are we still on for dinner tonight?"

"I have been looking forward to it all week."

"Good, I hoped as much, I am going to cook you anything your little heart desires."

She smiles, "Are we still going to the movies?"

"Yes, would you like to see another Hitchcock? I see that the classic theater is showing Vertigo."

She responds, "I don't know, they are also showing Breakfast at Tiffany's and I love Audrey Hepburn. Could we see that?"

McNally knows it makes no difference what they see. He just wants to be with her, although in reality there is no John McNally. He knows Jefferson Ripley really wants her now.

He says, "Sure, how about I pick you up at your house at 14:30 and that will give you time to get ready."

"Ok, that is 2:30 right? Just in case I am not ready I will leave the key under the mat."

"I'll see you then, and after the movie we will go to your house so you can relax and I'll get dinner ready. Do you want anything special or do you want me to surprise you?"

"I love your surprises."

McNally leaves there and goes directly to the local grocery store. He picks up fresh, thick cut, pork chops, rosemary, lemons, sea salt, coarse black pepper, minced garlic, olive oil, two pearl onions, shredded cheddar and a bag of red new potatoes. He is at Brandy's house about 14:25, he knocks a couple of times and there is no response so he uses the key to unlock the door and goes in. When he walks in he

188

announces he is there so as not to scare her. She is actually still in the shower at this point, this explains why she did not answer the door or even hear him knock.

McNally decides to use this time to prep some of the meal. He takes a sharp knife and cuts all but three-eighths inch of fat from the edge of the pork chops, and then places them in a mixing bowl. He then covers the pork with a solution of three tablespoons of lemon juice, one and one-quarter cups of water, and two tablespoons of coarse sea salt. He puts them in the refrigerator to brine while they are at the movies and he slices the potatoes into quarters and puts them in a bowl of water with rosemary, garlic, and onion. He then covers the potatoes so they won't turn black and puts them in the fridge as well.

He thoroughly washes his hands with soap, and goes into the living room to sit and wait for Brandy. He thinks of the gifts he bought her while on his trip to 'Nashville' and runs out to his vehicle to bring them in. He sets the wrapped box with the statue of Alan Jackson on the living room table. He wrapped it in newspaper because he was never good at that sort of thing. Since he has not wrapped the album he goes over to the console stereo and powers it up. Once the stereo warms up, he figures out how to switch it to turntable, and puts the record on. While Billie Holiday is crooning away, Brandy emerges from the back wearing a black kimono robe, panties, a bra, and nothing else.

She says to McNally, "John, welcome home. Do you want to switch that movie to an evening performance or do you really want to see the matinee?"

McNally sits there with his mouth slightly open, he simply blinks because he is unable to speak for a few seconds. He then says, "Movie, what movie? All I see is the most beautiful, sexy, woman I have ever laid eyes on."

She then points at John and curls her finger back in a come hither motion.

"Why don't you help me back here, I think there is something that really needs your attention."

McNally stands, wait till she turns, and removes his leather jacket and gun. He hides the gun in the stereo's album storage and quickly follows her to the queen size bed.

She is lying on the bed, wearing the robe that has fallen to the side exposing the black lacy panties and a matching bra. She looks like she is floating on a pillow on the bed but it is just McNally's imagination and the heat of the moment.

He says, "You are the most sensual, ravishing, woman I think I have ever known."

Brandy says, "Then why are you over there, and wearing entirely too many clothes?"

John responds "Good point." he then removes his clothes expeditiously as he walks across the room to slide into the bed beside her. Brandy makes love to John like a starving woman consuming her last meal. She absolutely devours him, and John in turn caresses every inch of her supple skin, wishing that it could be like this forever. Unfortunately, she is in love with John McNally, and it will by choice or design have to end. He wishes she had fallen in love with Jefferson Ripley but there is no way he can think of that reality to ever be in the realm of possibility. McNally hopes that she doesn't have these complex inner dialogues with herself while they are having sex. He only wishes that she enjoys the experience to the highest level, because although his mind is cluttered with thoughts, he most definitely enjoys the experience. His inner dialogue and over analysis of fact is a trait from his training he wishes would fade. The two lie in each other's arms holding one another silently. He cannot remember being with a woman that he wants to hold and caress as much afterwards as her. He holds her in a way that is both simultaneously soft and firm. Just as her body is soft and supple and firm at the same time, it seems to be an oxymoron but it is still the undeniable fact. McNally brushes her long hair away from her beautiful gleaming green eyes and tells her, "Now what is that thing that needs so much attention again?"

Brandy smiles and responds, "You showed plenty of attention and I think this is a much better time than we would have had at the movies even if it was Breakfast at Tiffany's. Although I don't object to again...."

They make love for another hour as both their bodies are like raw nerves tingling and the experience is an amazing dance between two people that fit like a key in a lock, at least for now.

McNally slowly, pulls away and gets out of the bed. He holds onto her hand until their fingertips finally, gently, pull apart.

"I hate to have to leave the warm bed but I did promise you dinner. Why don't you relax and cuddle up in the warm bed while I make us dinner. I will let you know when it is ready."

"Ok, I will get up in a few minutes and get dressed."

McNally smiles "Don't do that on my account, you look ravishing when you're naked."

She smiles and blushes from head to toe, "I will have to put something on for dinner but it is nice of you to say."

McNally leaves the bedroom and heads to the kitchen where he begins preparing the meal for the night. He drains the brine from the pork chops and the water from the potatoes. He puts the potatoes in a heavy glass baking dish and seasons them with salt, pepper, and rosemary and puts them into cook. He puts the pork chops into a flour breading and seasons them before sliding them into the oven to cook. Both dishes should take about forty-five minutes so that should give Brandy ample time to rest up from their earlier amorous activities. He cleans as he cooks so there will not be dishes to do afterwards. This also gives him time to think, 'Is this really right, she is in love with a man who doesn't exist. McNally cares for her a great deal but he doesn't know if this is love or if Jefferson Ripley is capable of such things.' McNally then thinks, 'Down time sucks if this is where my mind will wander to.' Right then he thinks being in love may be great, but love can suck too. It would be so much easier if he just didn't care. Why does he?

In forty minutes McNally walks into the bedroom to let Brandy know dinner will be ready in five or ten minutes. She is just getting dressed and puts on a pair of painted on jeans that show off her curves quite well, a white blouse, black boots, and a cable knit sweater in case they go out and it is cold. McNally stands there for a moment looking at her in the candlelight, he tells her, "Dinner is served."

They sit down to a nice dinner of broiled pork chops and cheesy rosemary potatoes. It is simple, but elegant and delicious. McNally serves Blue Moon Belgian Ale with dinner. He likes the fact that this woman isn't pretentious, and can just sit and drink a beer with a good home cooked meal.

McNally tells Brandy, "I wanted to make sure and tell you this time, I have got to go out of town tomorrow and will probably be gone until Saturday. I have a customer that I need to speak with about their order, and I want to do it face to face."

"Okay, it is a little weird that every time we are 'together' you have to leave the next day to go out of town."

"It is just a coincidence and a lot of my business is out of town. I would have never come to Cedar Creek if I didn't have to travel for business, and see how well that has worked out?"

Brandy smiles and says, "I guess I can't complain because you're the best thing to happen to me in as long as I can remember."

The two finish their meal in a soft silence and afterwards decide to take a late night stroll in the cold, crisp, autumn air under the stars. They walk for about an hour and Brandy never lets go cuddling up to McNally under his heavy leather jacket. They get back to the house and sit next to the fireplace for a couple of hours enjoying a warm fire and the silence of the night together. Later, when the fire has died down, they retire to the bedroom together and McNally sets his alarm for 10:30. They lie down together, and make love again just before slowly falling off to sleep in each other's arms. Another perfect evening with Brandy has come to a close. When will she find out what McNally is in reality and all of it will come to a finale?

Chapter 19

The next morning McNally rises and takes a long, hot, shower. Brandy hears him and decides to join him. He has the privilege of watching her naked, supple, body being covered in warm, soapy, droplets of water. He enjoys watching the warm sheets of water roll over her amazing curvaceous figure, but he does need to get on the road and the fact he must leave hinders any progression from that point. He finishes cleaning up, and puts on fresh clothes from his overnight bag, while she finishes showering. He checks his Webley revolver and stows it under his jacket over his right hip. Once she emerges from the shower wearing her red satin robe McNally softly kisses her goodbye. He tells her, "I hate to, but I have to go. I hope you enjoy your day off today."

She responds, "How could I not after last night?"

He smiles and dashes away in a moment. He gets into his explorer and John McNally is no more for now, Coswell is who has to take care of the issues of the day. With a new and clear goal in his head he drives towards Autryville through the back roads so he can turn east on county road twenty-four and make his way down to Wilmington. Driving through the back roads takes a little longer, but he should still arrive in Wilmington in about three hours. Louise Wilson is not scheduled to arrive at the rendezvous point until 18:00. Chances are she will be a little early because the fear of God, or at least the loss of her life, has successfully been put into her during the earlier phone call. Coswell should still be there more than two hours before she will arrive.

Driving down to Wilmington, Coswell can also plot where he will get rid of the weapon that will be used to remove the Colonel's scourge from this world. There are several rivers that run through the area, and he has narrowed down the best location to dispose of the weapon to two locations, either White Lake or the Cape Fear River. Both of these bodies of water are deep enough, far enough from the city of Cedar Creek, and remote enough, that they will likely not be searched by authorities for the weapon. According to his calculations, before the police are alerted to the fact of a possible crime, and long before they first arrive on the scene, he should be to Clinton, North Carolina. At least this is the plan.

197

Coswell is now driving through Clinton, and making a turn onto four twenty-one that feeds down to Wilmington. From Clinton to Wilmington is a little more than eighty miles. He left Cedar Creek at about 11:30, and it is now 12:45. By 14:30 he will be in Wilmington, and on the far side of town where he is to meet his employer, although she does not know she is meeting Coswell.

Soon Coswell will be in the Dockside Waterfront Restaurant and Bar in Wrightsville Beach. The good thing about meeting there is, this late in the season, the waterfront is not very crowded because tourist season is over. There are still enough people around to blend in, and he can still get a nice soft shell crab dinner too.

Coswell arrives in Wrightsville Beach outside of Wilmington and parks his vehicle around the back of the Dockside Waterfront Restaurant, by the loading dock where the deliveries are brought in. It is almost 15:00 and all deliveries should be done for the day. No one should see him, and there should be little activity back there until tonight when the trash is taken out after the restaurant closes.

Coswell disembarks his vehicle and walks around the boardwalk looking out at the ocean and sights to clear his busy mind. This woman that he is meeting cannot have even an inkling of an idea that he is the one she has hired for this job or she will have to be eliminated as well. That should not be a problem, Jefferson Ripley has played so many roles in his life he is really the only one that knows which persona is real and which is an alias. Right now there are four distinctly different characters he plays. He wonders if Jefferson Ripley is still the reality or has he become just another alias. To the rest of the world he is genuine, and as good as gold no matter which persona he shows them. He thinks Brandy has no idea that there is any other identity besides John McNally, but for now he wants to keep it that way. At least it is an escape for him, where he can sneak in some genuine feeling that involves another living being. Usually, the only ones who realize he is not who he seems, do so just before their life ends and they become another cold corpse in a long line of unsolved mysteries that Coswell has had a hand in.

The cold sea breeze blows in, there is a chill in the air as it is late October and the evenings on the

North Carolina coast can be bitter and harsh this time of year. Coswell looks at his watch, it reads 16:40. He thinks, 'I better make my way back over to the restaurant and find a booth that is secluded and has a line of sight facing the door.'

He walks in and surveys the restaurant to find his best spot. As he enters the place the long bar is directly in front of him with a stage for a live band, tables and a small dance floor to the far right of the bar. To the left of the bar is a cove of tables that are away from the music. In the back and to the left there is a hallway that leads to the bathrooms and emergency exit. Coswell goes to the bar and asks the bartender for a shot of maker's mark. He then tells him, "If anyone comes in asking for someone who knows Mr. Coswell please tell them to come to the table back here to the left. Okay?"

Coswell lays a twenty dollar bill on the bar and when the barkeep sees his tip he says, "No Problem buddy."

"Oh and when she arrives, make sure we have some privacy too."

The bartender is absently cleaning glasses and says, "Okay, shouldn't be a problem over there. Most everyone coming tonight is here for karaoke night, over by the stage."

Coswell settles into the cushy round bar booth in the far left corner and removes his knife from its sheath in the small of his back. He places it on the table under the heavy linen napkin. Coswell thinks to himself, 'Better safe than sorry and this will not make too much noise if it is called for.'

Soon a woman in her late fifties walks into the Dockside Waterfront Restaurant and begins to look around aimlessly. She is quite attractive, and this woman has the look of a woman maybe fifteen years younger. As old and withered with evil as Colonel Massengill is, his estranged wife is quite the opposite. She is a woman who is older, distinguished, and probably well respected, but as beautiful as the day she turned 35. She steps up to the bartender, and although they are out of earshot, Coswell sees him absently bob his head in the direction of the back hall where Coswell is seated. The bartender does so without even looking up from the glass he is wiping out. The woman, Louise Wilson Coswell assumes, walks toward him clutching her Valentino purse in front of her.

She walks up to the table and says, "Do you know a Mr. Coswell?"

The seated individual responds, "No one really knows Mr. Coswell, but I represent him. Please sit down ma'am."

She slowly sits and the creaking of the supple leather seats is heard as she sinks down into the padded booth. She sets her designer purse beside her and folds her hands gently in front of her. Next she asks "Who are you?"

The man sitting in the booth responds "Names are not important, and you need not be curious. You know what that can get you? Dead is what it will lead to."

"Yes sir, I'm sorry. I am just nervous. What does Mr. Coswell need of me?"

"He needs to verify that you still want this target eliminated and there have been no second thoughts when considering all the consequences."

"Yes, well I do, he is evil and this world will be a better place without him. Don't you agree?"

"I am not here to make judgments. I am here to verify that you are still adamant in your conviction to this job. I am here to make sure you can pay the remaining monies and that no mention of Mr. Coswell will ever be made once the target draws his last breath."

She responds, "Of course not, that could implicate me too."

"Just so you know, once this is done, it cannot be undone. I came here as a messenger from Mr. Coswell. This will soon come to an abrupt end and it will not be glorious or pretty. Death never is. Once you receive the final call you will have one business day to wire the remainder of the fee. Will that be a problem?"

Louise Wilson is a bit shakier now but utters one word, "No…."

In a moment she continues, "I have saved for this moment and the money is ready right now. I will send it as soon as I am told."

"Good, I am glad we have that out of the way, just remember never speak a word or the name Coswell or you will sign your own death warrant. Stay here and have dinner, I will pay for it and you may leave after 8:00 pm. not a minute before."

She looked at her watch 6:28 pm, "Yes sir."

Coswell removes his knife from under the napkin and puts it away. He rises from the booth and walks quickly to the bar. He stops and tells the bartender, "Here is eighty dollars to cover the meal for the woman in the back booth. She will need a menu and probably a drink menu too. You keep the change."

With that, Coswell walks out of the Dockside Waterfront Restaurant knowing that Louise Wilson may be nervous and scared, but she is genuine in her desire to end her estranged husband's life and just as interested in preserving her own life.

After walking down the boardwalk, making sure no one tails Louise Wilson or is helping her watch him, Coswell returns to the loading dock of the restaurant, gets in his vehicle and drives back west.

Just before 24:00 Coswell is pulling back into Cedar Creek and drives to the Shady Elms Motel for a well deserved night's rest. The next morning, he arises and knows the plan will come to completion in six days. It is Friday morning and Coswell has enough of the pieces to put together the real story. He could justify killing this man long ago, but now he can justify killing the man who was once awarded the CMH. He knows that they are one in the same, and he may have been a recipient of the Congressional Medal of Honor but it was not just or right.

Sitting in the room at the Shady Elms Motel, while going over all of his notes, he now has put together what troubled him about the different versions of the story of what happened in 1972. That piece that had always felt like a square peg in a round hole suddenly fit. It popped into Coswell's mind, the Captain's shoulder wound finally made sense. He knows why it was so traumatic and at the exact same time simply a flesh wound.

He remembered reading the dossier that had the official story and Louise Wilson's story in it. The official story claimed that Gunny Lopez was killed by enemy fire while running in full retreat. He had abandoned his post. Corporal Roosevelt was critically wounded by enemy fire and had a chest wound, and Captain Leslie D. Massengill was hit and had an injury on the ball of his left shoulder and a grazing flesh wound about an inch apart. Louise Wilson had told Coswell that in a drunken state Massengill told her that he had run and left his squad, Roosevelt was hit by enemy fire and the Colonel admitted he killed Gunny Lopez. This did not account for the wound he had on his shoulder or how he could drag a man the size of Gunny "Jumbo" Lopez to the tree line.

Coswell figured it out. When Massengill ran he had the M14E3 rifle, the full auto model. Lopez primarily chased Massengill to retrieve the rifle as it had greater firepower when it came to suppression. Roosevelt did get hit by SKS fire but Lopez did not. Lopez got shot multiple times in the chest, at the tree line, by none other than Leslie D. Massengill. Massengill didn't go back to get Roosevelt, he crawled his way over to the tree line after being hit. Finally the shoulder wound, it showed so much trauma because it was self inflicted to make the story believable. The only thing Massengill didn't count on was that the full auto M14 is very hard to control because of recoil, and although he only meant to cause a grazing flesh wound, he fired a two shot burst and planted a round firmly in his own shoulder. If he hadn't done that Roosevelt surely would have been killed on the battlefield as well. Massengill was a coward, traitor, sexual deviant and ended up shooting himself to obtain our nations highest honor and a trip home from the war.

Now that Coswell had put all of this together he is ready to act. Next Thursday is October 23rd and also the anniversary of Massengill being awarded the Congressional Medal of Honor. He decides that is when he will remove Massengill from this earth like a surgeon excises cancer. It is decided now, and Coswell begins to plan his escape route from Cedar Creek, and where he will dispose of any evidence that may be able to be tied to the crime.

Chapter 20

Lt. Bird is looking over the evidence the police collected from the murder and rape that occurred last week in the seedy sex district of Fayetteville. He is looking for connections and clues, and with the help of forensics has narrowed his list of possible suspects to about fifteen in a one hundred mile area. The one that is on the list that he reluctantly is looking at is Lt. Colonel Leslie D. Massengill, USMC Retired. He lives within a twenty minute drive of the crime scene, his print is a partial match to a smudge found on the doorknob, it is rumored but not confirmed, that he likes kinky sex and prostitutes, but as a former Marine, Detective Dallas Bird needs more than just the circumstantial evidence he has to tarnish the Colonel's reputation by bringing him in on a charge of rape and suspicion of murder. He is checking on other crimes in the surrounding area that are similar in nature, and he comes across the unsolved crime in Cedar Creek involving the rape of a fifteen year old girl who was restrained in bondage shackles, raped, and left for her father, a minister no less, to find. The M.O. is not specifically the same but similar and when Lt. Bird has the forensic files sent over he sees something that will require he give the Colonel some attention. A smudge of a print was left on the shackles used and Colonel Massengill is a possible match to that case as well, but it is the only evidence the sheriff has and not enough to bring someone before the grand jury.

Lt. Bird has been working feverishly on this case all day, it is Friday October 17th and he leaves for vacation starting tomorrow. He needs a rest, it has been two years since the last vacation and dealing with the depravity in homicide has taken its toll. That night at 22:30 he finally puts away the case for the evening. He tells himself, 'It is a cold case and it will be here when I get back.'

He sits at his desk and takes out a bottle of Jack Daniels from the bottom drawer and pours a coffee cup half full. He leans back and reads the brochure on the cruise he booked for his vacation. It leaves Sunday at noon and returns the following Thursday, the 23rd, at 6:00pm. He thinks, 'Gambling, food, fun, beautiful women, and Bermuda what else could a man ask for.'

He thinks of the two cases again and how are they connected, and then he says, "It will be here when you get back Bird, just relax and put it out of your mind dammit."

Then he thinks of Blackjack out to sea and it makes things better. He reaches up turns off his desk lamp and says, "Well I'll be back and I'll see you soon Colonel Massengill. I'll pull you in here to question, but not before a little R & R, and not before Monday October 27th."

With that Lt. Bird leaves the homicide division of the Fayetteville Police Department and heads to his home to do a little tinkering on his old Mustang. Working on a simple machine like an old Mustang always seems to clear his mind when nothing else works.

Lt. Bird Arrives home to his bachelor pad and goes to his workshop and garage. He pops the hood on his 1965 Ivy Metallic Green fastback 2+2 GT350 Shelby Mustang. He takes a moment to survey the beautiful work of art that powers this beast. It is a Hi-Po 289 that has been tweaked and massaged so it now pushes three hundred and fifty horsepower. It is backed by a manual 4-speed, only the grandma cars had automatics.

Lt. Bird always found peace working on his pony car. He decides to make sure she is tuned like a razor, so he can enjoy his Saturday off tomorrow, and cruise the back roads east of Fayetteville and let her loose. This engine needs to be set free on those back roads. An engine is like a wild animal and needs to breathe freely and run wild from time to time. It will also help to clear his mind and get ready for the well deserved time off, and the sea cruise the next day heading to Bermuda.

The morning that Bird's cruise leaves he gets up early, packs up the Mustang and makes the drive down to the coast, specifically Charleston, South Carolina. He heads down interstate ninety-five deep into South Carolina before turning east on interstate twenty-six that heads directly into Charleston, down to the harbor, and to the departure point for his well deserved vacation. The case and all his other worries are behind him for now, and will not even cross his mind again until Thursday the 23rd when he will arrive once again on U.S. soil. Until then he isn't Lt. Bird of the Fayetteville Police department, but just Dallas Bird, easy going bachelor and gambler. All Dallas Bird wants is good times, good cards, and easy ladies. He needs relaxation and to completely unwind, and this vacation should do the trick. He thinks of the wonderful moment once the ship has left port and it is twelve miles out. That is the moment the blackjack tables, as well as the rest of the casino open. Dallas however is a blackjack man. Blackjack has always been good to Dallas. It supplies him with entertainment, money, and there is always an overly friendly and flirtatious woman at almost every table he sits at. In his mind he is already on the boat and out to sea. He is nearing the coast, can smell the sea air, and can barely remember what he left behind, the case, the killer, the sick deranged man out there, all seem to fade for now. Everyone needs a little rest, he does so much for so little reward, he deserves this reward and with that everything fades from his mind as he pulls up to the parking deck for the cruise line, right by the ship.

Chapter 21

Monday morning, nice and early, Coswell gets up and takes a nice long, hot, shower. He needs to relax and make sure he is clear headed and covers all angles when it comes to the job. He is in the homestretch, and is ready to bring this to an end. By his estimation, the Colonel has a little less than 90 hours to enjoy breathing before he is shuffled off into oblivion.

Coswell gets out of the shower, dries himself off, and gets dressed expeditiously. He is wearing dark blue jeans, black cowboy boots, a red button down shirt, and his gun in his shoulder rig under his camel hair coat.

He walks down to the office at the Shady Elms Motel, and once again Wilbur the heroin addict is there. Coswell walks up to the desk and tells Wilbur "I am going to be in and out all week and want to make sure I am paid up. Here is my last week's payment. This should be enough to pay through Saturday."
Wilbur looks at the cash and his glazed over eyes almost gleam.

"Thank you for staying at the Shady Elms Motel."

Coswell sarcastically responds, "Yes it was such a wonderful stay, I will tell all my friends."

Wilbur is bewildered but says, "Thanks a lot man."

When Coswell turns and walks through the office door Wilbur puts twenty-five dollars in the register and the other cash he rolls up and stuffs in his pocket. Coswell walks back to his room and thinks to himself, 'That's one less thing to take care of, now to disassociate myself from some other connections.'

He gets into his Ford Explorer and rides out to Cedar Village Way to the Colonel's place, stopping along the way to fuel up and pick up coffee and some breakfast in a fast food drive-thru. He doesn't want to go to the Breakfast Nook this morning. There is nothing to be gained from doing so. If he were to go there it would not be for new information, Coswell thinks, 'That well has run dry, and I need to concentrate on bringing the job at hand to a close.'

On the drive out to Massengill's he makes a call to the Fayetteville Police Department.

Coswell opens, "Hello, I am calling to find out who the lead detective is on the case of the murdered call girl that was reported on television last week."

The Police switchboard operator tells him, "Hold one moment I will get you over to the Homicide division."

In a moment a female voice comes on the phone, "Homicide, Sergeant Carolyn Malanichi here."

"Are you the lead detective investigating the murder of the call girl in eastern Fayetteville?"

"Well, I am the current one investigating, Lt Dallas Bird is the lead investigator but he is currently on vacation until the 27th. Is there anything I can help you with?"

"It can wait. I wasn't going to be back in the Fayetteville area until that weekend anyway so I will just speak to him on Monday the 27th. Thank you very much."

"Sir what is your name and is there a message?"

"Just tell him Willie Roosevelt called and I will come by on Monday. Thank you."

With that the line went silent and Sergeant Carolyn Malanichi hung the phone up with a puzzled look on her face. She wrote down the message and stuck it to the computer screen on Dallas Bird's desk.

Coswell turns on the bugging monitor on his phone so he can listen to the interior of Colonel

Massengill's home. He is sitting there monitoring the bug and watching the house. He watches as the Colonel, once again, sits in his red flannel robe, pajamas, and leather slippers on his front porch. He is sitting there as he does every morning reading the paper, sipping coffee, and this morning he is eating a bagel. After two hours, three cups of coffee, and time to read the paper from cover to cover, the Colonel goes back inside. It is quiet for a while but then Massengill makes a call. "Hello, is the madam in?"

Gracie Greathouse answers her phone, "This is Greathouse, Attorney at law. Have some respect you slug. You don't deserve the madam, you need the mistress but you can't afford her."

"I really do need the madam, I know you said Madison and Cheryl don't 'entertain' but I am going to need some morally liberal entertainment for the night of the 25th and I wanted to have some variety for my guests. I would like a blonde, a redhead, and if possible a curvy Latina girl too."

Greathouse tells him, "That can be arranged but good 'entertainment' for your type of friends doesn't come cheap. I have a few girls who look very good and have little to no inhibition about what they do for the

216

money. However, it will cost top dollar for the night and all three, $5000.00 but I guarantee they are as kinky as you and your friends, maybe even more so."

"That is kind of high but if you can get a curvy Latina girl we have a deal."

"That should not be a problem, slime."

The line goes dead and now Coswell knows the Colonel is planning another sick party and Coswell thinks of that dungeon room in the Colonel's house. Coswell then thinks, 'You will never get the chance Colonel Massengill.'

Coswell sits and listens to Massengill making calls all day. He is setting up the party and calls James Willis, the owner of the hardware store.

Massengill tells him, "Get everyone together and be prepared for top notch entertainment. It will be a party to remember but the entry fee for this one is 500.00."

Willis tells him, "I know of at least 10 or 12 guys in town that will want in on this. It is on Saturday the 25th right?"

"This Saturday will be a night to remember Willis. I just don't know how I am going to make it through the next five days. I may have to celebrate a

217

little early, Thursday is my award anniversary. I may have to treat myself."

"Whatever you do, don't stir up any more trouble like before, the heat is just now dying down and I don't know how they didn't bring you in for questioning last time."

Massengill smiles as he responds to Willis over the phone, "Simple, I am untouchable. This is my town and I am of course a hero."

Willis tells him, "Right, well I will get everyone together and let you know who will be attending by Wednesday. Does that sound good?"

"That works, I will talk to you later. I have another call I must make. Bye."

Coswell thinks 'Maybe this could work out that I finish this job, make it look like revenge, close a police case and no one will even suspect a hit'. Coswell sits and smiles knowing exactly what he will do. This is because the Colonel has become quite predictable when it comes to how he likes to 'celebrate'. Just as his plan starts to form completely he hears another call from the Colonel's phone.

Massengill says, "Hello, Timothy. I am calling to see if you are ok after that horrible ordeal with your daughter. Is Chastity ok, has she recovered yet? Do they have any leads on who might have done such a sadistic thing?"

Chaplain Michaelson responds, "Thank you so much for calling Colonel Massengill. You don't know how much this means that you thought of us in this time of crisis. The police haven't any leads yet. A Fayetteville detective thought he might have something that might be connected but when I called and asked to speak to him they said he was on vacation for the next week."

Massengill says, "I don't believe it. He took his vacation when he has a case like this? What was his name? I will make a call to the Fayetteville police to complain."

"It's ok. There is someone else working on it. We are having another poker game this Saturday if you would like to come. The guys down at the VFW will be short because I won't be going for quite a while. I just can't leave Chastity alone again."

"Thank you Timothy but I can't attend this Saturday. I have a prior engagement already. Tell Chastity I called and will be thinking of her."

Chaplain Michaelson tells Massengill, "Thank you so much Colonel."

When Massengill hangs up an evil smile crosses his face as he thinks, 'He just thanked me for raping his daughter. I <u>am</u> untouchable.'

Chapter 22

After leaving port the night before, and enjoying a good night's rest, Dallas Bird strolls down the vast, beautiful, corridor of the Empress Sky cruise liner. He leaves his cabin near the forecastle of the ship heads down to the huge atrium, the sparkling crystal centerpiece of this ship. His cabin is on the 5th deck, which is the same level as the lowest part of the atrium. When he walks out of the hallway, and into the atrium, everything around him shimmers and is bathed in sunlight. Bright light filters in from the leaded glass ceiling six decks up and floods the entire area. From top to bottom it is like a palace, one level after another of wondrous entertainment and beauty. Dallas stands for a moment and silently takes in this sights and sounds that surround him. He stands at the bottom of the stairway that leads up to the glass elevator. As he looks from left to right there are five visible levels of the ship. At the bottom there are attendants at counters eagerly waiting to help the passengers with any desire they might have. They are there to point out all the wonderful choices of adventure. When Dallas peers up he sees the Karaoke bar to the left, a piano bar next to that and a disco all on the next level. Level after level has a platform overlooking the huge atrium with leaded glass and shiny brass rails guarding the edges.

On the level above the bar level is the restaurant level. There are two formal dining rooms, where the sky is the limit and rich food will be brought to a guest as long as they wish during the dinner hours. There is also a steakhouse on this level where one can indulge in Kobe and Angus beef. This is a steak lover's dream, indulging their fancy and eating a different cut of steak every night if it is their desire.

On the level above the formal restaurants is the place Dallas loves the most, the casino. He can walk in the casino and everything is right with the world. It has so many options and is like Vegas, only better. A myriad of games can be played there, roulette, craps, slots, Caribbean poker, Texas hold 'em, among others. However, Dallas has come for one thing and one thing only, Blackjack.

He will spend some time in other places so as not to feel he wasted his vacation. The deck above the casino is the lido deck with a bar, outdoor pool, dance floor, poolside café and of course a place to lie out and enjoy the sun. There are so many places to go and things to see on this ship, he wonders if he can see it all in five days. As that thought crosses his mind he realizes he hasn't even thought of the nightly shows in the theater or the late night comedy shows either.

Dallas looks over the great atrium again and takes a deep cleansing breath just before he climbs the flight of stairs that leads to the glass elevator. When he steps inside the elevator, and is watching everything below become smaller in aspect, he looks up and across the atrium to the entrance of the Karaoke bar. She is a vision he thinks to himself. The elevator cannot move fast enough to get to that level. He stares through the glass at an angelic face. She is about five foot four inches tall, strawberry blonde hair to her shoulders, a yellow mid-drift shirt is around her and tied under her perfectly rounded breasts, and to perfect the look she is wearing a sarong around her gently curved hips. She looks to be about thirty-five, maybe a few years older, but Dallas was never one for the much younger type.

The elevator reaches the level and just before he exits Dallas Bird checks his reflection in the shiny gold doors of the glass elevator. As he walks through the crowded groups of people all trying to find their calling on this ship, he has a purpose. He is determined as he makes his way to the front of the Karaoke bar called "High Notes". He hopes she will still be taking in the view of the incredible atrium and leaning on the freshly shined brass rail. She is gone.

Dallas smiles and thinks, 'C'est la vies' and walks into the Karaoke bar for a drink and to listen to the people singing badly. Dallas sits down at a dark table in the corner and when the waitress comes around he orders a Bahama Mama. As his drink arrives, an already drunk pudgy man is singing 'My Delilah' quite badly. Dallas sits sipping his libation, he enjoys the attitude of this crowd and how people on vacation let down their guard and lower their inhibition. It shows who people really are. After about an hour of drinking and listening to various singers, most that had no talent, he hears something quite different and looks up from his drink. Dallas changed to beer after his second Bahama Mama and that is when a voice grabbed him from across a room. He knew the song but had never heard it sung with such a velvety sounding female voice. The sounds of the words gave him that feeling you get when you are lying next to a lover brushing your hands gently on her soft skin.

He looks up from his beer and sees her as she sooths him, and the entire bar, with 'When the night has come, and the land is dark, and the moon is the only light you'll see.'

The hair on Dallas' neck stands up and he immediately thinks back to how he used to listen to Ben E. King on his old turntable as a teen. He knows right then he lost his first chance, but on a ship this big it has to be fate that she is in the one place he decided to go for a drink. When she finishes the room applauds and he gets up to meet her coming back to her table.

Dallas says, "Excuse me but I just want to tell you how wonderful that was. It took me back and I would love to get you a drink."

She smiles, "That would be lovely. Are you going to get up and sing?"

"Yes, I'll sing after our drink. I am Dallas, Dallas Bird."

Her cherry red lips spread across her face in a warm smile and she responds, "Charmed, I am Kelsey O'Quinn. Please join me."

"Thank you. What can I get you to drink?"

"I'd really love a tequila sunrise."

Dallas smiles back at her, "Coming right up."

Dallas walks up to the bar and orders a Tequila Sunrise and Sam Adams lager. He returns to the table and gently sets her drink in front of her. He slides into the booth and smiles. "You have a wonderful voice, where did you learn to sing?"

"I could lie and tell you in church like everyone else, but I was always getting in trouble for skipping church to go down to the river with boys."

"An honest and self aware woman, now that <u>is</u> refreshing. Do you do mostly rhythm and blues, or do you branch out to rock, country and jazz."

"If it has a good beat and a smooth sound I can sing it."

"What do you say you help me out with my song and we can sing a duet?"

She smiles, "Well I guess that's one way to see if chemistry is there."

They sit together enjoying their drinks and waiting for the DJ to call Dallas' name.
Dallas asks, "Where are you from?"

"Virginia, but I absolutely had to make the drive down to catch this cruise and get away from the beltway and all its headaches."

"You work in D.C.? What do you do there?"

"I am an actuary for a firm there but I used to be in the Navy years ago."

"Really, I was in the Marines, where were you stationed?"

"Technically I was stationed in Norfolk but was assigned to Quantico and worked in the JAG office there as an administrative clerk. How did you come to be on this cruise?"

"I am a homicide detective in Fayetteville North Carolina and just had to take a vacation. There comes a point where you just need to let everything go and relax. Don't you think?"

"Yes you can say that again Dallas."

Just as she is about to continue and Dallas hanging on her every word, they both hear his name called. She smiles and walks up to the stage behind him. At that point Kelsey is thinking to herself, 'This marine has got a cute butt.'

The DJ asks Dallas, "What'll it be?"

He responds, "We are going to do a duet. Do you have Johnny Cash and June Carter singing 'Jackson'?"

The DJ looks puzzled but looks it up. He says, "Oddly enough it is in here. Where the hell did you get this from? You are aware this is a Caribbean cruise."

Dallas tells the DJ, "Just play it." and the two are off and singing. Afterwards, they both run giggling away from the stage back to the table. Dallas wonders, 'Is it just the booze or could this be what he needs to really relax?'

After listening to a couple more singers perform Kelsey says, "What do you say we get out of here and go take in some of the fine dining before the formal dining room closes?"

Dallas thinks 'Why not all I have had today is beer and mixed drinks.'

"Yes, when you mention it I am famished and that will give me the chance to hear more about you too."

"Okay, let's do it up right, meet me in front of the dining room in the atrium in about forty-five minutes, I need to freshen up a little."

"Okay, I will see you then. Do you play blackjack by any chance?"

Kelsey smiles that warm inviting smile and teasingly says, "Is there another game in the casinos?"

Chapter 23

Brandy Potter is waiting behind the counter at the Breakfast Nook wondering about John McNally. As she absently wipes the counter, she thinks to herself, 'I really don't know too much about this man and now he has disappeared. I can't help but love him, he makes me feel so special, but does he really love me? He never has said it but men can be that way.'

She is daydreaming and waiting for her shift to end. She wonders why he hasn't been around to see her in the last couple of days. Brandy ponders, 'Will he come by and see me tomorrow? We always do something special on Wednesdays, I wonder is John really who he says he is? I just take him at his word any time he tells me anything. This is the first time I have ever been completely trusting since I was fifteen. I'm sure he is an honest man; no man would be so sweet, kind, and genuine as he has been and then turn out to be a complete liar and a bastard.'

Then Brandy buried her face in her hands and began to cry, "Why hasn't he called?"

At that point Carlos, the cook in the back, steps out of the kitchen and yells, "Brandy there is a phone call for you."

Brandy races over to the phone on the wall and as she is gasping for breath she hears a soothing voice, "Brandy, are you crying?"

"No sweetie I have just had a trying shift. Are you back in town now?"

John McNally says, "Yes, I just got back into town and I am completely worn out. Are we still on for tomorrow? I thought maybe we could make a day of it after you got off work. Does that sound good to you Brandy?"

"I so need some time off and would love to spend it with you John. What would you like to do?"

"Dinner and maybe a show would be nice, have you ever seen Casablanca? It is showing at the Valparaiso and it is one of the best romantic pictures of all time."

Brandy says, "I have only heard about it, never seen it but would love to. What do you want to do for dinner?"

"I have been dying for a steak since I got here, is there a really nice steakhouse in town?"

Brandy thinks for a minute and says, "The best one I know of is Angelo's but I have never been there, it costs about eighty dollars for dinner there."

John McNally responds, "Let's splurge Darling, you only live once right?"

Just then a customer is yelling for Brandy at the counter and she has to quickly bring the conversation to an abrupt close and hangs up. John McNally listens to the dial tone and the dead line as he presses end on his phone and thinks, 'Well Brandy, at least we will have a nice time this week.' He then looks up from behind the steering wheel of the Ford Explorer and down at the home of Colonel Leslie D. Massengill. "Colonel Massengill you won't be having such a wonderful week."

Back at the Breakfast Nook, Brandy's two best friends walk in and sit down for a late breakfast, but today Brandy is not their server. The twins, Madison and Cheryl Bridger are discussing something they thought they never would.

Madison says, "So you got a text last night from Colonel Massengill, the pervert who is always harassing us. What did it say?"

"He is having some sort of stag party this weekend to celebrate the anniversary of being awarded the Congressional Medal of Honor. He is especially interested in having us 'work the party' for him. He did specify that we would be naked, and I got the feeling so would everyone else there."

"Cheryl, how can we even consider such a thing? We are not whores. He wants to hire us to fuck him and any of his friends that are there. I am not ever doing that!"

"Madison, you don't understand, we are three months behind on rent, the landlord wouldn't even fuck us for payment right now, and the car is acting up, why do you think we walk everywhere? We are in a tight spot, and I hate to say it but one thing we can always use to make money is our bodies."

"With all those problems how is one party going to help? I am not going to become a prostitute Cheryl."

"Madison, he is offering six thousand dollars for the weekend, and I bet as bad as he wants us we can counter offer and get more."

"Six thousand dollars, I don't make that much in 3 months at work. You have got to be mistaken."

232

"What do you want to do? Should I text him back or would this be the perfect opportunity to get the police involved? I bet they could use this text and we could expose him for the sick perverted sadist he is."

"Cheryl you know he humiliated Rich and he has to work at that porno theater. I haven't seen Rich since then and I am ashamed to say it is because of what people would say. The fact is I still love him and have been talking to him recently about seeing each other again. I don't know if he would understand this. He hates that man so much because of how he tore his life apart."

"Madison, are you with him now? No, and Rich isn't going to fix our car or catch up our rent. If you do this you can get back together with your boyfriend and he will never have to know."

"That isn't the point Cheryl. What about dignity, self respect, and the fact that he is such a piece of slime?"

"I know Madison but we are in a tight spot and things are just getting worse. How do you purpose that we catch up the rent, fix the car, and buy groceries and gas? If Brandy didn't work here and give us everything for almost nothing we couldn't even afford to go to breakfast. What if something else goes wrong? We are at the edge now standing there looking into the abyss, and about to fall off. I hate the idea of Colonel Massengill and his friends leering and salivating over us. We always try to do things the right way and what has it gotten us?"

"Cheryl at least we are still respectable. Can you imagine how you will feel the day after you get home and shower and can still feel where Colonel Massengill and all his friends touched you anywhere and everywhere. Can you live with that thought? How did we get here? How did we sink so low?"

"Madison, I hate to think of that, but this is just a one time thing, and we don't have that much of a choice. If we don't do this soon enough we won't have to worry about the rent because we will be evicted, out on the street, and homeless. Which would you rather be a whore for a weekend, or a homeless woman who has to sell her body every night for a place to stay and something to eat?"

"Cheryl, I hate to admit it but you are right, after we leave here, call the Colonel and tell him we will be there Saturday and stay all weekend but it will cost him ten thousand. He has the money and we will just get a new car."

"Madison, are you sure?"

"Unfortunately yes, we have no choice. Everyone has skeletons in their closets, and this will just have to be ours. Clarify to him that this is just a one time offer. Make sure he knows that. Also tell him we want three thousand up front tomorrow and to meet us here at noon with the money. If he says that it is too much, tell him there isn't another set of twins in this town like us. I know this is wrong but the whole world seems to be against us. We will just have to think like a man, we are the best pieces of ass in North Carolina might as well get paid for it too."

Chapter 24

It was 19:00 and Dallas Bird is standing in front of the formal dining room, he leans against the gleaming brass rail in hopes that Kelsey is just fashionably late and hasn't changed her mind. Sometimes when the alcohol wears off and clearer thoughts prevail, people rethink their decisions. Dallas patiently stands there waiting and taking in all the sounds and sights around him. All of his senses are on high alert. He can hear the dealers shuffling and the slot machines ringing on the floor above. Everywhere around him is the constant hum of conversation. New relationships are starting, old ones being rejuvenated or rekindled, and all this is happening here in the one magical place. He goes on a cruise every time he needs to relax, unwind, and just tune out all of the ugliness in the world. Dallas believes this is going to be a great cruise. It is a vacation long overdue, and this is going to clear his soul of all the tarnish his career has applied.

Dallas is wearing his best suit. This is the one he knows he will be buried in one day because it cost him a month's pay. It is a tawny colored Armani suit. The jacket is double breasted and perfectly tailored for him. It has been tailored with a little extra room under the arms to hang perfectly even when hiding his prized Kimber 1911 pistol.

The slacks have a deep crease in the front and back and hang effortlessly down to a point just above his riding boots where they end in a perfect cuff. He is wearing a dark gunmetal gray Dolce and Gabbana shirt and a Zarrano silk tie. His whole ensemble, he thinks to himself, is really set off by his Tony Llama snake skin boots. As Dallas is nervously admiring his attire and waiting for Kelsey she comes breezing out of the elevator doors and he almost falls over.

She appears and is wearing a white satin gown that flows all the way to the floor, four inch high heels, and she is carrying a small matching white clutch purse. She would not be able to walk in this beautiful dress if it were not for the slit on the left side that comes nearly all the way up to her hip. When she is walking toward him he notices her beautiful hair is up now and he wonders how women ever get that done. He sees her sexy tan legs peeking out through the enormously long slit in this work of art that to her is just a dress.

She walks up to him and stands close and he puts his arms around her. She doesn't mind so apparently Dallas was stressing over nothing earlier. She leans in to whisper in his ear with all the noise around them.

"How do I look Dallas? I didn't make you wait too long did I?"

Dallas smiles, "Wait, not at all, you are right on time Kelsey. I have to tell you, I didn't know I was going to dinner with Audrey Hepburn. You sure know how to make an entrance."

"Dallas, I just threw on the first thing I came to, now let's see what they have for tonight's culinary delight."

Dallas and Kelsey stroll into the formal dining room and follow the waiter to the finely appointed table. They are sitting at a table for two. It has a thick linen tablecloth and taper candles in crystal candlesticks are set in the center of the table. The chairs are thick, heavy, cherry, high back chairs. Their table is situated next to a window, overlooking the blackness of the night ocean, which seems to be endless.

Dallas pulls the chair out for Kelsey and then takes his seat. He sits and stares at her watching the candlelight dance in her shimmering azure eyes. She has eyes that are uncommon, a dark sea blue. Just then the waiter approaches and hands them both menus. He begins to go over the specials for the evening and Dallas knows this is going to be a wonderful cruise.

The waiter begins, "Our special entrée for this evening is the Lobster with a rich creamy creole sauce. It is served with your choice of two sides but I highly recommend the creamy crab pasta and grilled asparagus, a truly divine selection. We also have a nice blackened red snapper, served extra spicy, and with a cup of creamy lobster bisque and mashed garlic red potatoes. Finally we have a special dessert tonight, a chocolate molten cake that is broken open and served with a scoop of finest vanilla bean ice cream inside."

Kelsey says, "Wow! That meal sounds like an absolute culinary orgasm."

Dallas cracks a huge smile, "I guess that is one way to sum it up."

The waiter never even misses a beat, "Shall I give you a moment to decide?"

Dallas looks over at Kelsey and she smiles back, "Yes just a couple of minutes to think about it."

"Well Kelsey, what sounds good to you?"

"I think I am going to go with the red snapper, I like a little spice in life."

"Then not to be outdone I will get the Lobster with creole sauce."

Dallas waves the waiter down and orders their dinner. He adds a Yuengling beer for himself and a piña colada for his lovely date. The waiter scurries away to bring back their drinks and place their order in the kitchen.

"So Dallas, you are a homicide detective? That sounds like such interesting work. It must be so exciting facing new and unknown challenges every day. You must have so many gruesome stories about cases that you have worked."

"Well there have been a few interesting ones, but it is Fayetteville, not New York. You are an actuary so you are in risk management right? I'm sure you have more interesting stories than me. That is a just a riveting field with everything always changing isn't it."

"Dallas I really hope you are teasing. My job is mind numbing but it does pay well so I can enjoy the other interests I have. I have a belief that your life is what you enjoy and what you do when you are not slaving away. So really tell me about one of your most exciting cases, if you can."

"Kelsey most of what I deal with is drug deals gone wrong, pimps who beat up and kill one of their girls, every now and then a robbery with a clerk who gets killed at the local rob and go convenience store. There is one case that is a recent one that you might find exciting. The only thing is it has gone cold. It technically is still an active case so I shouldn't talk about it, but technically the zodiac killer is still an active case and it is long cold. Right now it is on the back burner because it is beginning to ice over. There is a suspect out there somewhere that killed a prostitute and tied up another one near the combat zone area of east Fayetteville where the porno theaters and cheap motels are. The girl who was tied up never saw the man and couldn't give a good description because the killer applied chloroform and a blindfold while he raped her. I guess she was the lucky one because she didn't get killed. I am assuming the other prostitute was killed because she could identify her assailant. Is that too gruesome of a case?"

"Wow Dallas that is amazing. See you deal with life and death every day and the rest of us sit in our comfortable offices and stress about how bad we have it."

"I wouldn't say every day. It isn't as if I'm a soldier on the front lines of a war. I just have to figure out what happens afterwards and make sure justice is done. I think my job is more of a superhero role. Don't you think?"

"Really Dallas, superhero, I don't want you to get too big of a head, yet."

"Kelsey I am just teasing. What about you? Have you ever run across anything like that in your life?"

"Well as an actuary I haven't run into anything that exciting, but there was this one time when I was in the navy. It has been, wow, eighteen years ago. I went straight into the navy out of high school because of the G.I. bill and had been in for two years. I was working as an administrative assistant to a Lt. Commander in the Jag office at the Quantico base. There was an incident with the Base Commander's daughter. The B.C. was a full bird Colonel and while he and his wife were down at the Officer's club on a Friday night their house was broken into and their daughter tied up and raped. It was a scary time."

"Kelsey I had no idea, did they ever find anything, any suspects?"

"No one was ever formally charged, a couple of people were questioned about it and they had suspicions about this one major but all of the evidence was circumstantial and he had been a war hero of some note in Vietnam so he was never taken into custody."

Just then their dinner arrives and they take a break from the riveting story. The food looks delicious and they cannot wait to see if it tastes as good as it looks. The aromas swirl around the table and are not just a thought, but now a reality. Both Dallas and Kelsey greatly enjoy the culinary art that the chefs on the ship have created. After a few moments of pure dining ecstasy Kelsey starts back into her story.

"So Dallas, as I was saying, the only suspect was a major who had been seen by a neighbor. The neighbor was one of the high ranking officer's wives. She heard something outside and when she looked out the window she could see a man walking down the sidewalk in front of the base commander's house. It was only dimly lit outside so she couldn't positively identify anyone. However she was positive he had gold oak leaves on his collar."

"So what did the authorities do about that?"

"They called in several majors for questioning, and one said he was in the area but was walking home from the deputy base commander's house. The Lt. Colonel that lived three houses down was the deputy base commander and he was hosting a regular poker game that night. The man they questioned had gotten cleaned out and quit early. He was walking home because he only lived three blocks away. Many people thought he was guilty but with no physical evidence nothing ever happened."

"Kelsey that is quite a story you told. What was the major's name?"

"I can't remember it was kind of odd. He retired five years after that. He had made Lt. Colonel and moved out of state. I never heard anything about it again."

They finish their meal and as they are leaving Dallas asks, "Are you tired Kelsey?"

"No Dallas, are you trying to get rid of me already?"

"No, not at all, I am wondering would you like to head to the ballroom lounge and go dancing."

Her deep blue eyes sparkle as the lights flicker behind them and she responds, "I haven't been dancing in years. I would love to go dancing with you Dallas. Are all men from Fayetteville such perfect southern gentlemen?"

"No, you are lucky you found the only one on this cruise."

Chapter 25

Coswell drives out to the house on Cedar Village Way at 0900 on Wednesday morning. He sits there and surprisingly the Colonel is not sipping coffee and reading the paper as he routinely does. In fact he is nowhere to be seen. Coswell looks down the drive with his binoculars and sees the Colonel's Jeep is missing from the drive. This is a moment Coswell has been waiting for. Now he can take advantage of the Colonel's absence. Coswell exits his vehicle, puts his Webley revolver on his hip and stealthily makes his way down to the Colonel's porch. In a moment Coswell has removed his lock pick set from his pocket, and in another thirty seconds is inside. He slowly creeps around checking the entire house to be absolutely sure there is no one there. Once the house is clear he steps into Massengill's den. He reaches under the edge of the brass lamp that sits on the side table next to the Colonel's easy chair. He finds his microwave bug and removes it as he has no further use for it and doesn't want to leave anything behind for the authorities. He then walks over to the shadow boxes full of the Colonel's medals and ribbons. Coswell puts on his gloves, reaches up and turns the latch to the central box and opens it. He stands there for a moment in reverence of what is there but in no way the man who possesses it. Before him is the nation's highest honor, the Congressional Medal of Honor. Something very few men are ever awarded while they are alive. Usually a soldier only receives it when he bravely does something most would think is foolish and lives.

He reaches up and removes it from its resting place and then closes the shadow box frame. He puts it into a zip lock bag and slides it into the inside pocket of his leather coat. In another moment Coswell is gone and there is no sign he has ever even been in the house. Five minutes later he is in his vehicle again and starts the engine. He has a few errands to run and then he will go by this afternoon and pick up Brandy for a well deserved and relaxing night out.

Coswell drives down Cedar Village Way until he makes it into the main part of this quiet little rural town. He goes by the local post office and gets a priority mail shipping box and some packing tape. He is sitting in his vehicle and with a permanent marker writes the following on the box. Fragile Handle with

Care, then he addresses it to Sgt. Major Walker Ripley, P.O. Box 8766 Chaffee Lane, Ravenwood, Virginia 23322. He takes the zip lock bag out of his pocket and brushes it off, he then wraps it in bubble wrap and places it in the box and seals it up. He drives an hour away to the Steadman North Carolina Post Office and mails the package from there. While in town he fuels up, grabs some coffee, and then is back on the road again. As he drives down the desolate rural roads, with fields and woods surrounding him, he feels at peace. There is not much that brings him peace in this line of work. He is on his way back to Cedar Creek now to see Brandy at the Breakfast Nook. She should get off at about 14:30 hours, and he should be there by then.

Chapter 26

Lt. Colonel Leslie D. Massengill had been in the Breakfast Nook most of the morning, simply drinking coffee, eating a Danish pastry and reading his paper. At 10:45 Brandy came by and asks the Colonel "Is there anything else I can get for you today Colonel? We do need the booth and you are just one person sitting at a four seat booth."

"Young lady you are aware who you are talking to, right? I am Leslie D. Massengill and I will do what I damn well please. I am going to be here for a while today."

"Thank you Colonel. I am just asking if you would like to be courteous to some of the other patrons. I am sorry."

"No but you will be."

Brandy walks away and tells Carlos the cook she is taking her break. She begins to walk to the back. Down the back hall are the wash rooms, an office, and a small break room. As Brandy disappears from view the Colonel rises from his booth and heads in the direction of the restroom. Brandy is feeling the tension of her job today and she is not very observant to her surroundings when she feels a hand tightly around her wrist. It is the Colonel, and he spins her around and presses her to the cold concrete block wall. He holds her hands above her head with one hand and tears open her blouse with the other. He presses in hard and kisses her but she struggles away. Her breasts are bulging from the top of her bra and mostly exposed.

"Am I being courteous now Brandy?"

"Colonel please stop right now. I am going to call the police!"

"You can go I just needed to see how those breasts looked without that hideous waitress outfit. You can't do anything to me, who do you think the police will believe? I think they will believe the local hero and pillar of the community over the trashy little girl that works at a glorified truck stop. Now be respectable and go put on another top."

Brandy shoves the break room door open as she holds her top together with one hand and pulls another uniform top off the rack. She changes and then spends the rest of her break sobbing uncontrollably. When she returns red streaks run down her face and her make up is a mess. She asks one of the other servers to switch stations with her so she won't have to deal with the Colonel again. She looks at the clock and it reads 11:15 am, 2:30 pm can't get here soon enough.

At 11:40 am the bell rings at the front door and in walk the Bridger twins, two identical twins with the bodies of dancers, and until today high moral standards. This day is one that neither girl ever thought would come. They walk over and slide into the last booth. They are sitting across from the Colonel facing him, and at the same time facing their worst nightmare.

Colonel Massengill says, "I see you ladies are so eager, you even show up early for our 'meeting'."

Cheryl speaks as Madison sits quietly looking down, "Colonel you know we both come here almost every day for breakfast. It isn't like we are making a special trip."

"All the same I am so glad to see you both. I will be absolutely enthralled to see all of you this weekend."

Madison is still quiet and clearly ashamed of her presence there. Cheryl continues, "Colonel we agreed to this weekend, not to you making a scene here and trying to destroy our good reputation in this town."

"Oh you didn't, I most certainly think you did. You are sluts that I am buying and soon enough will be paid for. You are simply puppets for me to control with which I entertain myself and my friends. Don't think of it as destroying your reputation, think of it more as empowering you to be the most morally corrupt women you have always dreamed of being."

Madison finally speaks, "We do not enjoy this. We are doing it because we have no other choice. We do have the choice not to sit and listen to your insults. Pay us the agreed upon retainer now or we are leaving."

The Colonel smiles an evil smile, "Look who finally found her spine and her voice too. You know this money is nothing to me. I will throw in an extra thousand if one of you comes out to the Jeep to give me a taste of your talents. You will have to pass an oral exam to get it though."

Madison says, "You are disgusting I will never do anything like that, especially in front of a busy restaurant where everyone in town can see. There are boundaries."

Cheryl looks at her sister and leans over and whispers in her ear, "You know we could use the extra money. Should I tell him I will do it if he pulls the Jeep around back? We are both going to end up doing it Saturday anyway right?"

Madison stares at her sister in disbelief, "No Cheryl that is going too far."

Cheryl leans forward and tells the Colonel, "I will if you pull the Jeep around back, but this is just this once to show we are serious."

Colonel Massengill smiles, "Already becoming the whores you should have always been. I would pull the Jeep around back, but the offer is only good if your sister Madison does it. I want her to know what a powerful man is like, not that boy Rich O'Donnell."

At that point Madison gets up crying and dashes to the restroom. Cheryl then reaches down and takes the leather satchel with the $3000.00 in it. She gets up to go get her sister and tells Colonel Massengill, "I guess your lustful anticipation will just have to wait. I hope you get blue balls."

Chapter 27

It is late Tuesday evening when Dallas Bird walks into the Emperor ballroom of the Empress Sky cruise ship with the beautiful Kelsey O'Quinn on his arm. This evening alone has made the whole cruise worthwhile. Dallas walks in and is smiling like the Cheshire Cat. Kelsey gentle walks across the room, effortlessly gliding and floating across the polished wood floor. Kelsey checks her bag, then they find a table and a waiter comes by to take their drink order. The music playing is a live big band orchestra just like in the 1930's and 40's. In fact the band leader even plays the clarinet. Dallas thinks this is so fitting, like Benny Goodman or Artie Shaw. As Dallas takes Kelsey's hand to join the other couples on the magnificent ballroom floor the band leader raises his clarinet and starts into Begin the Beguin by Artie Shaw. Dallas and Kelsey are dancing away holding each other close. He is awash in the seas of sapphire that are her eyes. He is lost and at the same time knows he is right where God intends for him to be. As the soft sounds of the clarinet wail he cannot help himself any longer. He slowly, gently, softly, kisses her cherry red lips and feels the warmth as she gently kisses him back. They sway together for what seems like forever and then ever so gently their lips part. Dallas cannot help himself, he audibly says, "Ahhh…."

Kelsey looks back at this mysterious and intriguing man and says, "Isn't that what you always do after you take a drink of an ice cold coke on a hot summer's day?"

Dallas blushes a little, "Yeah but this is better than any coke I have ever had in my life."

They dance together for about forty-five minutes and the band plays one big band favorite after another. They play String of Pearls, Jump Jive and Wail, they seem to know every big band classic. After almost an hour of dancing, they take a break and walk back over to the table for two fresh drinks and some ice water. The two sit for fifteen minutes sipping their drinks as Kelsey curls up into Dallas' arms. She leans up and kisses his neck and makes a purring noise of contentment as they are quiet together among all the chaos around them. She asks Dallas, "Have you ever had an experience like this one on a cruise?"

Dallas smiles down at her and brushes a lock of her hair out of her blue eyes, "I can truthfully say I have never had this much of a good time on any cruise before. You are amazing Kelsey. You can sing like Stevie Nicks, dance like Ginger Rogers and you have the movements of a gazelle. Where did you learn all these talents?"

"Don't you know all women of good social status go to charm school? Well that would be one explanation, but not the truth. Each of us have our own gifts, it is just a matter of accentuating them properly."

"If you say so, but you sure did learn how to accentuate all of your positives Kelsey."

"Well, a girl does have to keep some trade secrets. What do you say we go show everyone else how it's done Dallas. Let's get back out on the dance floor."

Just then the band strikes up and plays the Glenn Miller classic 'In the Mood' and Kelsey is ready to dance like never before and Dallas gladly joins her. The night has quickly evaporated, and at 1 a.m. Wednesday morning, Dallas and Kelsey walk out of the grand ballroom. Kelsey's motor has begun to wear down a little. The new couple exits the interior of the ship, and walks out onto the deck to look at the star filled sky and feel the cool night sea breeze. Everyone else is in the theaters, clubs, or cabins in the interior of the ship. So the newly acquainted couple has the deck, and the romantic moonlight reflecting off the waves, all to themselves. Dallas is holding Kelsey in his arms next to the rail on the serenity deck that overlooks the stern of the ship. He tells her, "This has been one of the best nights I have had in as long as I can remember." She leans in and presses her head against his chest with her ear listening to his strong heart beat at a quickened pace.

"Do I excite you Dallas?"

Dallas responds, "More than any woman I have ever encountered. You look so beautiful bathed in this moonlight Kelsey. I must be the luckiest man on this ship."

"If you think you are lucky now, just think we have two more days, and it can only get better from here."

Kelsey smiles her sweet flirtatious smile and tells him, "The only thing is, it is getting really late.

Actually it is already early. Right now I have to say goodnight and go to my cabin so I get my beauty sleep." She leans up and kisses him deeper than she has all night, then she gives him her number and tells him to call her tomorrow a little before noon. "I promise tomorrow will be even more of an adventure. Goodnight Dallas."

He stands there as her angelic figure disappears in the darkness on the deck. All he can muster up to say is, "Goodnight Kelsey."

Chapter 28

John McNally pulls up at the Breakfast Nook at 13:50 hours on Wednesday. Brandy is scheduled to get off work at 14:30 hours however he sees her inside sitting at a booth crying uncontrollably. McNally dismounts his vehicle and walks through the door of the Breakfast Nook. He turns and calmly says, "Brandy, are you okay? What has happened?"

She gets up and turns to him burying her face in his chest. She stops sobbing long enough to catch her breath and tells McNally, "John, it is Colonel Massengill, I don't know what to do. He followed me to the back today and ripped my blouse open. I don't know if I could have stopped him if he would have wanted to do more. I am scared John. I am done here for today, I just told them to dock me the last hour. Can we leave here please? I want to go to my house and clean up. Would it be alright if I rested for a couple of hours? I really want to see you tonight, I just need to recover."

"That is perfectly fine, I am so glad you weren't hurt. I will stay with you, let you sleep and be there just to make sure. I won't bother you while you are resting or getting ready, you need to relax a little after this ordeal."

McNally drives the distraught Brandy home in silence, and when they arrive, she immediately goes into the back and lies down to relax. He sits quietly on the couch as she goes down the hall to her bedroom. Just before disappearing down the hall, Brandy leans her head out and says, "I don't know how I ever survived without you John. Give me a couple of hours and I will be as good as new. I love you John." Then she disappears into the back.

McNally thinks, 'She loves me, just great. What happened to disconnecting your attachments?' He goes to the bookcase and pulls a book from it. She finds Dashiell Hammett's detective masterpiece 'The Maltese Falcon', so he begins to read quietly about the adventures of Sam Spade and awaits Brandy's emergence from her bedroom.

While Brandy is sleeping and recovering in the other room John McNally makes a call to Angelo's Steakhouse. He looks at his watch, it reads 16:00 hours. The hostess at the restaurant answers the phone in a professional manner. "Thank you for calling Angelo's Steakhouse. How may I help you?"

"Yes, this is John McNally. I have a reservation for two at 17:30 and need to move that time back a little."

"Yes sir, what time would you like your reservation Mr. McNally?"

"I need to move that to 19:30 hours. Dinner shouldn't take longer than 2 hours should it?"

"No sir I do not foresee that to be a problem. Most ticket times run about 1 hour and twenty minutes barring any major issues. I have made that adjustment in your reservation time and we will be looking forward to your visit. Is there anything else I can do for you Mr. McNally?"

"No thank you, you have been very accommodating. Thank you so much."

McNally hangs up and returns to the story of Sam Spade. After about two hours have pasted, he can hear the shower running and assumes the steaming water is attempting to wash away the day's severe frustrations from Brandy's supple skin. In about thirty more minutes he hears the water shut off and in another half hour Brandy reappears. She is beautifully dressed, and there is a smell of vanilla in the air. It has been just slightly under three hours.

"Why didn't you wake me earlier John? Are we going to be able to make dinner?"

"I have already taken care of that darling. I made a call, moved our reservation to 19:30 and there is a showing of Casablanca at 21:15 at the Valparaiso so everything will be just fine. You needed to take it easy and relax. You don't need any more stress tonight and this night is going to be just perfect."

In another fifteen minutes she is ready and the two walk out the front door of her quaint cottage to head to the steakhouse. While making the drive to Angelo's, Brandy is surprisingly quiet. She is normally not a chatterbox, but she does not say a word. She does seem to be relaxing as she sinks into the cushy seats of the explorer. She seems at peace but McNally has no idea why or how.

"John, why is it that I feel so completely safe when I am with you?"

"I do not know Brandy, possibly because I have never given you any reason not to feel safe. You feel protected and secure with me right?"

"Yes John I have never felt like I do with any other man in my life."

McNally knows this is not a good line of questioning and immediately changes the subject. "You said you have never been to Angelo's right?"

"No I can't afford to go there with what I make, not if I want to buy groceries that month."

"Well you are in for a treat." As they pull up to the restaurant John McNally looks at his watch, 19:22, he gets out and opens the door for Brandy. He takes her by the hand and walks into the restaurant. They walk up to the hostess and he says, "McNally reservation for two at 19:30."

The hostess walks them to their table, and the ambiance is everything Brandy ever hoped it would be. Dark Mahogany wood tables and paneling, chairs and booths covered in a dark red leather material and each cushion overstuffed and the smell of well aged beef floating throughout the restaurant. They are seated at their table for two and their waiter approaches. The whole experience is surreal for Brandy. This is like a fairytale, like Cinderella going to the ball. The waiter goes over the different specials and hands McNally and Brandy both menus. Brandy is puzzled because she has never seen a menu with no prices before. There is a dish on the menu known as steak Milan that Brandy questions the waiter about. He explains that this a dish with two five ounce filet minion medallions served with a rich peppercorn gravy and choice of side. Brandy smiles, "That sounds wonderful. I will have that with a baked potato and a glass of Chianti as well."

The waiter turns to McNally and says, "What will the gentleman have?"

"I will have the ten ounce filet minion, medium rare, with a twice baked potato and extra sour cream. Please bring me a Michelob with my meal."

The waiter responds, "Very good sir." and walks briskly to the kitchen.

Brandy smiles and says, "John, thank you so much for being patient earlier and taking me out tonight. This is such a treat I really appreciate this. You are such a true gentleman."

McNally thinks to himself, 'If she only knew the true nature of the man I am would she be so smitten with me?'

"It is nothing Brandy, you have to live life, and to the fullest when you can. I have always lived for the moment. I enjoy this night and every night as if it is the last."

Soon their food arrives and Brandy has never experienced such a masterpiece of flavor. This is nothing like any steak she has ever eaten. She always thought her uncle, who grills out constantly, cooked a good steak. However, it is nothing compared to the fine dining she is having tonight. They finish their entrees and soon enough the waiter brings an exquisite dessert for two. McNally and Brandy both order a nice cup of Cuban coffee to accompany dessert.

McNally looks at his watch as they are finishing up the dessert, a rich crème briolette, and he notices it is 20:45. The timing seems to be perfect, they have a couple of moments to sip the rich coffee and let everything settle before making the short drive to the Valparaiso Theater. John walks with Brandy clinging to his arm as they leave the restaurant and make their way to John's Ford Explorer. The Valet staff at the restaurant have pulled it around and warmed up the vehicle so the heater is blowing a comfortable temperature when John opens the door for his lovely date. John gives the valet twenty dollars and slides into the driver's side of the SUV.

"Brandy, we should be just in time for the movie. I really hope you enjoy Casablanca, it is one of my all time favorite classics."

"I'm sure it will be delightful John. Almost every minute I spend with you is wonderful. You always pick romantic movies, treat me to fine dinners and take such good care of me. When we get back to my place tonight I have something very special planned for us."

"What would that be? You are so sensually amazing are you sure I can survive it?"

"If you don't, you will die happy darling."

Just then they pull up to the theater and in moments are in the mezzanine as the large red velvet curtain opens to reveal the movie screen. They sit there and enjoy the movie together. Brandy with her head leaning on the left shoulder of McNally. He has his arm around her pulling her up close. They are in perfect harmony as she listens to his strong pounding heart and he listens to her quiet sighs. McNally thinks, 'I am going to enjoy this night in the theater, it always seems that so many things in life happen in a theater.'

The movie comes to a close and it is 23:00 hours. Brandy and John quietly shuffle out of the theater and back down into the now frigid fall evening air. It is a shame the theater doesn't have valet service.

"Well Brandy what did you think?"

"It was so wonderful, the story of star crossed lovers, like a modern day Romeo and Juliet. I do wish it would have had a happy ending for the lovers but she did love two men and made the right choice even know it was hard."

"Well art imitates life, love is not always cut and dry or a clear choice. There are always gray areas."

"Yeah I guess I know what you mean. I was talking with Madison a few days ago and she is thinking about getting back together with Rich O'Donnell. She is ashamed of the fact that she didn't believe him before about why he got fired. I know him too and don't think he is a thief. It did ruin his reputation in this town and he has to work in that awful area of east Fayetteville. Madison says she doesn't care where he works she just cares about who he is."

"Brandy it is true, you only live your work if you want to, and love doing it. The lucky ones in this world will find a calling they enjoy. I love my job so I don't see it as work, just what I do."

"I wish I did. You know I really would enjoy my job if it wasn't for Lt. Colonel Massengill. He always sits at my station and harasses me. If he didn't come in I would love it. I get to see people I know, meet new people and brighten their day with a smile and a cup of coffee."

McNally points out, "People usually get what is coming to them Brandy. The Colonel will have to pay the piper some day."

Just then they pull up to Brandy's quaint home and she tells McNally, "John, wait out here for ten minutes. I just need a few minutes to get things ready. I will turn out the living room light to signal you to come in."

"Okay. I will be waiting. I know whatever it is will be wonderful."

John McNally sits quietly watching for the lights to go out. After about fifteen minutes of patiently sitting in anticipation he sees the living room darken. He thinks, 'What could she plan that she hasn't already done?"

He walks in and there is a note on the table. He picks it up and it reads, 'Take off every stitch of clothing, and put on the satin blindfold before you enter the bedroom.' McNally is a little leery of this, but has grown to trust this woman. He removes his jacket and hangs it up on the coat rack and removes his shirt, boots, places his gun in the boots, removes his pants, and boxers and leaves them neatly folded on the couch. He carries the satin blindfold and just as he reaches the bedroom door puts it over his eyes and knocks on the door. Brandy answers the door and walks him to the bed. There is dim light in the room from what must be dozens of rose scented candles. She lays him down, still blindfolded, and begins to massage his entire body with warm almond scented oil. Her hands are warm and soft as they glide over his entire body. She starts with his chest, shoulders and arms. Then she moves down to his stomach, hips, thighs, calves and even the bottom of his feet. His entire body is in ecstasy and completely relaxed. She comes up and kisses him deeply. He reaches up to where she should be and begins to cup and caress her breasts through the fancy lace gown she is wearing but she tells him, "Not yet we aren't rushing anything. You have to keep your hands to yourself until I tell you that you are allowed. Now be a good boy."

She begins massaging back down on his legs and rubbing the inside of his thighs. She runs her fingernails even further up and he moans with pleasure. McNally thinks, 'This woman sure knows how to get a man charged up.' He doesn't think he can be anymore turned on until he feels her warm wet mouth where her fingernails had been. He is losing his mind at this point. After about six or seven minutes she crawls back up where he can feel her now naked breasts against his chest and she kisses his neck. Her thighs are straddling his waist and she reaches back to put everything where it should be and he once again feels very intense warmth like never before. He reaches up and kisses her round ample breasts as he thrusts deep inside her. Then uncontrollably he says something and he even surprises himself. He tells Brandy, "Oh God, Brandy I love you." She tears his blind fold off and he sees her naked undulating body as they both reach climax simultaneously. In a few minutes an exhausted Brandy rolls off from on top to curl up beside the now spent McNally.

"I had a feeling you'd like that, and I knew you loved me. You just needed the proper motivation to coax the words out."

McNally is quiet and as he holds Brandy's naked body close to him. His head is swimming with thoughts but the most prevalent one is, 'What have I done?'

Chapter 29

Dallas leans on the edge of the railing staring at the ocean off his balcony. He looks at his Submariner Dive watch and the illuminated dial reads 09:45 hours. He crashed immediately after arriving at his cabin at 02:15 early that same morning. He had slept quite deeply and soundly and was awaken at 08:15 by the smell of Kelsey's vanilla sky perfume. It was still lingering on the shirt he was wearing from the night before. Dallas had already taken a shower, shaved, brushed his teeth, dried his hair put on fresh clothes and sent his Italian suit to the dry cleaners on the ship and it is not yet 10:00. He is going to wait until at least noon to call Kelsey simply because he does not want to seem too eager. The dance has just begun although they both went headfirst into the deep end last night. They didn't do anything too foolish, just what anyone would do on a boundless, limitless adventure like this cruise. A cruise is a vacation designed to let your inhibition melt away and just be yourself. Dallas is just lucky enough to have found a woman on this boat that shares the same belief.

Dallas decides to go to the casino and see if his luck is as good there as it has been on the rest of the cruise. He strolls from the forecastle, down the corridor, and into the enormous atrium that is flooded with mid morning sunlight. He climbs the stairs that are covered in a thick red velvet runner all the way up to the casino level four decks up. He walks into the casino and surveys all around him. Looking from left to right there are slot machines along one wall, in the back left corner roulette and craps tables, the far back wall has more unique games like Caribbean poker and Keno but directly in the middle of the floor sit six Blackjack tables. Dallas walks around the tables and watches the dealers and the players to find a table with strong players and a weak dealer. Most players are average, the kind you find on cruises and not in Vegas. There is one table that has mostly adequate players but the house keeps winning because the person playing third base, the last player next to the dealer, doesn't know when to stay and make the dealer bust. If the right player is on the third base position the whole table will benefit. The woman playing in that position at one table has done nothing but win for the house in the last five hands. She clearly doesn't know how to play but it looks like she is getting up because she has lost the small amount of money she brought with her to the table.

Dallas decides to sit down at that table, he slides two fresh one hundred dollar bills across the table and the dealer yells, "Changing two hundred." Dallas is sitting with forty, five dollar chips in front of him and decides to start light. He lays down a ten dollar bet and the dealer begins dealing the cards. Most of the cards dealt at first are low ones, seven and below. Then the first face card comes out, a king in the position in front of Dallas. He has a feeling luck is with him. More cards come out and Dallas is sitting on sixteen and the dealer is showing a six. If that other woman was still sitting there she would probably hit. Dallas waves his hand to stay and the dealer rolls over his bottom card and it is a jack. The dealer must hit sixteen and rolls over an eight. That is twenty-four and the table wins. Dallas keeps playing for the next half hour winning about eighty percent of the hands. He looks down at his dive watch and before he knows it the time is 11:40. One last hand, He is up one hundred and sixty dollars so he bets two hundred on the next hand. His first card is a queen and Dallas is quite pleased with that one. When the dealer spins his second card across the table and it is the Ace of spades Dallas only has only one thing to say, "Winner, winner, chicken dinner." He collects his three hundred dollar pay off and says the phrase no casino ever wants to hear, "Color me up."

Dallas cashes in his chips and takes his winnings back to his cabin to put them in the in room safe. Once the cash is safely put away he picks up the phone and dials the number Kelsey had given him the night before. It is 11:58 when the phone begins to ring and the smooth voice on the other end answers. Kelsey says, "You sure have impeccable timing lover, I almost had to wait."

"We sure wouldn't want that would we?"

"Good things are worth waiting for I have been told. Of course, I wouldn't have any experience in that area, men don't make me wait."

"So Kelsey what would you like to do this wonderful sunny midday?"

"What do all women come on a cruise to do? Meet me up on the Lido deck at the bar across from the main pool. I will be there in thirty minutes, if you are there early grab a couple of chaise lounges for us."

"What sort of attire is required Kelsey? Are we just going to be lounging or swimming, or dancing to the reggae band?"

"Come prepared, I would just answer 'Yes' to those questions. Aren't you detectives supposed to be like boy scouts? Always be prepared."

"Ok I will see you very soon Kelsey."

"Not if I see you first darling."

Dallas finds this woman intriguing, intoxicating, and at times frustrating as hell but that is women for you. He goes to his closet and pulls out a swimsuit and puts it on. He thinks for another minute and grabs a pair of baggy cargo shorts to go over the swimsuit. He grabs his favorite Hawaiian silk shirt and dark shades. Then he slides on a pair of heavy leather sandals, the kind some people hike in, and is ready for anything Kelsey can throw at him.

Dallas thinks, 'I'll show her who is always prepared.' He steps out of his cabin door with a huge smile on his face and ready to confidently strut up to the Lido deck to meet this wonderful and mysterious woman. Just then as he turns the first corner she steps out and wraps her arms around his neck and kisses him in the same way as she did when she left him the night before. Dallas almost falls backwards.

Kelsey says, "I thought you were going to be prepared? Doesn't that include a surprise attack and changing the plan mid-stream?"

"You are what people refer to when they say they know someone who is unpredictable, aren't you?"

"What fun is it if you always know what's going to happen? I live life as an adventure where anything can change at a moments notice."

They stroll up the hall together and Dallas takes her hand to help her up the steep stairs leading to the lido deck. He notices two things, one is that she looks fabulous in the banana yellow bikini and sarong wrap she has on, the second is that she has a small cross tattoo on the inside of her right wrist. He thinks a beautiful woman who not only is talented but when she gets body art it is even something well thought out and not a drunken mistake on spring break. They get a small bite to eat and a couple of bottles of water as they lay out in the sun to gently give a bronze tone to their skin. Dallas applies suntan lotion to her back and neck and in return she applies it to his back and neck as well.

In addition she carefully applies heavy SPF sunscreen to his face and nose.

As they are lying in the sun quietly enjoying each other's company, and the warmth of the Caribbean sun, Kelsey breaks the silence.

"Last night was just magical Dallas, I can't believe I haven't met a decent man in all of Washington D.C. in over a year and I decide to get away to forget about all those troubles and end up meeting you."

"Life is funny how things work out but they say life is what happens when you are making other plans."

As they are both lying face down on the chaise lounges, she reaches up with her hand and ever so lightly runs her fingernails back and forth on his bare back.

Just then she says, "I don't want to get sweaty. What do you say we go inside, I'll throw on a top, and we can grab a couple of Margaritas and play some blackjack? She doesn't have to ask Dallas twice as he is pulling on his cargo shorts and Hawaiian shirt in seconds. He takes her hand and begins to lead her inside. Just then he realizes he doesn't know where she is berthed on the ship. He turns and asks, "Where is your cabin Kelsey?"

"She takes a step back, I don't believe it. I must be the luckiest girl on this ship. I found a man who will ask for directions. It is deck seven aft, the Coronado Suite."

When they arrive she opens the door and lets Dallas in while she goes in the other room to change clothes. He is looking around and tells her, "You know your cabin makes mine look like a gym locker. My cabin is so small when I stuck the key in the door to the cabin I thought I was going to break a window. This place is fabulous."

"Well when I am on vacation I like room to breath, even if I am only in the cabin for a short amount of time."

"Well Kelsey I'll have to remember that for the future."

She steps out of the other room and is now wearing a slinky, but very comfortable black knit dress that comes down just above her knees. To complement the dress she is wearing black sandals and has put her hair down. They both walk back to the atrium and then up to the level the casino is located on. They slowly stroll in and survey the gaming tables. Dallas follows as Kelsey leads him to a Blackjack table she apparently feels is lucky. Just as Dallas is about to take his normal position at third base on the table, Kelsey taps him on the shoulder and tells him, "You're in my chair."

Apparently this is a woman who takes her gambling seriously. She throws down three hundred and Dallas follows suit. The dealer yells, changing three hundred twice and they are off and gambling. She is quite skilled in Blackjack and even sometimes has the arrogance to split tens. She does it twice and wins three out of the four hands, once with a blackjack. Any time Dallas is gambling, time always seems to just fly by. The old adage is true, 'Time flies when you're having fun.' The only unfortunate part about that is he is having so much fun with Kelsey and their time is slipping from his hands like sands through an hourglass. Dallas hopes this will not be just a fling for a couple days. He wonders if she is interested in possibly continuing their blossoming relationship after they once again reach the shores of Charleston.

After playing for a couple of hours and winning a couple hundred dollars apiece they decide to take in some of the other sights of the ship. Dallas and Kelsey head to the central tiki bar behind the casino. It has a huge picture window overlooking the main deck railing and beyond that are the endless waves of the Caribbean. They sit and stare at the ocean and sip frozen drinks. After about another hour Kelsey asks Dallas, "How would you like to go to the Jazz and Blues club this evening?"

"I love the blues and a there is nothing like a really good jazz singer."

"Well I want to run back to my suite and catch up on some sleep and I have a couple other things to do. What do you say I meet you in the atrium tonight at 8:00 pm?"

"Sounds good I can't wait to see how you are going to surprise me tonight."

"Well I guess you will just have to wait, now won't you? Remember patience is a virtue."

With that Kelsey rises and strolls out of the bar heading for the stern of the ship where her comfy suite is located.

Chapter 30

McNally lies wide awake in Brandy's bed still not understanding how he could have lost so much control the night before. He was on the right track and now has headed back down the wrong one. He cannot worry about such things now. He knows that today is the day of reckoning for Lt. Colonel Leslie D. Massengill. He knows that he will be making preparations for his get together on Saturday. McNally already knows the Colonel's plan for this evening, a little pre-party celebration for himself. He knows that Massengill will leave to go to Fayetteville around 17:00 and McNally will be there to track him like a bloodhound. What seemed like such a simple job at first has become quite complicated. It was originally a cut and dry case of find out the truth, and simply do what needs to be done. Now it seems the lives of everyone in this little town are all intertwined because of this evil man who is a blight to humanity. McNally rests comfortably and looks at the clock beside the bed. It reads 12:00. Just then Brandy stirs and presses her wet lips to McNally's.

"Are you having a good morning my love?"

"Yes, it has been a long time since I have slept in like this. After last night I think we both needed the rest."

"I didn't wear you out did I?"

"No but you sure did try."

"Yes, I always aim to please."

"Brandy this afternoon I have some business over in the next town and will be gone tonight. What do you say I make us some lunch and we can relax here at the house for a few hours before I have to go?"

"That sounds just great. I'll throw on my silk robe to lounge around in today. What are you going to make?"

"I don't know, that depends on what you have."

"How about you make meatloaf? I have everything for it and it shouldn't be a lot of trouble."

"Okay, you relax I'll get to work on our lunch."

McNally went to work in the kitchen quickly putting together lunch. All the while, he is putting the final touches on his plan for the evening. Brandy sits in the living room flipping channels on the TV. She is wearing a floor length red satin gown and matching robe. McNally takes a look out of the kitchen and sees her on the couch. He thinks, 'I do have to hand it to her,

283

she always knows what looks sexy on her.' He quickly goes back to cooking to clear his mind because he knows he should have never become attached to Brandy the way he has. It isn't fair to her and he normally isn't one for breaking hearts. He should have just done what is necessary for the job and no more. Brandy just has an irresistible quality and McNally has to be more careful in the future.

When their lunch is ready, McNally sets the table, and carries the serving dish over to the table. He then lets Brandy know and she comes over to the table and sits across from him at the formal dining table. John McNally smiles at her, "It is nice to just be able to relax and enjoy an afternoon isn't it?"

"More than you know sweetie. Before you were around I would just sit around in this lonely house, no one has every made me feel so much like a woman in love than you John McNally. You are truly a gentleman in every sense of the word. You are the finest, gentlest man I have ever known. There are not many men in the world like you."

John McNally is quiet for a moment while he finishes his lunch. "Brandy I am flattered you think of me that way, but you are far too complementary of me.

I am just a man, and unfortunately the first one that you have had in your life treat you like a real woman. I know there are much better men out there than me Brandy."

John McNally looks at his watch and it reads 14:30. He says to Brandy, "I have to be going now if I am going to make my appointment. Last night was amazing and I have enjoyed our day today but unfortunately it has to come to an end."

"It is ok John we have all the time in the world. Give me a call when you are back in town okay."

"I'll be sure to call you as soon as I am back in Cedar Creek."

McNally walks to the door and she follows him. When they reach the door they embrace and she kisses him deeply for what seems a long time. He then walks out to his explorer, gets in and in a moment is driving down the road. He thinks at that point, 'That wasn't really a lie. She just won't hear from me again because I just won't be coming back to Cedar Creek.'

McNally drives out to the Shady Elms Motel and pulls the explorer next to the building. He goes to his room to verify that everything is cleaned out and not a single trace of his existence has been left behind. Once he has swept the room completely he cleans all the surfaces that could hold prints like the bathroom, toilet, shower, door knob, mirror, and chest of drawers. Then he strips sheets off of the bed and leaves them in the middle of the floor. The last thing he does is call the front desk and ask that the room be cleaned and new sheets placed on the bed. After hanging up he cleans the phone and will never be seen there again. McNally gets back into the explorer and pulls away from the motel. He drives about a block away and watches the room he had rented on the corner of the main building. After forty-five minutes he sees a middle-aged Hispanic maid wandering in its direction. After another thirty minutes she emerges with the old bed clothes and he can see her pushing her cleaning cart in the vicinity of the laundry room. Once he sees this McNally starts the explorer to make the drive out to Cedar Village Way. It will not be too long and the Colonel should have all his plans in place and be ready to go out and celebrate in his favorite sleazy way. McNally thinks, 'Hope this is all you hope it will be Massengill. Chances are this will be your last hoorah.'

Chapter 31

After a mid-afternoon break for rest, a shower, and a change of clothes Dallas is getting ready to walk to the atrium to meet Kelsey for an evening of bliss. It is 7:45 pm and he is only a five minute walk from the shimmering centerpiece of the ship. He arrives in the huge atrium at 7:52 pm and it is quite crowded. Movement along the different floors is not as free and easy as it was the day before. The place is bustling with people all trying to make it to different destinations on the ship and trying to get there quickly. Unfortunately, there is not an unfettered pathway to his destination.

Dallas wants to make sure he is visible for Kelsey whenever she appears from her suite in the aft of the ship. The best, most central place, he can think of is to stand next to the white Steinway grand piano that is on a platform in the middle of the atrium. Currently the pianist is on a break so Dallas is not disturbing him. This turns out to be a good plan because he sees Kelsey as she emerges from the deck that houses the casino. She looks around for a moment but quickly picks Dallas out of the crowd. This could have also been helped by the fact Dallas is waving his arm in the air at her. She comes down and meets him on the piano platform. Kelsey is wearing a red pleated evening dress with a skirt that reaches a couple of inches below her knees. She is also wearing matching red high heels, and a gold pendant with a ruby set in the center. Her blonde hair is straight now and flowing down onto her shoulders.

"Is there anytime you don't look like a woman that just stepped out of the latest copy of Vogue?"

Kelsey smiles a wry smile, and her beautiful blue eyes wink at Dallas and she says, "Maybe, but it is very rare."

"Well all I can say is Wow! Of course that is what I thought the first night up on the Lido deck and every time I have seen you since."

"I do try. So where is this Blues and Jazz club we are supposed to be going to?"

"It is on the same deck as the formal dining room, but two doors over from it. There is an entrance from the main deck and the atrium."

The Blues and Jazz club is fittingly named Ellington's, after the great Duke Ellington, a Jazz and Blues legend from Birmingham Alabama. As they walk in, the sultry, gravelly, voice of a female jazz singer in a slinky

288

sequined dress can be heard belting out 'Sophisticated Lady.' Dallas and Kelsey walk through the darkness to a corner booth that still has a good view of the stage, and cuddle up together. Soon the spotlight goes dark on center stage and the house music comes up. They both watch as a thin, well attired, older gentleman strolls to the center of the stage. He comes to the microphone and in a deep voice says, "Let's hear it for the musical styling of Holiday Rae. She is going to take about fifteen and if any of you have any requests please let her know. I am Calloway King and am honored to be your Master of Ceremonies for the evening."

Dallas looks up and sees Holiday Rae walking off stage left down to a small table in the corner. She is a tall, slender, woman with long dark hair, black and shimmering like a starless night. She glides like a cat walking effortlessly to her table. Dallas thinks, 'I wonder what Kelsey would like to hear?' Dallas asks Kelsey, "Would you excuse me just a moment?"

"You're heading over to the singer? Didn't anyone ever tell you blondes have more fun?"

"It isn't that, I am going to request a song. Anything in particular you would like to hear?"

"Surprise me hon, I'm sure you will pick something suitable."

Dallas strolls over to her table and instantly Holiday's soft brown eyes perk up.

"Well hello. What can I do for you?"

"I just had a request. I wanted to see if it is something you knew."

"If it is 'let's go back to my cabin and see who can get naked first' I know that one by heart."

Dallas blushes a little, he is usually the aggressor. He hasn't had too much experience with women that just come out and say what they are thinking. "I am very flattered, you are strikingly beautiful, and I normally wouldn't turn that offer down, but I am already here with a special lady."

"I had to give it a shot cowboy. I have always found, you don't know until you ask. So what would you like me to sing for you and your special lady?"

"I would love to hear the Jazz standard All of Me."

"Slow like Billie Holiday or fast like Joanna Hudson?"

"I was always partial to the slow sultry sound of the Billie Holiday version myself. Can you do a dedication to Kelsey?"

"Sure cowboy, I just wish you were coming back to ride in my rodeo, instead of hers."

Dallas walks back to the table, still a little flushed from his encounter with the lovely jazz singer. He sits down next to Kelsey and she lays her head on his shoulder. The waiter comes around and takes their drink orders. Soon enough the waiter brings Kelsey a tall Mojito and Dallas gets a Sam Adam's Lager in the bottle. In another five minutes the house music goes back down and the lights dim a little. Holiday Rae steps back out onto center stage and the spotlight envelops her. The sequins on her dress are shining like diamonds and she leans into the microphone and says, "This next song is a special dedication. It is dedicated to one of luckiest women here tonight. This is for Kelsey, you are lucky to have the cowboy you are with. The next song tonight is Billie Holiday's version of the old standard All of Me."

Kelsey listens and smiles from ear to ear. "How did you know I like this song?"

"Just a feeling I got Kelsey. So I guess I did pick something appropriate?"

Kelsey leans in and kisses Dallas and then leans up and whispers in his ear.

"I know this may not be the best time for this but I have something important to tell you."

"Okay what is it?"

"You know that story I was telling you last night at dinner about my time in the navy?"

"Yes, how could I forget?"

"It is funny how the mind works. I could have sat at the table all night racking my brains and never come up with some of the details. However, after being completely exhausted by someone, my mind relaxed while I was sleeping and this morning I remembered everything about it."

"What else is there to the story, you told me everything."

"I told you the major that was a suspect was a Vietnam hero of some note. He actually was awarded the Congressional Medal of Honor. I was right that he had a peculiar name. It came to me in the night as well. His name is Leslie Massengill. Have you ever met a man in your life named Leslie? It is an uncommon man's name, like naming a boy Beth it is asking for an ass kicking. I guess that's why he was awarded the CMH. He must have had to overcompensate for that feminine name."

"You are sure, Leslie Massengill? Oh Jesus, this can't be. You have got to be shitting me, right?"

"What's wrong, did I say something I shouldn't have? I'm sorry Dallas. I didn't mean to upset you."

"It is not that, I shouldn't tell you but you know so much already. Lt. Colonel Leslie D. Massengill is the man I am supposed to bring in for questioning upon return from my vacation on Monday."

Kelsey props herself up on her elbows and while looking at Dallas her mouth drops open.

"So you are supposed to question him in the case of a murdered prostitute and the other girl that was tied up raped?"

"Yes and it gets worse."

"How is that possible? How can anything be any worse?"

"There is also a possibility he may have a connection to another rape that recently occurred in the town he lives in. The M.O. is almost exactly what you described to me happened in Quantico. Another

293

military officer, a former Marine Chaplain, was at a poker game and while he was there his fifteen year old daughter was bound, raped, and left in a compromising position for her father to find her. Reports have Colonel Massengill at the poker game but the exact times he left or arrived at the game are fuzzy at best."

"O my God, so he has been out there doing this, and possibly getting away with it, for twenty years or more? I need another drink."

Kelsey orders a tequila sunrise and Dallas gets another beer. Kelsey looks at Dallas for a moment. "I didn't mean to kill the mood of our evening Dallas."

"It is okay, how could you have known you were going to tell me about the Major in your story and he turns out to possibly be the Lt. Colonel Massengill I am supposed to question? You were just telling me something that came to you in the night. I know how those eureka moments can be, when something pops back into your mind that you thought was gone forever."

"Still I feel like a buzz kill. What are your plans when we pull back into port tomorrow?"

"The only plan I have is to load my luggage up in my Shelby Mustang and drive back to Fayetteville. What do you have in mind?"

"Just think about this tonight and let me know in the morning. What would you say about us driving north of Charleston and spending a night at one of the resorts on the Isle of Palms? Now don't answer now, just think about it and tell me in the morning."

"Okay, I will think about it, but I think I know what the answer might be."

Holiday Rae sings for another hour, and a Jazz Saxophonist plays smooth, sexy, music in the background for an additional hour after that. It is now midnight and another day has slipped away from Dallas and Kelsey. She is an exquisite, mysterious, physically perfect woman that intrigues his mind. He knows there are no women like this in Fayetteville, and he hopes that everything isn't slipping away, like the days on this cruise seem to have slipped away from him. The evening ends utterly too soon. Dallas and Kelsey part once again, Kelsey heading to her palacial suite and Dallas heads to his cabin that compares to the steerage class on the Titanic.

Chapter 32

Coswell is sitting outside of 1313 Cedar Village Way watching the house with his binoculars. It is almost 16:30 and he hasn't seen Colonel Massengill yet, but both of his vehicles are there, and lights in the living room have turned on and off periodically so he knows he is inside. Coswell reaches back on his right hip and removes the Webley .45ACP revolver from its holster. He opens the console to the explorer and reaches inside to retrieve the Smith & Wesson model 18 revolver chambered in .22 long rifle. He places it in his holster on his hip after checking to make sure it is freshly loaded. He places the Webley revolver in the console. He then checks the pocket of his coat to be sure that his silencer is with him. He pulls it out, checks it, and blows through it to check for obstructions and make sure the threads are clean and will easily thread onto the model 18's barrel. Once all the equipment is checked, he is ready. An hour later at 17:40 Colonel Leslie Massengill steps out onto his porch and surveys his front yard. He is dressed in dark blue jeans, a checked flannel shirt and timberland style boots. He walks to the edge of the porch, and then down the stairs, and over to his long driveway. He looks at the Chrysler sedan and the Jeep Wrangler. He thinks to himself, 'I took the 300 last time, don't want anyone to recognize my vehicle. Better take the other one to be safe.' He climbs into the Wrangler, starts it up, and turns it around in the driveway. He drives up his long driveway and at the end of the drive turns right onto Cedar Village Way.

A moment later Coswell starts the Explorer and begins to follow him at a safe distance. The Colonel drives out of Cedar Creek heading west for Fayetteville. The drive seems to take longer than the thirty minutes it normally takes to cover the distance. This is because ten minutes into the drive the Colonel pulls over and spends five or six minutes fueling up his Wrangler, he then goes into the gas station to pay and spends another five minutes shopping in the convenience store. He comes out of the store with a small brown paper bag in his hand. He continues his drive down the highway, and before he enters the Fayetteville city limits, stops at Smokey's Package and Tobacco. He is inside for about ten minutes and Coswell parks across the street and is standing in front of a local barber shop watching for the Colonel to once again get into his vehicle and continue along his way. He looks at his watch to check the time, it is now 18:15 hours and the sun has set. The Jeep Wrangler starts back up and the headlights come on now. The Colonel continues on to the combat zone in eastern Fayetteville with Coswell following along. This is the same area Coswell had tracked the Colonel to before, when the incident had occurred with the hookers at the motel. The Colonel drives immediately to the Bushy Hills Motel and walks inside to get a room. The clerk comes over and asks, "What can I do for you?"

"I need a room for the night. Something away from the street so I can sleep in peace and quiet."

"Okay, I'll give you room 191, it is the last one on the end."

"That will be fine." Just then the Colonel grabs the pen on the chain and signs the register, Alex Hidel.

Coswell is sitting across the parking lot and sees Colonel Massengill as he walks out of the motel office and down to his Jeep. He gets in and drives to the end of the building, parking in front of room 191. Once the Colonel has gone inside Coswell starts his vehicle and moves it down closer to Massengill's room so he has a clear line of sight to the door of room 191. Coswell thinks, 'I know where you are going later. Your predictable behavior will be your undoing Colonel Massengill.'

Coswell sits patiently and waits in the cold, dark, Explorer. He knows soon enough that Massengill will not be able to resist the call of the Blue Danube Theater, the question is will it be before or after he desires live entertainment. If he follows his pattern of predictability he should head to the Blue Danube at or around 22:00 hours. Last time he stayed there for a little over an hour and then moved on to the hooker's row on his way back to the Bushy Hills Motel. Coswell thinks to himself, 'A half dozen of one or six of the other. It does not matter.' Coswell will be there, and there is nothing that Massengill can do to stop the inevitable course of fate. It is 20:00 hours and Coswell has seen no movement, but he knows that will change soon.

Inside the room Colonel Massengill picks up his phone and dials a familiar number. A sultry voice answers the phone, "Gracie Greathouse here."

"This is the Colonel for the madam, is she in?"

"She is always in you slime. Do you have anymore special requests?"

"No, in fact I am going to have to cancel the redhead and blonde from you. Just send the Latina girl to the party on Saturday."

"No one ever cancels. There is no one better at supplying special entertainment than me. Why could you possibly want to cancel?"

"Because I corrupted the Bridger Twins enough so they agreed to attend my party and entertain."

"Impressive slime, how on earth did you do that?"

"I told their landlord to go up on their rent so there is no way they could make it every month and they got behind. Then I told him not to accept if they offered 'other' ways to pay him off. In return he is being allowed to attend the party for free. He will get to have his way with both of them as well as maybe a favor from me in the future. At the same time I bribed the local mechanic to cause small difficulties with their car while fixing whatever they brought it in for. These small annoyances eventually drive them crazy and make them think at any moment they may need a new car. It has taken months to set this up but it has all been worth it."

"You are truly evil, this impresses me. Maybe you have even earned a session with the mistress, maybe!"

"I am flattered mistress Gracie."

The line goes dead and the Colonel reaches over and clicks the cradle to get a dial tone. Next he has one more call to make. He dials Cheryl Bridger's number. After four rings she answers, "Hello? Who is this?"

"This is Colonel Leslie D. Massengill. Are you looking forward to Saturday? Has the excitement and anticipation begun to build yet? I expect your sister to be just as quivering with anticipation as I know you already are."

"Colonel we are doing this because we have no choice and we have to do this or become homeless. Your misconception is revolting. We will do our jobs when we are at the party but you cannot make us desire to be there."

"After you have started at the party you will not want to stop. You will want nothing but for it to continue over and over. The ecstasy will be more than you can possibly imagine. Just make sure your sister is ready to be the slut she has always desired to be. Not that little good girl Rich O'Donnell dated."

With that the line goes dead again as Massengill places the receiver on its cradle.

Chapter 33

Dallas lies on his bed staring at the ceiling of his cabin. He knows today is the last day of the cruise, and the ship is scheduled to arrive in Charleston at 4:00 pm. He is resting, although he cannot sleep anymore. He was able to get about six hours of good sleep but after that all he did was lie in bed and watch whatever movie the ship's movie channel played. He has checked all the TV channels, nothing there, read everything about the huge Empress Sky ship in the brochures available, and even gone over the last day's newsletter and itinerary for the day. Let's face it, he is killing time. If he doesn't hear anything from Kelsey by noon he will give her a call. He might head up to the casino bar and grab a beer and a Monte Cristo sandwich about 11:00. He can play a few hands of Blackjack too while he is on that deck.

It is 10:50 so Dallas decides to stroll up to the casino bar and have a bite to eat. He arrives right at 11:00 and quickly eats. By 11:20 he is finished eating and makes his way over to the Blackjack tables. He plays well enough for the next forty-five minutes. Cards have seemed to be coming for him the whole cruise. In fact he cannot think of one instance on this cruise that has been unsatisfactory. He cannot blame the bomb Kelsey dropped at the jazz club last night on the cruise. That was just an unfortunate coincidence that led to the change in the mood of the evening. At 12:05 Dallas walks over to the bar phone and dials Kelsey's cabin extension. Ironically, the live band playing in the bar is playing REO Speedwagon's 'Should I follow my Head or my Heart'.

She picks up the phone and speaks, "Good morning hon, nice of you to let me sleep in."

"I am a gentleman as you know."

"We only have about four hours of cruise time left and I think I am just going to relax and get some sun on the serenity deck."

"Okay."

"What do you say about just meeting in the atrium before disembarking?"

Dallas understands wanting a little alone time, "Sounds great, I will see you when we dock. If you can't find me just call my cell. See you then Kelsey."

Dallas thinks, 'Back to the tables. Winner, Winner, Chicken dinner.' He looks to see what he has in cash and it is quite adequate so he heads for a table. The dealer is a beautiful eastern European girl named Svetlana. Dallas smiles at her and thinks, 'Hate to do it but I am going to break this dealer.'

Three hours later Dallas gets up from the table up four hundred and fifty dollars and cashes in. He thinks about the fact that the cruise has flown by, and decides in his last hour to go and try some of the cuisine he hasn't had the chance to yet. He heads for the all you can eat buffet restaurant in the stern of the ship. He is quietly sitting looking out of the huge plate glass windows enjoying the view that is visible on three sides of the restaurant. He looks out over the back of the ship watching the wake churn up behind the massive cruise liner. He is eating jumbo fried shrimp, steak tips, mashed potatoes and gravy, as well as macaroni and cheese. Needless to say, Dallas likes protein and starch. After finishing that feast, a small fruit salad, and a soft serve ice cream dessert, he feels the ship make a course adjustment. Right then, he looks out of the starboard side window, and he sees the coast line and cityscape of Charleston, South Carolina. He begins the walk back down to his cabin and takes a thorough look around the cabin. All of his bags are packed and sitting on the bed. Upon looking around Dallas gets a sinking, empty, feeling inside. This same thing happens every time he is at the end of an adventure. Whether it is a cruise, vacation to the mountains, the beach or just a city he has never visited, the end always has a moment of fleeting sadness. This time could be different. The cruise is over, but his budding relationship with Kelsey could have just begun to blossom. He will know soon enough. He listens to the captain as he calls the different decks to disembark the ship. He hears his deck and is soon carrying his bags through the halls of the ship on the way to the atrium. This moment, oddly enough, reminds him of humping his alice pack through the jungle when he was in Grenada years ago. He is one of the passengers who elect to carry their own luggage. A grunt just can't fathom having someone else carry his stuff.

Kelsey is waiting in the Coronado suite for the porter to come and collect her things. She has three large suitcases that must be carried off the ship and back to the port parking area. Just as the porter arrives and loads her luggage she reaches for her cell phone. She makes a quick call, "Dallas, hon, I am on my way to the atrium now."

"I'll see you when you get here. I'll be counting the moments. Bye now Kelsey"

In a few minutes the two are together and walking down the gangplank with the porter in tow.

"So Kelsey I made my decision and as anticipated it is a resounding yes. I would love to spend another night with you here in port. Where is it that you want to go to?"

"We can drive a piece north of here to the Isle of Palms. There are some nice resort hotels there and we will get a suite. How does that sound?"

"Sounds wonderful, what hotel are we going to? We are in separate vehicles and I don't want to get lost."

"I have a friend that works at the Wild Dunes and will get me the corporate rate. I'll call him on the way up. Just follow me and stick to my tail if you can."

"Yes ma'am. The last time I went to the Isle of Palms, and it has been a while, there was an excellent restaurant there named the Boathouse. Do you know if it is still there?"

"It is there and it is fabulous, I'll call the hotel and you call the restaurant. Make us reservations for 7:30. I hope that they aren't booked up because I love their spicy shrimp and grits and their bananas foster."

Once Dallas has loaded up his Shelby mustang with his luggage he fires the motor to life. It has an untamed, throaty, growl like a lion roaming free on the Serengeti. The porter has loaded all of Kelsey's belongings in her AMG Mercedes and the sound from the Mercedes is smooth, powerful, yet completely refined. They are both on the way north up the coast from Charleston to the Wild Dunes resort on the Isle of Palms. Dallas calls the Boathouse and is able to secure a reservation for two. Kelsey, with much less trouble, calls the concierge, her friend Andre, at the Wild Dunes and he tells her that the penthouse suite will be ready and filled with her favorite white roses upon her arrival. Dallas feels good back behind the wheel of his fastback and running eighty miles an hour with an evening of great potential in front of him makes life even better. He is glad he won all the money he did on the cruise. It will probably take all his winnings to pay for the suite Kelsey reserved. That is no matter, this has been a great vacation, a wonderful adventure, and he has tonight and the morning before heading back to Fayetteville. Dallas slides the car from fourth gear down into third to accelerate and catch up to Kelsey. He thinks, 'She must not worry about cops too much, she is doing ninety miles per hour and she knows the man behind her is a cop.'

In just a few minutes they are at the Isle of Palms Wild Dunes resort. Kelsey in her sleek black AMG Mercedes C63 coupe pulls up first followed by Dallas in the Shelby Mustang fastback 2+2. Both pull up to the valet station, Kelsey swings the door of the AMG open and she is a picture of grace as her long sexy legs appear from behind the wheel of this well tuned machine. She hands the keys to the valet and he gives her a ticket and unloads her luggage. She is standing on the curb waiting for Dallas, but the valets seem to ignore him at first. They cannot pry their eyes off the radiant beauty that is standing there in a yellow cotton sun dress. Dallas is thankful he is not a man dying of thirst in the desert, because he would have no chance of survival. One of the valets, named Earl, remembers he has a job and is apparently a big muscle car buff too. He walks over and talks to Dallas about the Shelby mustang. "Is this really a GT350? Man this is one awesome Mustang."

Dallas gives him the keys and tells him, "Earl, it is a GT350 and this car is my pride and joy. There is an extra fifty dollars in it for you if you show it some special attention and park it away from the other vehicles."

"Gladly sir, anything I can do to help. You just let me know if you need the car. Just call down here and ask for Earl. Is that your girlfriend over there?"

"That Earl is the woman I am staying here with. Anything else is yet to be determined. However, it is nice that your pals can't pry their eyes off her and I am going up to the penthouse suite with her."

Earl smiles as he slides behind the wheel of the Shelby, "I bet it is sir."

Dallas grabs his overnight bag, throws it over his shoulder and walks over to Kelsey. He turns to the valets and tells one of them, "Have the bellhop bring Miss O'Quinn's bags to her penthouse as soon as possible." He hands the valet a ten dollar bill and the valet tells him, "Yes sir, right away."

Kelsey and Dallas walk through the grand hotel lobby of the Wild Dunes resort and across the highly polished stone floor to the elevator bay. The elevators in this place are even ornate with brass facings, mother of pearl, and a seashell motif inlaid in the wall above the doors. In moments the elevator races to the top floor and Kelsey leads the way to the penthouse. Dallas gets the feeling she always reserves this room when she comes to this hotel. She seems quite familiar with everything here. They are soon at the door and in another moment have stepped inside. Dallas looks around the suite and is amazed with the luxury of the accommodations. There is a sixty inch plasma television on the wall, a huge corner sectional couch, a large coffee table and credenza with an espresso machine, and a full kitchen just in the first room when he walks in. Dallas walks back and sees that it is a two bedroom suite. He takes his overnight bag with him to the smaller bedroom with the queen size bed. Attached to that bedroom is a modest but full bath that one would find in most nice hotels. Dallas walks back out of the smaller bedroom and across the living room to the master bedroom and knocks on the open door. Kelsey is standing there putting her small carry bag in the chest of drawers. This room has a California king bed, another huge credenza with a standard coffee maker, the honor bar, and what looks to be a huge bathroom with a garden tub and his and her sinks.

"Kelsey, you sure know how to spend a night away from home."

"Like I said, I like to be able to relax for the short time I am in the room. If you will excuse me I am going to take advantage of the Jacuzzi tub in here. I need a nice hot relaxing soak."

"I know what you mean, I was just about to hit the shower too, the showers in the cabins on the ship are a little small and I am going to enjoy using a full sized one again."

"Okay, well give me about an hour, I like to take my time and let everything relax."

"Okay then, I might catch a few z's too while you are in the tub. See you in an hour or so Kelsey."

Just then there is a knock at the door and Dallas walks over to answer it. Kelsey's luggage has arrived and the bellhop delivers it. Dallas carries it to the master bedroom and he tips the bellhop as he leaves.

Dallas closes the door gently and notices she does not lock it. He walks over to the smaller bedroom, goes in the bathroom and turns on the shower. In just a minute he is naked and the warm water is washing away any stress he might have had. He notices a switch on the wall of the shower stall and small jets everywhere on the tile walls. He thinks, 'What the hell.' and throws the switch labeled rain room effect. He has never experienced a shower like this in his life. There is a pulsating wave of water coming from three directions and massaging every muscle in his body. Dallas thinks, 'Wow, I got to get me one of these!' He takes about thirty minutes to shower and dry off and then lays down on the queen size bed, face down, covering himself with a bath sheet just in case Kelsey accidentally comes in while he is napping.

In the master bathroom, with the tub run full and the heater going Kelsey's naked glistening body slides into the Jacuzzi tub and presses the button to activate the jets. She has her hair up to keep it from getting too wet and lies back as the water jets massage her body like the strong hands of a masseur. She lets her mind wander and it drifts to Dallas. She thinks, 'Dallas has been such a gentleman, it is so nice to meet a true southern gentleman who presumes nothing. When we walked into the hotel suite he immediately went to the smaller bedroom to store away his bag. He assumes not that we will be spending the night together in the big king size bed, but that we will be enjoying each other's company. He doesn't rule this out of course, but takes nothing for granted. He knows that if that is what I want I will give him the proper signals. I don't know how I am going to tell him what I need to tonight at dinner and not ruin our new friendship. I just hope he can forgive me and still trust me. I should have told him before.' She, once again, leans back and lets the jets of hot water envelop her body and massage away the stress. 'Well there is no way but just to come out and tell him and hope that he can find a way to forgive me. He will have to know that I had to do it. My feelings that I acquired for him on the cruise are genuine and he will know that they are not a lie.'

She has been soaking for over an hour now and it is 5:45 pm. She gets out, drains the huge garden tub, and slowly dries her soft skin and slides on a short silk night gown.

Kelsey walks across the master bedroom to the small desk in the corner and puts her makeup mirror on it. She then pulls her makeup bag out and begins to skillfully apply her makeup. Soon enough her makeup is done and she looks like one of the classic beauties from the 1940's with the look of pale skin, cherry red lips, and just a dash of pink color on her cheeks. She takes off the gown and puts on a matching panty and bra set, and another dress, one that Dallas hasn't seen yet. It is an eggshell color dress that is Japanese in style. It wraps around and buttons at the side with wooden toggles rather than buttons. She finishes off the ensemble with Japanese wooden sandals for that sexy, sophisticated, and exotic look.

She walks out of the bedroom and across the living room to the other bedroom and gently knocks on the door. There is no answer so she checks the knob. It is unlocked, so she quietly opens the door. To her surprise Dallas is still asleep, naked on the bed with the bath towel barely covering him. She shakes him a little and he immediately awakens realizing there is a significant difference in her attire and his.

She smiles, "Nice, naked and asleep, were you hoping I would come in here?"

"No, nothing like that, I just have not been able to sleep in clothes since I was about eighteen years old. If I am asleep, I am always naked."

"I hope you don't fall asleep too soon when you are naked with others."

"That is a little different situation. If you would just give me a couple of minutes I will be dressed and ready and we can go to the 7:30 reservation."

She walks into the living room and closes the bedroom door behind her.

As she leaves he thinks, 'Wow she looks better every time I see her.'

In just a couple of minutes Dallas has thrown on a clean pair of khaki pants, a nice charcoal gray shirt, and the only pair of boat shoes he owns. He walks out of the bedroom and Kelsey is sitting on the couch with her legs crossed. She gets up and walks over to him. Dallas asks, "Shall we go?"

"I am ready when you are hon."

Dallas is looking puzzled for just a moment and Kelsey says, "Is there something wrong?"

He says, "Yes." Just then he leans in and tenderly kisses her. "You needed to blot your lipstick, but I took care of it for you."

"Very cute, I have to give you points for that line, it is very original."

They head downstairs and Earl pulls the Shelby Mustang around for Dallas and his beautiful date. Dallas opens the door for Kelsey and she slides into the passenger's side. Dallas closes her door, walks around the back of the Mustang to the driver's side, and they take off heading for yet another adventure. In a matter of minutes they are at the Boathouse restaurant.

Once they are seated, and have placed their orders, Kelsey seems quiet and much more serious than before. Dallas asks, "Is something wrong Kelsey? Why are you so quiet?"

"Dallas, do you trust me? Have we had a good time together so far?"

"Of course Kelsey, I have had a wonderful time with you. We haven't known each other but a few days, however I have begun to trust you in that short time."

"What if I had lied about something? Would you forgive me if I came clean and told you the truth? I ask because I have had so much fun with you and have begun to develop feelings for you and I don't want that to all be for nothing because of a white lie."

"What is it Kelsey, I can't guarantee I will, but I will try my best to forgive you. I can't say yes or no until I know the lie. Please tell me."

"Well, you know how I said I remembered the name of the suspect from Quantico?"

"Of course I do."

"Truth is I will never forget that name. The fifteen year old daughter of the Base Commander at Quantico was my baby sister. I am not just an actuary, I own an actuarial firm that also has a division that is a think tank. I know you probably wondered how an actuary could afford so much. I knew who you were when you stepped onto the cruise ship. I have been following and hunting Leslie Massengill for twenty years now trying to find a time when he slips up and can be brought to justice. I knew you were my best chance because I looked up your arrest record and you don't give up. You were the only one to connect the dots between the incident in Fayetteville and the one in Cedar Creek that was so close to how things happened in Quantico. I saw you that first day and watched you go into that Karaoke club. I went and changed clothes and knew that I had already drawn your attention from the moment you saw me. I knew I had to meet you and be able to give you the information on Massengill to lead you where you needed to go in the case. The only problem is after the first night I really liked you and couldn't stop seeing you if I wanted to. I know this is a lot, but I figure if I come clean, and if you really care about me, you may be able to find it in your heart to forgive me. Otherwise everything has been a lie."

Dallas sits silent for a moment. She can see the rage build up a little. He sits there, closes his eyes and breathes deeply for about five minutes. She doesn't know what to do, but watches as his body and mind ease as the waves of anger dissipate and flow gently away.

She says, "I understand Dallas, I will have my luggage moved to another suite and leave tomorrow the suite is paid for two days, please enjoy it with my complements. I wish it could have been different but I used you. I am so very sorry."

She gets up and as she is walking past him, he reaches up and grabs her hand. He pulls her down so she is face to face with him. He quietly says, "I will forgive you this time Kelsey. Just trust me in the future, don't lie to me. I deal with enough of those in my line of work and I don't need that in my love life, and I do want you in my love life."

"What was the purpose of the slow controlled breathing?"

"A meditation technique that I have learned works quite well to help alleviate undo stress and tension. Now how would you like to continue our evening? It is up to you, but I do see our dinner coming this way."

She softly kisses him and tells him, "Where did you come from Dallas Bird?"

Chapter 34

Lt. Colonel Leslie D. Massengill steps from the light of room 191 across the threshold and into the darkness and calm of the night. He looks around observantly and begins walking toward the office. He is now dressed in black slacks, leather wingtip shoes, a black oxford shirt and a black suede hat. He walks past the office and calmly across the street. Once he reaches the opposite side of the street, Coswell, who is watching calmly, dismounts his vehicle, puts on his camel hair coat, and begins to follow the Colonel to his next destination. Coswell keeps him in sight, about fifty to seventy-five yards away. The Colonel slowly strolls along the side walk leading to the Blue Danube Theater like a man without a care in the world. He is a man who has every aspect of his existence completely under control. As far as the Colonel is concerned, the world around him belongs to him because he is untouchable and the rules governing society do not apply to his life. It may be true that the Colonel has lived his life above the law, but not for very much longer. He, like all the others that Coswell has been hired to eliminate, will pay for his evil discretions very soon.

Coswell follows along behind the Colonel and all of his senses are heightened. He can hear every car horn, siren, conversation, and confrontation taking place on the mean streets of this city, but he dismisses all around him because of his singular purpose that is being brought into focus. This is the night and time for Coswell to eliminate Colonel Massengill. Now all Coswell needs is the proper setting and timing for his plan to be executed. Coswell has thought this over in his mind and knows that, if his plan is executed properly and efficiently, it will serve two purposes simultaneously. He will complete his mission and disgrace this once highly revered man. As an added bonus, the justified disgrace of Colonel Massengill will restore peace to the small town of Cedar Creek and the many lives of its citizens. Honor will also be restored to all Congressional Medal of Honor recipients, removing the tarnish put there by the unjustly awarded.

Colonel Massengill is about a block away from the theater. He is walking by hooker row with all the street walkers in the city of Fayetteville. Coswell thinks, 'These girls are too good for a bastard like Massengill.'

Colonel Massengill only yells at the hookers and does not stop. He is walking with purpose toward the Blue Danube Theater and Coswell sees the marquee and knows instantly why. On the marquee sign it reads, 'The Resurrection of Eve', and Coswell knows where the Colonel will be with his love for classic pornography. Once the Colonel arrives at the theater he immediately steps through the big double glass doors and disappears inside in a moment. Coswell knows to give him a little time. He does not want to be noticed now so he gives the Colonel a thirty count before he enters. Once inside, Coswell mills around looking at the unique magazines and movies sold in the theater for home consumption. He knows that this is a scathing indictment of society today. People might say the same thing about his profession because he does not follow all of the laws set out in society, but it is nowhere as depraved as this dark underworld. There is one thing that justifies Coswell's existence. If he is coming to see you, you did something to bring him there.

At that moment, Coswell notices Colonel Massengill at the ticket counter. He is, once again, making the life of ticket taker Rich O'Donnell a living hell. After ten minutes of berating and belittling Rich

O'Donnell, the Colonel has had his fill and walks toward the theater entrance to enjoy his night's entertainment. Coswell can tell that Rich O'Donnell is frustrated and angry just by the look of him. He hears him tell another employee, "I'm going to take my break watch the counter for me."

Coswell looks at this as a prime opportunity as none of the other employees have ever seen his face. Coswell walks up to the employee now selling tickets and purchases one. This employee has much less ambition and pride in his work. In fact, he reminds Coswell a great deal of Wilbur back at the Shady Elms Motel.

Coswell steps quietly into the back of the theater showing 'The Resurrection of Eve'. He stands for about ten minutes, not looking at the screen but staring intently at the floor of the aisle. While staring into pitch black darkness his eyes begin to adjust and his vision is razor sharp. His eyes now draw in the smallest ray of light. Most people who enter the theater are enveloped in darkness but the room is a sea of detail to him. At this point, his eyes are as sharp as an eagle, his mind is centered on a singular purpose, his breathing is quiet and even, and his pulse is slow and

323

steady. He knows that the Colonel will want his privacy in the theater but also want the best view of the screen. Coswell slowly scans the crowd for the Colonel's face. In the center row, eight rows from the back wall of the theater, Coswell spots the highly decorated Lt. Colonel Leslie D. Massengill. Coswell looks at the row behind the Colonel. In this row, there is a man sleeping in the last seat on the end. Coswell will need to enter that row from the other side of the theater. He steps outside and walks to the doors on the opposite side of the theater and begins again. He stands in the back and once again let his eyes readjust to the darkness. After ten minutes he is ready. He quietly walks from the back of the theater counting the rows. As he counts them he verifies there are no occupants that will see him. Most of the occupants are sitting up front with their eyes glued to the scene flickering across the faded silver screen. Others are seated on the side rows and are mostly drunk or asleep. Colonel Massengill is sitting precariously alone, near the back third of the theater, in the center of the row.

Coswell walks past the sixth row and makes a ninety degree turn smartly on the ball of his left foot and walks down the seventh row. He sits down one seat to the left and behind Lt. Colonel Massengill. Massengill is enthralled in the movie. He not only enjoys the depravity of this genre, he watches the classic pornography because he even is deep into the attempt at a plot.

Coswell takes his time and wants to time this moment properly. It will be best if he can do this during one of the louder scenes so not even the whisper of the .22 long rifle will be heard as it spins its way down the rifled barrel, through the silencer, and into the awaiting skull of Colonel Massengill. Coswell reaches into his left jacket pocket and retrieves his silencer. He shifts quietly in his seat and removes his Smith and Wesson Model 18 revolver from his right hip. This is the perfect weapon for this kind of work. When it is up close and personal you want something quiet, small, easy to conceal, and of course no recoil. This revolver is the perfect tool for such a job. He slowly begins to thread the silencer onto the threaded barrel of the revolver. He turns it one turn at a time. It takes about a minute because he is being careful not to make any noise. He is only about an arms length away from Lt. Colonel Massengill and this is the closest he has been to this man since arriving in town. After about a minute, the silencer bottoms out on the threaded barrel and Coswell is ready. Colonel Massengill is sitting straight up in his seat, engulfed in the scene that is unfolding upon the screen. Coswell takes a quick look around to make sure there are no other patrons that have joined them in seats nearby. The only one is the man down to Coswell's extreme right who is soundly sleeping at the end of the row. Coswell leans forward ever so slightly. He slowly, gently, and with no sound rocks the hammer of the revolver to the rear position, so a hair's breath of pressure on the trigger will send the bullet cascading to its intended target. He places the revolver's barrel onto the middle of the Colonel's seatback at a thirty degree upward angle. On screen the movie has entered one of the more vocal scenes and Coswell could not ask for a more perfect concert of events. Just then, Coswell leans forward and quietly whispers to Lt. Colonel Massengill, "Alpha, Mike, Foxtrot (Adios Mother Fucker) you evil bastard."

Lt. Colonel Massengill slightly turns his head to the left putting it in the perfect position and before he can even respond, 'What?' the Smith and Wesson has whispered its own farewell. Lt. Colonel Leslie D. Massengill's head gently slumps forward. Coswell looks to the end of the row and the sleeping man has not even stirred. Before the .22 caliber slug finishes rattling around inside the skull of Lt. Colonel Leslie D. Massengill, Coswell rises, puts his revolver away, smoothes his jacket so it cannot be seen and quietly walks out of the movie theater.

Coswell walks out from the darkness of the theater and quickly to the glass doors leading to the street. Just before leaving, for some unknown reason, he is compelled to look back. He sees Rich O'Donnell standing behind the counter of the theater. Just then, Rich looks up and notices a man that he thinks he may have seen once before. That man is Coswell. As Coswell pushes open the door and strolls down the street one of his favorite Shakespearean quotes pops into his head, 'All the World is a Stage, and the men and women merely players'. He crosses the street calmly and just after passing the site the Colonel had propositioned the two prostitutes the last time he followed him through this wasteland. Once on the other side of the street, he takes his time to calmly walk to the Bushy Hills Motel. He appears calm but does not take too much time to arrive there. Once at the motel, he walks across the parking lot and quickly gets into his

Ford Explorer. Coswell spins the engine to life and begins his drive eastward. He drives down county road 53, southeast out of Fayetteville, and is on his way, via the back roads, to Elizabethtown, highway 87, and eventually Wrightsville Beach past Wilmington. Coswell drives through the darkness of the cold rural county roads. They lead him southeast to White Lake, the Cape Fear River, and once he disposes of his weapon in that river, freedom. By the time Lt. Colonel Massengill is discovered, and the authorities are notified, Coswell will be in another town and well on his way to the coast on his roundabout trip back home to South Carolina. It takes Coswell about forty-five minutes to make his way down the winding, two lane, country road on his way to Elizabethtown. About seven miles outside of Elizabethtown, Coswell arrives at the point he has been most eager to reach. The road begins to run along a large grove of trees that are at the edge of a forest. On the other side of that thin grove Coswell can hear the rushing waters of the Cape Fear River. He pulls the Explorer well off of the road and kills the lights and engine. He quickly exits the vehicle after checking that there are no other vehicles as far as the eye can see. Coswell carefully makes his way through the narrow grove of trees and once out of sight removes the Smith and Wesson Model 18 from his holster. Coswell kicks the cylinder out to the side on the revolver and removes all the ammo. He then scatters it to the wind and the small .22 shells fall into the rushing water. Coswell is wearing gloves, but he still takes a microfiber cloth and wipes the handle, cylinder, trigger, hammer and barrel of the revolver. He looks at the weapon that performed so well for him one last time and then drops it into the Cape Fear River. Authorities will never look for it here. Soon enough it will be sunk into the muddy murky bottom of this river and will be a part of this place. He creeps back up to the edge of the narrow tree line, and while crouching looks down the road each way. He is assured there is no traffic and quickly makes his way back to the Explorer. He climbs inside the truck, starts the motor, and turns on the lights. As soon as it is possible, he slowly eases back out onto the road, and drives toward the intersection of highway eighty-seven. Once he reaches highway eighty-seven, he drives another desolate stretch that seems much longer than it is in reality, but soon he reaches his destination of state highway seventy-four. It is another forty-five minute drive until he finally enters the city limits of Wilmington. It is strange seeing the lights of a large coastal town again. It seems like so long since he has been anywhere but a small town, however it was only a matter of weeks ago he was in Arlington, just outside of Washington D.C. That seems so far in the past to Coswell for some reason.

He takes the bridge that crosses the bay and in twenty-five more minutes he is in Wrightsville Beach, right on the coast. He drives down near the pier. He parks on Oceanside Street seven blocks from the Dockside Waterfront Restaurant. He parks across from a nice home that has the lights on in the den, and the name Wilson on the mailbox.

Coswell picks up his satellite phone and dials the number of the Louise Wilson's burn phone.

The phone rings three times and a woman answers, "Hello?"

"It is time to complete the final payment."

"Mr. Coswell? Are you saying it is done?"

"I don't need to say anything. It was done as soon as I agreed to take the job, and you can make the transfer now."

"Yes Mr. Coswell."

"I trust the funds will be there by the close of business tomorrow, if not I will have to come visit you. That's on Oceanside Street isn't it?"

"How do you know where I live? I never gave you any of that information."

"Just to let you know, I will make good on my promise one way or another. If my payment is not there that will be a problem, I eliminate problems. Now follow the instructions given to you and destroy this phone Miss Wilson. Goodbye."

With that, Coswell slides the Explorer quietly into gear and drives away. He does not foresee any chance that Louise Wilson will not make good on her end of the contract. Fear, especially of one's own life, is a great motivator.

Chapter 35

Rich O'Donnell is hard at work and diligently doing his job. Even though he hates working at the Blue Danube Theater, his work ethic and ambition will not allow him to do anything just half way. Part of his job, after the movie is over, is to go through and roust all the drunks, stoners, and other unconscious patrons. He wakes them up and shuffles them out of the theater, at least for the night. 'The Resurrection of Eve' is finally over and the lights have come up in the house. Rich begins in the right rear of the theater, and moves around the perimeter of the seats first. Most of the patrons who are asleep usually sit in the wings of the theater seats. The center aisle usually does not have that many people to wake or run off because the people that sit in the center row do so for the best possible place to view the movie. It takes Rich about twenty minutes to clear out the perimeter seats of the theater. He walks down the main aisle and only sees two sleeping patrons, both of whom are near the back. He walks to the back and wakes one man, who is sleeping in his own vomit on the end of the row. Just in front of him Rich sees a familiar, repulsive, patron, a man he has grown to think of as his nemesis and he approaches him from the rear. Rich thinks, 'It is awfully strange that Colonel Massengill sat through the whole film, and fell asleep at that.'

Rich walks up to the unconscious patron, who has been the bain of his existence for years, and gently shakes him and there is no response. He shakes him again, however when he shakes him does not stir from his slumber. Rich looks more closely and when he shakes him a third time he notices a reddish brown, slightly crusty, substance on the back of the Colonel's neck. Rich yells at him, "Colonel Massengill wake up. Are you alright?" Right then the Colonel's head heaves forward and Rich can see the entry wound. He realizes the red, crusty substance on his neck is blood, not quite dried yet. He knows the Colonel is dead. Rich throws his head back and looks up, stands tall, crosses his arms, and a wide, devilish smile races across his face. Rich even throws his head back and laughs.

Rich audibly exclaims, "I guess that's what you get when you treat everyone like shit you old bastard."

Rich turns and calmly strolls to the counter. He picks up the phone behind the counter and with a great deal of pleasure dials '911' on the phone.

The Fayetteville police arrive after about half an hour, and swarm around the building. They tape off the exits, detain all the people still inside, and begin to take statements. They scurry around like ants rebuilding a freshly destroyed ant hill in an attempt, no matter how pathetic, to apprehend this assailant. Rich O'Donnell cannot help but smile. He wonders who could have done this wonderful deed. He knows that if anyone knew how he felt, suspicion might be cast on him so he tries to keep his feelings to himself. He would like to know who killed Colonel Massengill, so he can shake their hand and thank them. Apparently it is possible to cut off the right hand of the devil.

An attractive, well toned, olive skinned beauty of a female police detective corners Rich O'Donnell. She asks, "Are you the one who made the call to the police about this homicide?"

Rich looks at her and responds, "Yes, I am Rich O'Donnell. What is your name detective?"

"I am Detective Sergeant Carolyn Malanichi. Has the body been moved or touched?"

"I did shake him because I thought he was drunk or asleep, but the body is still in the same

334

position I discovered it in. It is still in the same seat it was in when he was alive and watching the movie."

"Mr. O'Donnell we will need to take your statement and exclusionary fingerprints from you to rule you out as a suspect. I assure you this is just a formality. Are you able to come down to the precinct and run through what happened tonight?"

"I can come down to the station and tell you what I know, but I really have no idea what happened."

"Did you see anything strange, um, let me rephrase that, out of the ordinary tonight?"

Rich thinks over the entire night for a moment, the one thing that comes to his mind is the split second when he saw Coswell. He knows that the man he saw had been in there once before, the night when the Colonel was in the theater and the prostitute down at the motel was killed. Maybe there is a connection, but if anything he has done a great service to the citizens of both Cedar Creek and Fayetteville. For that he should not be punished, rather rewarded. Rich responds to the detective, "Yes, I saw a man in here I have never seen before, and he is the only one that left the movie early."

"Can you describe this man?"

"Yes, I got a really good look at him. He was a shorter man, maybe five foot seven inches tall. He wasn't very big, a very slight build and probably weighed about one hundred and thirty-five pounds. He had a thin, pale face, short, sandy, blonde hair, and wore round wire rim glasses. Does that help you any Detective Malanichi?"

"It is a very good start, with detail like that we should be able to pick up a suspect and close this case. We will call you to come down to the station tomorrow and give a full official statement and a description to our sketch artist."

Rich O'Donnell thinks, 'Whoever you were that did this, thank you. I hope I have thrown the police off your track with a description of such a polar opposite.'

Malanichi rounds up her men and tells them to finish up. She motions to the assistant medical examiner to collect the body. She tells the medical examiner, "Get the body back to the morgue and set up an autopsy. I am going to give Dallas a call in the morning. I hate to cut his vacation short but he will want in on this."

The Fayetteville Police pack up and leave the now deserted, Blue Danube Theater with a great deal less pomp and circumstance, in comparison to their arrival a couple of hours prior. The police are always like that, come in like a lion, and leave like a lamb.

Rich finishes his closing duties and at 02:30 in the morning walks to his car. He climbs inside his Nissan and sits in the comfortable leather seat for a moment. He exhales deeply, "Thank you God. Maybe my life can get back on track now." He starts the engine and makes the drive in the cold darkness back to his small home in Cedar Creek. On the way back home he makes a decision, "I think I will have to go out for breakfast tomorrow. I have not shown my face in the Breakfast Nook in over a year, and things are about to change."

Chapter 36

Dallas Bird, after thoroughly enjoying a cruise and a nice night at the Isle of Palms, is driving his fastback Shelby Mustang, from Charleston, up interstate twenty-six Friday morning. As he opens up the throttle and tears up the open four lanes of interstate, his phone cell phone rings. He knows from the number on his caller I.D. his vacation is really over. Dallas pushes the button on his Bluetooth earpiece. He answers, "Dallas Bird, what do you want Carolyn?"

"How did you know it was me calling Dallas?"

"Caller I.D., and the fact you are the only woman in my life that would actively try and ruin my wonderful vacation."

"Well I'll try to make this worth it then. Just after midnight last night a call came in from the Blue Danube Theater, there was some major trouble there." Dallas listens, "Okay, you have my interest, what happened over in the trenches of the combat zone last night? Did a pimp kill a girl, or a pervert get caught with his pants down in public?"

"No this call was much more serious. There was a body found in the

338

theater, a man was found sitting in the back, with a small caliber hole in his head."

"That doesn't sound like some thug and a drive by shooting. That sounds a lot like a professional hit, thugs use nines and forties, and couldn't make a headshot to save their lives. Who was the victim or are we still identifying him?"

"He was easily identifiable. Unlike most, he still had his wallet, driver's license, and money on him. This is going to floor you Dallas so get ready."

"Damn it Carolyn, this isn't a reality show, just tell me who was killed so I can come in and start the investigation. By the way, thanks Carolyn for finding a reason to cut my vacation two days short."

"Okay Dallas, the victim last night was Lt. Colonel Leslie D. Massengill. Is that short, concise, and to the point?"

"Massengill's dead? I was going to call him in for questioning on Monday. I ran across some new information that connected the case at the Bushy Hills Motel to one that happened about a month ago in his home town. I guess Karma, just like payback, really is a bitch."

"It's going to be kind of hard to question him now Dallas, you may have to call in one those mediums for assistance."

"Very funny Carolyn, were there any messages while I was on vacation?"

"I almost forgot. Let me get it off your desk." The phone goes silent while Carolyn steps away for a moment. "There was one message that was kind of odd, a guy called and asked who the lead detective was on the case at the Bushy Hills Motel. He did say he would come by on Monday to talk with you about the case, he was kind of cryptic and said he had some information for you."

"What was his name?"

"He said to tell you that Willie Roosevelt called. Does that name mean anything to you?"

"No, but I will find out by the time this guy shows up. Thanks Carolyn, I am still about three hours away so I will be in around lunch time."

"Did you have fun on the cruise, I mean before I called and brought you back to reality?"

"Yes I did. I met a vibrant, beautiful, woman who was an absolute joy to spend time with. She is the exact opposite of you sometimes Malanichi. Maybe I'll get to see her again. I'll tell you all about it when you come over and help me work on the case this weekend."

"Dallas, I am supposed to be off this weekend."

"You ruined my weekend, I am ruining yours. Don't you know turnabout is fair play Carolyn?"

Dallas hangs up, and is roars up the interstate, when Kelsey crosses his mind. He reaches down to his phone and dials her number. After several rings she picks up the call.

"Hello? Dallas is this you?"

"Yes Kelsey I thought I would give you a call once I had arrived back in Fayetteville, but this just could not wait."

"Is there something wrong? Has something happened?"

"No, I have news that you will probably hear soon enough, but I wanted you to hear it from me first. I got a call from my partner and she told me that there was a murder last night over in the east section of Fayetteville. That is where the Colonel allegedly killed the prostitute before."

"He didn't rape and kill another girl before you could even get back to question him did he? I cannot believe he committed another heinous act before you could even get home and stop him. If we wouldn't have spent that night for ourselves you could have stopped him and it is my fault."

"No Kelsey, he didn't do anything like that, don't put the weight of the world, and the consequences of the Colonel's actions, on your conscious. In fact this should lift the weight you have been carrying for much too long. The only way to say this is just to tell you. Lt. Colonel Leslie D. Massengill is dead."

The line went quiet for a moment. "What did you say?"

"Lt. Colonel Leslie D. Massengill is dead. He was murdered in an adult theater, sometime after midnight last night. There is an eye witness that gave a description of a possible suspect but the description could match hundreds, maybe thousands of people."

"Dallas, I hope you don't think ill of me when I say this, but I hope you don't find his killer. Whoever did that should not be locked up. He did the world a favor."

"I thought you might feel that way, but I still have to look into it. I have to serve the law not justice. We will just have to wait and see. I did want you to know about it. Your hunt is over now and you can get on with more productive things in your life. The most important one I can think of is: when can we get together for another getaway weekend?"

"You have to work a little harder than that Dallas, but we will see about it really soon. Give me a call next week. Does that sound good to you?"

"Fabulous, it sounds just fabulous."

Dallas pushed the end button on his phone, and just at that moment he had reached the interchange with interstate ninety-five heading north back to Fayetteville. He steered the big Shelby through the cloverleaf and roared up interstate ninety-five. Dallas thinks to himself, 'You have made the turn down the homestretch, a hell of a long one, but the homestretch.' He slides the Shelby into third gear and has the throttle to the floor, as he shifts to fourth at ninety miles per hour and the Mustang immediately winds up to a hundred miles per hour, and keeps on winding up. Dallas smiles, "A cool car, smooth tunes, and a disregard for public safety. What else is there in this world?"

Chapter 37

While Dallas Bird drives up interstate twenty-six, Coswell is, at the same time, driving down highway seventeen that runs parallel to the Intracoastal Waterway and the Atlantic coast of the Carolinas. They are only about a hundred miles apart, but nothing links Coswell to the murder or the town any longer. It is ironic that Coswell is tracing the same route from Charleston to escape and return home that Dallas is taking to return to Fayetteville and the scene of the crime. Coswell drives down the sleepy coast on his way to the interstate twenty-six interchange that will take him back to Columbia. There he will check James Winchester out his extended stay at the Holiday Inn, return his rental car, and drive his Suburban back that night to the small town south of Lake Marion he calls home. Coswell has to keep razor sharp focus now so as not to make any minor mistakes. This profession of his does not forgive mistakes. He only hopes that it forgives the one with Brandy. He should have never let himself get so deeply involved with a woman, especially one that was so closely connected to the target and the job. Coswell thinks, 'Just don't do that

344

again. You cannot afford those types of connections, if you want that sort of life, you don't need to be in this business.' With all of the thoughts swimming through Coswell's head, the time and the drive seem to pass quickly. He is already making the turn up interstate twenty-six and is on the long haul to Columbia South Carolina.

Coswell takes his time making the long, easy, one hundred and thirty mile drive from the coast to Columbia, South Carolina. He makes sure not to do anything that may attract attention. The closer and closer he comes to the end of this job, and his eventual arrival back at his lake cottage, the more cautious he becomes. Once everything has been brought to a finale, and no connection can be drawn between Coswell and Colonel Massengill, then and only then, he can relax and file this escapade away as another successful target eliminated. Within an hour, Coswell is crossing the interstate ninety-five interchange and moving closer to the end. He picks up his satellite phone and places a call to Templar.

"Templar, you can put it in motion now. Operation plain brown wrapper is a go."

Templar responds to Coswell by simply speaking two syllables, "10-4."

In another fifty minutes Coswell's Explorer makes the turn up interstate twenty heading east. He has only a short drive to his exit and the Holiday Inn. It is late afternoon, and in the south this late in the fall, the sun is just hanging over the western horizon. Long shadows are thrown easterly and one looms from the back of the hotel and completely encompasses the back parking lot where Coswell's Suburban is parked. He pulls in beside it, and quickly walks to the back of the Explorer. He removes the North Carolina license plate from the Explorer, and stashes it under the front seat of the Suburban. He walks to the back of the Chevy and removes the rental plate from the Chevy Suburban returning it to the Explorer. Finally, and with little haste, he returns his South Carolina license plate to his Suburban. Coswell takes a few moments to clean out his belongings and wipe down everything in the interior of the Ford Explorer. He has to wipe all the surfaces just to make sure he has covered all his bases. He wipes the mirrors, inside and out, the door handles, the steering wheel, shifter, radio, console, seats, back window, tailgate, and of course the gas door and cap.

Coswell puts on a pair of surgical gloves and gets back into the Explorer to make the short drive across the street to the rental agency. Once he arrives there, he removes the surgical gloves and puts his leather ones on. Lastly he removes his Webley 45ACP revolver from the console and holsters it on his hip. He walks slowly but intently into the agency and assumes the persona of James Winchester.

He tells the counter worker, "This was a mighty nice ride y'all rented me. Got to hand it to you, she didn't give me a minute of trouble."

The attendant smiles and says, "Thank you Mister....." She looks at his license and rental agreement, "Winchester. I am glad to hear you enjoyed it. It looks like you had it out for three weeks and four days. I will go ahead and give you the monthly rate and save you about a hundred dollars."

"Well thank you darling, thank you so much. I drove that thing all over tarnation and I'll tell all my business associates to rent from y'all. I'd be happy to do anything I can to help a fellow American company. You know we are darn big on the American way in Texas."

"You came all the way from Texas? Hope you enjoyed our fair state."

"Darling, you never have to ask a Texan if they are from Texas. That is a fact we are proud of and will let you know. I am going back there in the morning, you know deer season is starting there now and I got to get out this year as much as I can. My name's not Winchester for nothing."

"You have a nice day sir."

James Winchester turns and walks out the door and back across the street to the Holiday Inn. He walks directly to the hotel office, and asks the clerk in his down home Texas way, "What's the damage sonny?"

"What room sir?"

Winchester gives him the room and the clerk takes a moment to look it up.

"I can give you the weekly rate on your extended stay, your total comes to $784.59."

"Well cheap service ain't good and good service ain't cheap, right sonny? Put it on this card, I get double points and frequent flyer miles with this one."

He runs the card and the approval registers almost instantly. He hands the credit card back to James Winchester and he turns and tells the clerk,

"Adios partner." In another moment he is across the parking lot and fires up the Chevy Suburban which has lay dormant for this month long adventure. After the rumbling 454 V8 warms up, and the heater begins to function, Coswell is back on his way down interstate twenty on a short jaunt to the interstate twenty-six interchange.

Coswell drives southeast along the interstate twenty-six corridor, for about an hour, until he nears the interstate ninety-five interchange. All of the posturing and planning have come to fruition, and it seems, at this point, Coswell has gotten away without a single loose end that can tie him to the murder of Lt. Colonel Leslie D. Massengill. He makes his turn northeast on interstate ninety-five and drives just south of Lake Marion, South Carolina. He starts to unwind and the excitement of the job begins to dissipate. He is, for now, returning to his true identity. His identity of Coswell begins to fade as he drives down the country back roads on the way to his lake house. Once again, this man is Master Sergeant Jefferson Ripley, US Army Retired. He pulls into his long gravel drive, up through the path that is beset on both sides with southern live oak trees forming an arch, this winds up to his three bedroom log home that backs up to the lake. He pulls the Suburban up next to the house, dismounts the vehicle, retrieves his travel bag from the back, and walks up onto his porch. He unlocks the door, walks through it, and has finally arrived. With a deep exhale, Jefferson Ripley sets his gear down next to his coffee table and exclaims, "Home at last."

He walks into his quiet study and looks over at his easy chair, the bar, and his reference book he had been reading on commercial Mauser hunting rifles. He walks to the bar, has one shot of 16 year old, single malt scotch, and walks to the master bedroom for a well deserved rest.

Chapter 38

Dallas Bird and Carolyn Malanichi have spent the entire weekend researching, investigating, and collecting evidence in the case of the now suspected, serial rapist and killer Leslie D. Massengill. After going through all the statements about the connected sexual assaults, Dallas runs across a scribbled post it note.

"Carolyn, what the hell is this? Is this in English?"

Malanichi looks at it, "I told you about this. This guy called and said he would come by on Monday to talk to you about this case."

"What does the name say?"

"Um…. Roosevelt, this is the note from Willie Roosevelt."

Dallas has been researching the Colonel's background all weekend and the last twenty years of the Colonel's life have all run together in Dallas' sleep deprived state.

"I saw this name in Massengill's military record."

Dallas looks through several stacks of files and finds the names of the soldiers killed and mortally wounded in the battle for which the Colonel received the Congressional Medal of Honor. He looks at the members of the squad and quietly says, "I'll be damned..."

Just then he realizes the message being sent. There is no way Willie Roosevelt, or at least the Willie Roosevelt from Massengill's past, could be coming in to see Dallas about new information on the serial rape case. This is because Willie Roosevelt is dead and has been since the Vietnam War.

Dallas also wonders why only one person at the scene of Colonel Massengill's murder gave a description of the possible murderer. Rich O'Donnell gave a detailed description of a man leaving the theater, and although most patrons in blue theaters do not want to be seen, they will answer questions when cornered by a police officer. No one else saw anything, or could give a description of anyone, that came near Rich O'Donnell's detail and precision. Dallas goes over the description and compares it to anyone that is in any way connected to the case. The only person the description comes even close to is Chaplain Timothy Michaelson, father of Chastity Michaelson, second alleged rape victim of Leslie D. Massengill. Chaplain Michaelson has an alibi for the timeframe, he is a respected and highly regarded citizen of Cedar Creek, and there is no way he could have murdered Massengill. He may have been able to have it done, but not do it himself.

Dallas looks at Carolyn, "Hey Malanichi, I know I ruined your weekend, and this looks like a dead end. What do you say we call it quits, box this stuff up and I'll take you for pizza and beer."

"Dallas, I didn't know you cared. That would be great."

"Carolyn, I don't care, I am sick of tracking a murderer's killer and I want a slice and a brew. Are you coming?"

"Always the gentlemen aren't you Dallas?"

"Sometimes I am, not always."

Chapter 39

The door opens at a small clapboard house in Jacksonville, North Carolina, just outside of Camp Lejeune. An attractive, but aging, Hispanic woman steps out onto her porch and looks down at a small brown box wrapped in a plain brown wrapper with U.S.M.C. stamped on the outside of it. She picks it up and takes it into her small, quaint, living room and begins to unwrap it as she sits on her faded floral pattern couch.

Inside the small box there is a white envelope and a flat black box with a U.S.M.C. Anchor, Globe, and Eagle seal on it. She opens the envelope and removes the letter inside. The letter is written on letterhead from the United States Marine Corp Public Affairs office. It reads as follows:

To Lucia Lopez,

Enclosed is an award, which by all rights, should have been bestowed upon Gunnery Sergeant Luis Juan Lopez. This award was mistakenly, and unjustly, awarded to another marine. This grievous error was recently discovered and the

U.S. Marine Corp would like to extend its deepest apologies and sympathies to you and your family. Your husband was an exemplary marine, and example to all other marines everywhere. It is with a heavy heart, we posthumously award Gunnery Sergeant Luis Juan Lopez, the Congressional Medal of Honor, for conspicuous gallantry above and beyond the call of duty.

Sincerely yours,

General James F. Amos, USMC

Commandant of the Marine Corp

Lucia looks down in the cardboard shipping box, removes the long black box with the U.S.M.C. Anchor, Globe, and Eagle Seal on it and opens it. When she looks inside the box she finds a ribbon, and the highest honor any U.S. soldier or sailor can be awarded. Inside is the Congressional Medal of Honor….

www.ingramcontent.com/pod-product-compliance
Lightning Source LLC
Chambersburg PA
CBHW021438240626
47153CB00001B/201